Praise for
CHRISTMAS IS AL

"Christmas Is All Around is everything I w[...] woman from big city travels to another big c[...] her occupation, has nothing nice to say about carolers, falls in love with bespectacled Englishman, saves Christmas. Charlotte and Graham's banter sparkles, the strong cast of secondary characters is such fun, the picturesque English settings are DIVINE, and the demonic baby is written-word birth control. Martha Waters, never stop writing books just for me."

—Sarah Hogle, author of *Just Like Magic*

"*Christmas Is All Around* is a festive riot of marvelously eccentric characters, witty banter, and swoony romance. Perfect for fans of Emily Henry and all things Bridget Jones. I loved this book!"

—Jenny Bayliss, author of *The Twelve Dates of Christmas*

"I want Martha Waters to write whatever she wants, but I also kinda want Martha Waters to only write cozy Christmas romances until the end of time because she does it SO WELL. From the moment of their felt reindeer costume striptease meet-cute, Graham and Charlotte's banter absolutely sparkled. Their story was also such a lovely meditation on figuring out what you want your life to look like, letting go of some of the past while still honoring it for how it's brought you to where you are. I already look forward to rereading this book every Christmas season!"

—Alicia Thompson, *USA Today* **bestselling author of**
With Love, from Cold World

"Simultaneously a hilarious send-up and a delightful homage to Christmas romances, *Christmas Is All Around* had me laughing, swooning, and rooting for Charlotte the whole book. Waters is the queen of historical rom-coms, and here she proves she's just as adept at crafting contemporary stories. An all-time favorite Christmas romance that shouldn't be missed!"

—Alison Cochrun, author of *Kiss Her Once for Me*

ALSO BY MARTHA WATERS

The Regency Vows Series

To Have and to Hoax

To Love and to Loathe

To Marry and to Meddle

To Swoon and to Spar

To Woo and to Wed

CHRISTMAS IS ALL AROUND

MARTHA WATERS

ATRIA PAPERBACK

New York　London · Toronto　Sydney　New Delhi

ATRIA
PAPERBACK

An Imprint of Simon & Schuster, LLC
1230 Avenue of the Americas
New York, NY 10020

First Atria Paperback edition October 2024

ATRIA PAPERBACK and colophon are trademarks of Simon & Schuster, LLC

Simon & Schuster: Celebrating 100 Years of Publishing in 2024

For information about special discounts for bulk purchases, please contact Simon & Schuster Special Sales at 1-866-506-1949 or business@simonandschuster.com.

The Simon & Schuster Speakers Bureau can bring authors to your live event. For more information or to book an event, contact the Simon & Schuster Speakers Bureau at 1-866-248-3049 or visit our website at www.simonspeakers.com.

Interior design by Erika R. Genova

Manufactured in the United States of America

1 3 5 7 9 10 8 6 4 2

Library of Congress Cataloging-in-Publication Data

Names: Waters, Martha, 1988- author.
Title: Christmas is all around / By Martha Waters.
Description: First Atria Paperback edition. | New York : Atria Paperbacks, 2024.
Identifiers: LCCN 2024021481 (print) | LCCN 2024021482 (ebook) | ISBN 9781668069516 (paperback) | ISBN 9781668069523 (ebook)
Subjects: CYAC: Christmas—Fiction. | BISAC: FICTION / Romance / Holiday | FICTION / Romance / Contemporary | LCGFT: Romance fiction. | Novels.
Classification: LCC PS3623.A8689 C57 2024 (print) | LCC PS3623.A8689 (ebook) | DDC 813/.6—dc23/eng/20240510
LC record available at https://lccn.loc.gov/2024021481
LC ebook record available at https://lccn.loc.gov/2024021482

ISBN 978-1-6680-6951-6
ISBN 978-1-6680-6952-3 (ebook)

For Kristyn,
who hates Christmas

FIVE WEEKS
TO CHRISTMAS

CHAPTER ONE

Whenever Charlotte was feeling particularly gloomy about the state of the world, finding herself at the arrivals gate at Heathrow Airport inevitably made it even worse.

"Don't mind me," she muttered darkly, swerving around a couple that was enthusiastically kissing directly in front of her and narrowly avoiding hitting them with her overstuffed weekender bag. Considering she'd booked this plane ticket with approximately forty-eight hours' notice, she had not managed the world's most efficient packing job; however, the couple in question was still making out, showing no sign they even noticed that one of them had nearly been accidentally assaulted by a fellow passenger.

"Charlotte!" She peered around at the sound of her name, spotting her sister's blonde hair, identical in hue to her own. That was before she registered the hand frantically waving in the air or the bright green, flowing dress that looked impossibly chic amid a sea of weary, sweatpants-wearing travelers just off a red-eye from New York. Clutching her bag and tugging her wheeled suitcase behind her, Charlotte made a beeline toward Ava and soon found herself engulfed in a hug.

"I told you I could just catch the Tube," Charlotte said, once Ava drew back enough to allow her to breathe.

"But where's the fun in that?" Ava said brightly, and Charlotte was immediately suspicious. She loved her sister, but Ava was not the sort to go out of her way. Charlotte considered the options Ava had weighed to arrive here.

a) Pay the exorbitant cab fare to get to and from Heathrow;

b) Brave London traffic, in an exceedingly small car, while driving on what Ava still, after several years' residence in the UK, insisted on calling "the wrong side of the road";

or

c) Take the Tube all the way to Heathrow herself, merely to keep Charlotte company on the return journey.

In other words, Charlotte smelled a rat. She considered how to broach this topic delicately, but delicacy had never been one of her particular virtues.

"What's this about?" she asked bluntly, allowing Ava to relieve her of her bag as they made their way to the cabstand.

Ava frowned, attempting to look hurt; Charlotte was not convinced. "Can't a woman want to spend a few minutes with her baby sister without her motives being questioned?"

Charlotte considered for approximately 0.2 seconds. "No."

"Fine." Ava waited until they had secured a cab, loaded Charlotte's bags into the trunk, piled into the back seat, and inched their way out of the frankly terrifying milieu of Heathrow before she continued. "It turns out that the flat on the floor above us has been turned into a holiday rental."

"Okay?" Charlotte was mystified as to how this related to anything, unless Ava was going to launch into a lecture on the evils of capitalism and the devastating impact of short-term rentals on the property market, in which case the timing still seemed a bit odd. A grim thought occurred to her. "Wait. Are you asking me to stay there instead of with you?" She started calculating how much a six-week rental, in West London, at Christmas, would be, and then wondered how much it would cost to change her plane ticket instead.

"No! No!" Ava said hastily, looking contrite. "Charlotte, you're *my sister*. I would *never*." Her eyes went misty; Charlotte was unmoved, because Ava had been adept at working up a tear for dramatic effect since she was about five.

"Ava." Charlotte sensed that someone needed to take this conversation in hand, and, per usual, that person was not going to be her elder sister. "Explain."

"Kit's parents have rented it!" Ava burst out.

Charlotte frowned. "For how long?"

Ava leaned forward, with the foreboding air of someone about to deliver a terminal cancer diagnosis. "From *now until New Year's*."

"Good god."

Ava slumped back in her seat—a clear sign that she was upset, because she was usually irritatingly conscious of her posture, and constantly badgering Charlotte about hers. "I love Kit's mom, you know—"

"Because she's your future," Charlotte said with an angelic smile at her sister. "I deeply do not want to psychoanalyze your husband, but there are undeniably similar . . . vibes."

Ava narrowed her eyes at her, but wisely decided not to open that particular line of debate. "*But*," she continued determinedly, "six weeks is . . ."

"A long time?"

"Yes." Ava sighed. "And I wanted to warn you that Simone is very keen on . . . activities." She paused dramatically. "*Christmas* activities."

Charlotte allowed a single, muffled whimper to escape her lips.

"It's just that it's Alice's first Christmas, you know," Ava said hurriedly, naming the very round, very loud offspring she'd produced that summer. Charlotte had already visited once since then; she was not much of a baby person, but she did think—in her totally unbiased opinion—that Alice was quite obviously the most adorable baby on earth. She also, however, happened to be possibly the most demonic. "So Simone thinks we need to take her to meet Santa, and to tea at Fortnum's—"

"She's a *baby*," Charlotte said, appalled. "She can't *eat*."

"No," Ava said with a fond smile, "but she can look adorable in a Christmas dress while *we* eat." She paused to consider. "If we shove a bottle in her mouth, she might give us five seconds of peace and quiet, and I can try to remember what an adult conversation feels like."

"I am going to kidnap your baby and spare both of us from this fate," Charlotte said gloomily.

"Well, it's still a better option than Mom and Dad coming to visit for the holidays—"

"Wait," Charlotte interrupted. "Are they together again?"

"Apparently," Ava said airily, waving a hand as though this was not of particular interest. Their parents' relationship was infamously tempestuous; they'd never officially divorced, but had spent a great deal of time and money moving houses, then moving back in together, then repeating the entire cycle over again. It was, Charlotte had been informed on numerous occasions, part of their *artistic temperament*, although she, who made a living off her art, personally thought it could simply be chalked up to being the two most self-centered people on the face of the planet.

"My point is," Ava said, "a holiday with the Adeoyes sounds considerably nicer, so I'm not going to complain too much." A speculative gleam lit her eye. "Besides, they *adore* Alice, and if that means that I can finagle some free babysitting out of them so that I can seduce my husband—"

"No! No! No!" Charlotte yelped, clapping her hands to her ears. From the front seat, the cabdriver cast a stern look at her in the rearview mirror, but she stared back at him, unrepentant. After a moment, an exasperated-looking Ava tugged at her hands until she lowered them.

"Will you be good?" Charlotte asked severely.

Ava pouted. "I *was* being good. It's not my fault you're a prude."

"Yes," Charlotte agreed, deadpan. "That's exactly the word I would use to describe myself. Should we revisit the string of torrid affairs in my twenties?" She was joking, but also *not* joking; after her last relationship, years earlier, she'd informed her best friend, Padma, over expensive cocktails that she was swearing off anything serious indefinitely, and she'd been true to her word. Vacation flings? Definitely. One-night stands with life-ruiningly hot bartenders? Sure. But nothing more.

"It has been absolutely *ages* since I heard someone use the phrase 'torrid affair,' and I really think it's time it made a comeback," Ava said approvingly. "But if we could return to the point of this conversation—and the whole reason I schlepped all the way out to this godforsaken airport so I could get a moment alone with you—"

"What happened to *I just want to see my precious baby sister*?"

"I just wanted to *warn* you," Ava said, undeterred. "And if you want to suddenly find yourself unavoidably busy on certain days while you're here, just to escape for a bit, I understand." She delivered the offer with the air of someone who clearly expected to be sainted any day now, though by Ava's standards, this *was* pretty considerate. "I know how you feel about Christmas."

"Last time I checked, *you* weren't the world's most festive person, either."

"It's true," Ava conceded. "But I am a *parent* now. Sacrifices must be made. Plus, I don't have the lingering childhood-career-associated holiday baggage that you seem to be carrying."

"What a sentence."

Charlotte leaned back in her seat, watching the London suburbs creep slowly by as they inched through heavy traffic. She yawned; god, she was so tired. She'd turned twenty-nine this past summer, and was convinced that it had destroyed her ability to sleep properly on a plane, like some sort of horrifying aging switch had been turned on in her body's wiring.

"Besides, given recent events, I think I'm well within my rights to be a bit of a Scrooge."

Ava reached over to pat her on the hand consolingly. "Absolutely." A pause. "Also, that reminds me: the primary school down the street from our flat is putting on a production of *A Christmas Carol* featuring all the children in costume as Muppets, and Kit's mom wants to go."

Charlotte blinked. "You mean, using actual puppets?"

Ava shook her head firmly. "No, the children are going to be dressed as *the* Muppets. I'm looking forward to seeing a very small child performing Robin the Frog *as* Tiny Tim—this might be how we spot the next generational talent in the theater world!" She paused, frowning. "I'm not sure how this isn't going to end in a lawsuit, but a bit of litigation does tend to liven up amateur theatricals, wouldn't you say?"

"I don't know how to answer that," Charlotte said, and Ava laughed.

❄

Padma: Did you make it? Are you okay? Did anyone attack you on the plane???

Charlotte: Padma ffs

Charlotte: It was one teenager

Padma: Exactly!

Padma: If teenagers are accosting you in public parks, who knows what's next!

Charlotte: Don't worry, if anyone tries, I'll take them to court and hire you as my lawyer

Padma: Charlotte, I'm not licensed to practice in England.

Padma: You understand that, right?

Padma: Charlotte????

Padma: I don't even understand the difference between a solicitor and a barrister!

Charlotte: 😬

Charlotte set her phone down on the bed in Ava's guest room, leaning back against the headboard and resisting the temptation to go to sleep right now. By the time they'd made it back to Ava's flat, Alice had awoken from her morning nap, giving Charlotte plenty of time to bond with her niece (read: place a ginger kiss on her fuzzy head, then hold her at a safe distance and watch her warily, alert to any sudden movements, like some sort of skittish animal) before lunch. Then it was time for another nap—could Charlotte be a baby, please? They just ate and slept; it truly seemed like a dream life—which at least gave Charlotte time to shower, then a long walk around the park once Alice had awoken, which seemed to have done nothing but give her extra strength so that she could scream loud enough for four babies.

The point was: after all that, plus a transatlantic flight, she was *tired*, and the thought of twelve or so hours of uninterrupted, horizontal sleep was extremely appealing at the moment. Experience had taught her that going to bed at—she checked her phone—five thirty would be a mistake, though, so she instead dragged herself down the hall to the holiday cheer that awaited.

"All right, Charlotte?" asked Kit, Ava's husband, as soon as Charlotte dared to poke her head into the kitchen. He was wearing an apron in a William Morris print without a hint of self-consciousness, frowning down at a cookbook in a way that Charlotte found worrisome; she adored Kit—he was, truly, one of her very favorite people, and she had shed actual tears of joy for possibly the only time in her life when he and Ava had gotten engaged—but he was a bit . . . scattered. She wasn't sure she loved the idea of him attempting a recipe he hadn't tried several times previously—although she, who largely subsisted on takeout, salad kits, and meal delivery boxes, wasn't exactly going to offer up her services as sous chef.

"Hi, Kit," she said, crossing the room to drop a quick kiss on his cheek before heading for the fridge to see if there was any wine already open. "Where's—"

"*Waaaaaaaa!*" came the howl of a banshee, or perhaps someone possessed by a demon, or even a bird of prey.

"Never mind," Charlotte amended hastily, retrieving an open bottle of sauvignon blanc and waving it in Kit's direction. "Want a glass?"

"Go on," he said amiably, returning his attention to the cookbook. He looked, as usual, a bit disheveled: his curly dark hair, several shades darker than his brown skin, was in a state of disarray, and although he couldn't have been home from work for more than fifteen minutes, there already appeared to be a disturbing, Alice-generated substance on the shoulder of his white oxford shirt. "It sounds like I'll need the fortification."

"Why does she sound . . . like that?"

He cocked his head to the side as another yowl sounded from the living room, a thoughtful expression on his face. "That's a hungry cry," he said wisely. "Not to be mistaken for a sleepy cry, or a needs-a-nappy-change cry, or a general *fuck you, parents who put me on this earth* cry."

Charlotte stared at him in horror, handed him his glass of wine, and said, "Parenthood is a gift. Treasure this time." She offered a serene smile in response to his frown and ducked out of the room. Two seconds later, she heard the clicking of the gas stove, followed by a slight yelp. She immediately poked her head back in, only to find a sheepish-looking Kit hastily turning the knob. "More flames than I was expecting!" he said brightly upon seeing her. "Not to worry! I've sorted it!"

Not feeling remotely soothed, she retreated again; in the living room, she was greeted by the sound of screeches and baby talk mingling together, which had to rank pretty low on her list of favorite noises. At some point while she'd been settling into the guest room, Kit's parents had arrived, and they were presently standing huddled together, cooing adoringly over the unhinged monster flailing in the arms of Kit's mother. Simone, for her part, seemed unfazed by the fact that a small, chubby fist narrowly avoided direct contact with her eye, and she beamed down at her granddaughter. "That's the spirit, darling!" She was a petite, elegant woman in her sixties, her auburn hair mostly having faded to silver, which she somehow managed to make look like the absolute height of fashion. She was wearing a simple black dress and Chanel flats, and made Charlotte, in the leggings and oversized sweater she'd changed into after her shower, feel distinctly underdressed for Ava's living room.

John, Kit's father, reached out to capture the fist in his hand. "Perhaps she'll be a boxer!" he said cheerfully. He paused to consider. "Might be best to practice on someone other than your gran, though." He was a tall, lean Black man, several years older than his wife, currently wearing an extremely cheerful red-and-green striped Christmas sweater that felt like a harbinger of the festive nightmare that Charlotte was about to be sucked into. He glanced over at Ava, who was sitting on the sofa—an elegant vintage settee upholstered in beautiful pink silk—with a baby bottle in one hand and a glass of wine in the other. "Perhaps we ought to let you feed her, Ava dear?"

"Only if you value the sound of peace and quiet," Ava informed him, extending her arms to reclaim her daughter. After a further moment of adoring exclamation—which Charlotte thought was reck-lessly bold on the part of John and Simone; she valued her personal safety far too much to get that close to a creature making that much noise, even if that creature weighed only about fifteen pounds—Alice was passed to her mother, a bottle was offered, and a moment of silence, punctured only by the eager grunts of a feeding baby, descended upon the room.

"I'm not sure my ears are working after that," Charlotte said, daring to sink down on the sofa next to her sister. It dawned on her, a bit belatedly, that she hadn't had a roommate in over four years, and had come to cherish her solitude, but was about to spend the next six weeks in close quarters with multiple other adults *and* the world's loudest baby.

"You'll get used to it," Ava informed her with battle-hardened weariness.

"Hello, Charlotte!" Simone said brightly, perching on an armchair opposite the sofa with impressive posture. "Was your flight all right?"

"Were you hounded by any Christmas film enthusiasts on the plane?" John asked, a twinkle in his eye.

"Apparently no one on my flight had seen *Christmas, Truly*," Charlotte said.

"Ha!" Ava said darkly. "Unlikely. What's *more* likely is that they either didn't recognize you as that adorable, wide-eyed nine-year-old—"

"You truly did master the art of not blinking for extended periods of time," Simone contributed; Charlotte was honestly unclear on whether this was intended to be a compliment. It was true, however, that given her resting bitch face and general disinclination to sugar-coat anything she said, she hadn't been described as "adorable" in a long, long time.

"—or at the very least they're not unhinged enough to approach a perfect stranger on an airplane to harass them about their professional choices," Ava concluded.

"One has to admire the forthright American spirit," John said thoughtfully; this was a man who was prone to putting a positive spin on nearly everything, but Charlotte did have to draw the line somewhere.

"One does *not*," she objected fervently. "At least, not when that means that complete strangers are sending me death threats on Instagram, and a girl who can't possibly have been older than six-teen is approaching me in Central Park to tell me that I have ruined Christmas for her."

"Her parents will buy her a new iPhone and she'll forget all about it," Ava said absently, looking down at her daughter with a soft, tender sort of expression that made Charlotte feel slightly uncomfortable every time she caught sight of it. It was strange, after nearly thirty years of knowing her sister, to watch her morph into something new before her very eyes.

"Heartwarming," Charlotte deadpanned.

"Scrooge," Ava murmured, smiling down at Alice.

"I'm sure it will blow over soon, dear," Simone said, rising and making her way toward the doorway leading to the kitchen; Kit had been alarmingly silent for several minutes now, which Charlotte hoped meant that he was preparing a simple meal with no great drama, and not that he was dead. Simone leaned down and offered Charlotte a comforting pat on the shoulder in passing.

Simone was probably right, Charlotte knew objectively—the internet had a collective attention span of approximately twelve seconds, and no doubt someone would creepily live-tweet innocent interactions between strangers on an airplane or make a TikTok about a kid who liked a vegetable any day now, and Charlotte could retreat into peaceful anonymity. However, the entire experience of the past week had thrown her for a loop, and she was feeling a bit rattled at the moment.

The problem, in short, was this:

Twenty years earlier, Charlotte had appeared in a movie.

This wasn't as surprising as it sounded—her father was an acclaimed director of critically beloved, commercially underperforming art-house films, but his closest friend directed commercial hits, and he'd been looking to cast a precocious, well-spoken, extremely adorable kid in his ensemble holiday rom-com. It had taken nothing more than a look at Charlotte—quietly working on her math homework at the kitchen table—for the wheels to be set into motion. She had not particularly enjoyed the experience—the number of people who stared at you every time you had to recite a line was not something she'd been warned about, and she'd found it mildly terrifying—but it had been easy enough to put the whole thing behind her. Her parents had been—continued to be—disappointed that she'd had no further interest in an acting career, but she *should* have been able to move on and never think about it again.

Except for one problem: the movie in question—*Christmas, Truly*, which Charlotte continued to believe was the stupidest title for any movie made this century—had been a hit.

A big, big hit.

The sort of hit that appeared on television multiple times every holiday season, that people quoted from, that was the subject of endless memes on the internet. That sparked countless think pieces on whether the various plotlines were sexist, fatphobic, deeply problematic on every level. (To which Charlotte could have easily replied: yes, yes, and yes. It was made in 2004! It was not a good time for The Culture!)

All of this ultimately didn't affect Charlotte's life much, particularly once she grew older, cut her long mane of blonde hair to her shoulders, and got contacts. She'd changed her look just enough, and been just young enough at the time of filming, that she got recognized far less frequently these days than she had in middle school and high school, which was just how she liked it. She'd completely ignored her parents' dreams for her future, studied at RISD, and then, after graduation, used the padding in her savings account provided by the residuals she'd earned from the movie to set up her own business as an artist. She hadn't been above using her minor fame at times in the past when it was convenient for her—a splashy profile in an online magazine about "Tallulah from *Christmas, Truly*'s adorable new stationery line" had caused a bump in much-needed sales as she was starting out, to be honest—but, for the most part, her brief career as a precocious child star hadn't had much of an impact on her life as an adult.

Until now.

Until *Variety* had published a piece absolutely bursting with quotes from an "anonymous source" who was "well-placed at the studio" that revealed that the entire cast of *Christmas, Truly* had been convinced to sign on for a reboot of the original.

Except for one Charlotte Lane. (Or, as she'd been credited in the original movie, in horrifyingly cutesy fashion, "Charlie Rose Lane.")

And since a large part of the vision for said reboot involved Charlotte's character, Tallulah, marrying the other former child star from the original movie, this had cast a huge wrench into these plans. Charlotte didn't see why they couldn't just write around her—or *recast her*, for god's sake; it's not as though there wasn't a bountiful supply of blonde actresses in Hollywood who'd be delighted to land this job—but the entire article had been written in such a way as to cast blame on her for the reboot's failure to get off the ground

Charlotte hadn't predicted this level of hysteria. The people had already been appeased with a *Mean Girls* reboot—how much more tepid revisiting of early aughts pop culture was necessary? But her Instagram—which had a sizable following, since she used it to promote her artwork—had been flooded with messages ranging from disappointed to distraught to hostile to extremely disturbing. Charlotte had utilized the block button with cheerful abandon and told herself that the entire thing would blow over soon enough.

Until the encounter with the wildly indignant child (*fine*, teenager) in Central Park, which had been the last straw; before she'd even arrived home that afternoon, Charlotte had been on the phone with Ava, confirming that it would, in fact, be all right if her weeklong visit at Christmas turned into a six-week vacation instead.

And here she was.

And all she could do—aside from hoping to god that Kit and Ava had been exaggerating the extent of Alice's current sleep regression, because Charlotte did not function well on anything less than eight hours of uninterrupted slumber per night—was hope that it would blow over soon enough.

She was in London, not New York. Surely no one here cared. Surely she could have a peaceful English respite, get ahead on work, and return to New York in the new year feeling refreshed and— crucially—no longer fearing for her safety at the hands of rogue sixteen-year-olds.

Surely.

CHAPTER TWO

P lease don't complain," Ava began, which was an absurd thing to be asked by a woman who had once gone into hysterics when her favorite eye cream had been discontinued.

Charlotte blinked up at her from her coffee mug. The tiny guest room in Kit and Ava's flat was directly next to the nursery. This was hardly surprising, the realities of the London real estate market being what they were, but it did make for a less-than-ideal night's sleep. She spared a passing, longing thought for her cozy apartment in Brooklyn, with the blue bedroom she'd painted herself, and the alcove nook she'd converted into a desk and studio space. It was the first place she'd ever lived alone, the refuge she'd created for herself after her last, terrible breakup. Until recently, Padma and her new husband, Andrew, had lived a couple of blocks away, their proximity more of a comfort than she'd fully realized, until they were gone. It was, admittedly, eye-wateringly expensive, but it was *hers*, and her bed was exactly the right firmness and her next-door neighbor was a divorced jewelry designer who threw fabulous dinner parties but, blessedly, had zero children.

"But Simone wants to go to visit some stately home out in the countryside this afternoon for their Christmas lights switch-on," Ava continued.

Charlotte resisted the urge to groan by taking another large sip of coffee. It was Saturday, only three days after her arrival, and she'd already been subjected to a series of breathless monologues from Simone on the subject of the Christmas merriment that awaited them over the next month. Charlotte, who liked Kit's parents but generally attempted to tone down her bluntness in their company, had done her best to nod politely and make noises of vague encouragement that went some way toward disguising her actual feelings on the matter.

She knew from previous visits to see Ava at the holidays that London was extremely enthusiastic about Christmas. But she lived in New York! All of Midtown Manhattan was a terrifying, glistening, Christmassy nightmare from Thanksgiving through New Year's Eve, so it wasn't as though she wasn't used to it.

One thing that the English were inescapably, dementedly fond of, however, was the ceremonial switching-on of Christmas lights—and these festivities had been in full swing this week. Charlotte didn't know if she had it in her to attend another such event, and was just beginning to attempt to formulate an excuse that she could offer for staying home instead, when Ava added this tantalizing detail:

"It's at the house that belonged to Christian Calloway."

Charlotte's head shot up. "*The* Christian Calloway?" Calloway was a Victorian-era artist who had been involved in the Arts and Crafts movement, and had been famous for his intricate prints, used on textiles and wallpapers.

"I don't know how many others there are." Ava winced at the sound of a squawk from the direction of the nursery. "*Kit!*" she hollered at a pitch that Charlotte personally thought should be illegal at eight fifteen on a Saturday morning. "Your offspring is awake!"

There was a thump, followed by some mumbled cursing from the living room, where Kit was attempting to wrestle a Christmas tree into a stand, Ava having awoken that morning determined that the tree move indoors from its spot in the back garden, where it had languished for two days since being acquired, no one being able to face the task of decorating with a maniacal baby.

"Coming!" Kit called back, and Ava poured hot water from the electric kettle over a tea bag in a mug, looking unconcerned.

"Didn't Kit do all the feeds last night, too?" Charlotte asked, impressed by whatever witchcraft Ava had mastered to bend her husband to her will.

"Only because it's a weekend," Ava explained. "I do them on Sunday through Thursday nights, since he has to work weekdays and I don't, at the moment. Or any days," she added wryly. Ava had wrapped up her last show, at a theater in Richmond, when she was six months pregnant, and had not returned to acting since. Charlotte was uncertain how long of a maternity leave she planned, though she supposed that living in a country that didn't expect mothers to waddle from the delivery room straight back to the office likely made the urge to return to work considerably less pressing. Plus, Kit was an architect—and if their flat, full of vintage furniture and expensive rugs, was anything to judge by, a successful one—so there was likely no urgency to Ava's search for her next role.

"Anyway—Calloway. The house is called Eden Priory—it's in Hampshire, outside some quaint little village." Ava sighed happily, sipping her tea and completely ignoring the frankly horrifying screeching now emanating from the nursery and Kit's attempts at singing some sort of soothing lullaby to calm the baby. "It should be a scenic drive. We can admire all the handsome farmers."

"Please stop, I beg you," Charlotte said. "You're starting to sound like Mom." Last year, while Charlotte and Ava were spending Christmas together, their mother was romancing an inappropriately young Spanish sailing instructor.

Ava scowled and pulled a box of muesli from the pantry. Charlotte rose to fix her own breakfast.

"Calloway," she said dreamily as she poured some muesli into a bowl, then went to the fridge for yogurt. "Have you seen his wallpaper patterns? They're incredible."

Charlotte's own artwork leaned heavily toward patterns and details—lots of twining vines and roses and the like; her bestselling print series ever had depicted various citrus fruits surrounded by cleverly arranged leaves and blossoms—and she'd always loved Calloway's work, even though he had never been as famous as William Morris and some of the other leading artists of that movement.

She supposed that she could brave a bit of Christmas cheer for the sake of *art*. And, besides, an afternoon in the countryside would be a perfect excuse to ignore her phone, and the DMs she continued to be flooded with each time she checked Instagram. (She'd turned off notifications days ago, but the knowledge that the messages were piling in, regardless of whether she checked them every five minutes or not, was not soothing.)

All she wanted was a single afternoon in which she didn't have to think about *Christmas, Truly* and her current status as a minor internet villain. And while a Christmas-themed activity wouldn't have been her top choice, at this point . . . she'd take it.

❄️

The drive from London to Eden Priory was as scenic as Ava had promised; once they left the motorway, they traveled down a series of winding country lanes through a landscape of gently rolling green hills and bucolic villages. John was at the wheel, exclaiming in delight each time a new Christmas song came on the radio, and Charlotte kept her gaze fixed out the back seat window as they snaked their way through the village closest to Eden Priory—it was, ridiculously, called Upper Larkspur, and featured a tiny, two-platform train station, a couple of pubs, a few small shops, a church, and a number of thatched-roof cottages. Charlotte was not generally charmed by things that could be classified as "cute," but even she recognized that this was, basically, the romantic ideal of a quaint English village.

Eden Priory itself was just outside the village proper, down a long driveway lined by thick clusters of trees forming a canopy overhead that must have been stunning in the summertime, though now, in late November, the branches were nearly bare. After a couple of minutes, however, the trees cleared and the house suddenly came into view, perched on a hillside they were now inching their way up, surrounded by woodland. There was an ornamental lake on one side of the house and, just at the edge of the woodland, a folly. The house itself was a romantically ramshackle stone building that looked as though it had been cobbled together over the course of several decades—or possibly a few centuries. As soon as she saw the house, however, Charlotte felt the strangest niggling at the edge of her mind, like she was seeing a vaguely familiar face that she couldn't quite place.

"Does this look familiar to you?" she asked Ava in an undertone as they climbed out of the car with John, who was whistling cheerfully. A sectioned-off portion at the bottom of the lawn had been marked for parking, and they waited patiently as Kit and his mother emerged from the other car and attempted to extract Alice from her complicated-looking car seat.

"What do you mean?" Ava asked distractedly, holding out the baby carrier for Kit to wrestle Alice into, an ambitious operation that seemed to require both of their full attention.

"I don't know," Charlotte said, but quickly realized that Ava wasn't listening. She frowned slightly as they approached the long gravel path leading up to the front door, wondering where she could possibly have previously seen this house. It sported a dramatic turret, rising above the gables of the roof. Where had she seen that turret before? Probably in some period drama about pale women who took long walks and the brooding men who loved them. Not her favorite genre of movie, but Padma adored them, and so Charlotte had watched her fair share. She pulled out her phone to take a photo to send Padma later.

They found themselves plunged into a cheerful flurry of activity as soon as they entered the front doors and paid the entrance fee to the smiling, albeit slightly harried-looking woman about Charlotte's age who was running the front desk, dressed in a Victorian-era gown that Charlotte was almost certain was supposed to be a reference to something. There were hordes of people wandering around, a brass band offering renditions of Christmas carols in one corner, and a station selling mulled wine and mince pies set up along one wall. The room they found themselves in was enormous, featuring a soaring, timbered ceiling and a floor done in black-and-white tile that clicked satisfyingly under Charlotte's heeled boots as she made her way through the crowds. A sign at the base of the staircase noted that Christian Calloway's descendants still lived in the house, but that select rooms were open to the public with decor that had been preserved to offer visitors a glimpse into what the house would have looked like during Calloway's lifetime. She turned in a slow circle, taking in her surroundings, and her gaze landed on the unlit Christmas tree occupying much of one wall.

She froze.

And suddenly realized, with unfortunate clarity, why this house looked so familiar.

There was a swear from behind her, and Charlotte realized that she'd stopped in her tracks so suddenly that Ava had nearly walked directly into her.

"What is wrong with you?" Ava asked, irritation creeping into her voice, though Charlotte charitably decided not to take offense at this, given that Ava was currently having her hair tugged by her spawn. Charlotte already knew from experience that Alice had an astonishingly firm grip.

"Oh my god," Charlotte said, still not moving, staring ahead of her at the Christmas tree with something akin to horror. It was so obvious. The dark blue wallpaper. The worn, ancient-looking chaise directly to the right of the tree; the impressive marble fireplace beyond it. Even the ornamental china dogs that graced the mantel. Was this what post-traumatic flashbacks felt like?

"*What?*" Ava asked, more sharply this time. "Are you having a stroke?"

"I wish," Charlotte said fervently, tearing her eyes from the scene before her at last and turning to face her sister. "Ava, this is the house where they filmed Pip's scenes in *Christmas, Truly*."

Pip had been the counterpart to Charlotte's character, Tallulah; where she was the lonely daughter of a workaholic single dad on the Upper East Side who spent long evenings sitting in her bedroom window seat, writing letters to the English pen pal she'd been assigned through some sort of program at her elementary school, he was the lonely son of a single mother in a literal English manor, who alternated between staring wistfully out of his turret (she *knew* that turret looked familiar!) and sitting on a fabulous chaise by a large fireplace, writing letters by the light of the Christmas tree.

Ava blinked, then burst into laughter.

"Oh my god," she cackled. "I promise I didn't know."

Charlotte shot her a filthy look.

"Very convincing," she said darkly. "I really appreciate the empathy, by the way. Nice to rely on family."

This sent Ava into another round of cackles, at which point Kit materialized, looking politely puzzled, and Ava managed to explain the situation to him, which set her off laughing yet again.

Kit squinted at the tree, and then his expression brightened.

"You're right!" he said excitedly. "That's right where Pip sits—there on that chaise, right by the fire!" He paused to look at Charlotte, entirely serious. "Do you think the dog that sat at his feet is still alive?"

"*Kit*," Charlotte said, horrified by this betrayal.

"Probably not," he conceded. "It was twenty years ago—that would be an incredibly healthy dog."

"Maybe he gained immortality through the magic of Christmas," Ava managed to get out before collapsing into giggles again.

"I thought you were my *friend*," Charlotte said to Kit, ignoring her sister entirely.

"Kit *loves Christmas, Truly*," Ava confided. "I've convinced him never to bring it up around you, but I guess it's too late now."

Kit shrugged apologetically. "I can't help it," he said earnestly, spreading his hands. "The scene where Pip finally moves to New York and into the brownstone next door to Tallulah, and he sets his stationery away in a desk drawer, because he won't need it anymore . . ." He trailed off, his eyes going misty. "I don't see how you *don't* like it."

"I don't like any Christmas romances," Charlotte said stonily.

Kit looked crestfallen. "But *why*? Love and Christmas? My two favorite things!"

Ava gave her husband a sideways look. "Ahem. Aren't *Alice and I* your two favorite things?"

"Two favorite *people*," Kit corrected. "An entirely different category." He pressed a kiss to Ava's temple, and she appeared mollified; Kit, meanwhile, looked back at Charlotte. "I know you were a bit traumatized by *Christmas, Truly*, but surely you don't need to be prejudiced against the entire genre?"

"I do," Charlotte insisted. "Because Christmas romances are *bad*.

The meet-cutes under implausible circumstances! The elaborate festive tasks that require the protagonists to join forces and discover the joy of Christmas! The quirky, borderline-contrived Christmas rituals! The meddling supporting characters! The third-act fights! The sudden, improbable snowfalls! Kissing in front of Christmas trees! It is *all terrible.*"

Kit shook his head. "I think you just need to meet a handsome man from a small village whose family livelihood is tied to the festive season and who teaches you to view the holidays through new eyes," he said solemnly. "You'll be discovering the joy of Christmas in no time!"

"If that happens, please take it as a warning sign that I've suffered some sort of head injury," Charlotte said darkly; at that moment, John and Simone reappeared, bearing an entire tray of mugs of mulled wine, one of which Charlotte seized eagerly, taking a hasty gulp and then immediately spitting a mouthful of scalding-hot wine into her mug.

"Jesus Christ," she coughed, barely managing to avoid upending the entire mug.

"The steam rising from the surface is often viewed as a warning," Ava said sweetly.

Charlotte shot her a look, then took another, more cautious sip. When she wasn't burning the roof of her mouth off, it was delicious.

"Isn't this nice?" Kit asked cheerfully; Charlotte had already realized, over the course of the past few days, that the Adeoyes' enthusiasm for all things Christmassy must be some sort of genetic trait that they had passed down to their son, because Kit seemed genuinely delighted by every single decoration he spotted. In this instance, however, Charlotte had to grudgingly admit that he was correct: once she recovered from her initial horror at her unwitting visit to a hub of *Christmas, Truly* nostalgia, she could appreciate that their current surroundings held a certain degree of charm.

The soaring entrance hall in which they found themselves was a holiday wonderland: there was the Christmas tree—still unlit, of course, though not for long—and also the oak banisters bedecked with greenery; the (also currently unlit) fairy lights strung from the timbered ceiling; and the antique vases overflowing with sprigs of holly berries that were placed on nearly every available surface.

It was Christmassy without being cloying—and it was the latter quality that so often set her teeth on edge whenever she was being forced into some sort of holiday activity.

"Is something going to actually . . . happen? At some point?"

"What do you *need* to have happen?" Kit asked earnestly, sipping from his own mug of mulled wine with frank delight. He appeared to be a man entirely in his element: surrounded by his family, drinking mulled wine, and wearing a Christmas sweater featuring all eight reindeer. (Rudolph, notably, was absent, because Kit considered Rudolph to be a "corporate invention.")

"Well, when are they going to switch on the tree?" Charlotte asked. "That's why we're all here, isn't it?"

"They have to *build* to the moment," Kit informed her earnestly; next to him, John nodded eagerly, and the resemblance between father and son was almost unsettling. "Also," he added, more practically, "they wait until it's fully dark—I don't think the switch-on itself is until five thirty."

Charlotte checked her phone and noted that it was only four. "How are they possibly going to keep us entertained for this long?" She glanced down at her mug of mulled wine and decided to carefully ration it.

A few seconds later, as if summoned by her words, there was a slight commotion at one end of the room, near the Christmas tree; the brass band had wrapped up their rendition of "Santa Baby" (which felt like an odd choice for their current setting, but Charlotte wasn't the Christmas police), and a woman who looked to be about Simone's age, dressed in a floor-length red dress and a snowy-white apron, stepped forward, clutching a mic.

"Hello, everyone! I'm Elaine Calloway . . . but for today, you may address me as Mrs. Claus!"

There was a great deal of enthusiastic applause in response to this.

"And this," she said with a dramatic wave of the hand, "is—"

"Mrs. Cratchit," said the woman who had taken Charlotte's money at the entrance. She had a heap of messy dark hair that had been somewhat tamed into a braided knot at the back of her head, and at some point since Charlotte had last seen her, she appeared to have smudged flour on her cheeks for dramatic effect. "Naught but a humble housewife, suffering the effects of my husband's employer's greed." She offered a lip wobble; Charlotte glanced sideways at Ava, who was watching this performance approvingly.

"And *this*," Mrs. Claus declared cheerfully, waving another hand, "is Cindy-Lou Who!"

Charlotte blinked as a girl who appeared to be in her early twenties appeared from behind the tree; her dark hair was a bit shorter than Charlotte's, and she sported a blunt set of bangs, but the rest of her hair had been wrangled into two pigtails, and she was wearing a green shift dress. She looked unhappy about her current circumstances, and Charlotte couldn't blame her. "Who will carve the roast beast?" she asked, scowling, and Mrs. Cratchit elbowed her in the side, presumably to encourage a better display of holiday cheer, which merely had the effect of causing Cindy-Lou's scowl to deepen.

"We are delighted to welcome you to Eden Priory for the annual Christmas lights switch-on," Mrs. Claus continued with a determined smile, "and this year, for the first time, we are *thrilled* to offer a complimentary photo opportunity for anyone who wishes to have their photograph taken with a famous Christmas character!"

She paused, beaming, and there was further appreciative applause; Charlotte suppressed a sigh.

"And it is not just us who are here to welcome you," she continued cheerfully, "but a *very special visitor* that I've brought with me from the North Pole!"

"If Santa appears, I'm leaving," Charlotte muttered to Ava, who hissed, "Shh!" Being shushed by Ava was somewhat galling in and of itself; as the far more melodramatic and attention-seeking of the Lane sisters, she had been known to monologue on a wide-ranging array of topics, despite Charlotte's usually not-at-all-subtle attempts to get her sister to shut up and leave her in peace. However, it was *particularly* irritating now, when, prior to her conversion from normal human into mother, Ava had been perfectly happy to indulge Charlotte with a healthy bit of Christmas complaining.

"My husband, Father Christmas, is of course very busy this time of year," Mrs. Claus said now, and Charlotte didn't think she was imagining that the smile of Mrs. Cratchit became a bit strained at these words, "but he was good enough to send one of his helpers down to see you—yes," she added dramatically, beaming at a small child who seemed to be actually quivering with anticipation at the front of the crowd, "it's *one of Santa's reindeer!*"

There was considerable oohing and aahing at this news, followed by a burst of applause when a reindeer—or, to be clear, a human in a felt reindeer suit—emerged from behind the Christmas tree. The quivering child seemed to actually be blinking back tears, though Charlotte was unclear on whether this was a positive reaction.

"Do you think they're hiding anyone else behind that tree?" asked a guy standing in front of Charlotte to the man whose hand he was holding, who himself was wearing a pair of extremely bright green trousers.

"Maybe Pip from *Christmas, Truly*," Green Trousers Man muttered back, causing his boyfriend to clap a hand over his mouth to stop a laugh.

This, obviously, was Charlotte's cue to make herself extremely scarce, lest anyone else have that godforsaken movie on the brain and happen to notice something familiar about her. She turned to Ava. "I'm going to poke around upstairs," she murmured in her sister's ear, and Ava nodded distractedly, her attention still focused on the events at the front of the room. Charlotte was experiencing extreme secondhand embarrassment on the part of everyone involved, so it was a relief to slip out of the crowd and slowly climb the stairs. She half expected the next floor to be blocked off, but it wasn't; some of the rooms had signs on the closed doors marking them as private, but there were several with open doors that she wandered through; these were all decorated in period style—wallpaper, lavish rugs, worn-but-elegant furniture—and featured a number of pieces of Christian Calloway's art in frames on the wall, including plenty of sketches and unfinished works that Charlotte had never seen before. She occupied herself reading the informational placards in each room that explained how the house had been used during Calloway's lifetime; he'd apparently inherited the house from his father, as he'd been born into family money, but had undertaken extensive renovations following the success of his home furnishings company in the late nineteenth century.

She was so caught up in her self-guided tour that she wasn't sure how much time had passed when she realized that she was not alone. She stepped back, having been immersed in a lengthy placard about the contents of Calloway's library, to find a woman a bit older than her with curly blonde hair and glasses watching her with an avid expression.

"Holy fuck," she muttered under her breath, and then immediately clapped a hand over her mouth. "Sorry! Sorry! That's 50p to the swear jar!"

Charlotte blinked. "The . . . swear jar?"

The woman nodded fervently. "My husband told me I swear too much—I'm a pediatric nurse, and I keep swearing in front of the kids—and I'm trying to work on it, so I'm charging myself 50p each time I swear."

"Well," Charlotte said warily, "I'm sure an occasional slip of the tongue—"

"But holy *shit*. You're *her*."

Oh, dear god. "I don't know what you mean," she said, plastering a polite smile on her face (not a thing she excelled at, generally) and slowly inching away from the woman.

"You're Charlie Rose Lane. From *Christmas, Truly*!"

"I don't think—"

"No, I saw you downstairs and thought I recognized you from your Instagram, and I was right!" the woman said triumphantly, and Charlotte sighed. She'd been meaning to replace her profile picture with a sketch she'd done of herself instead, and this was clear proof that this step was overdue. The woman's expression darkened. "And I read that *article* about you, you know. Did you really ruin the entire reboot?"

"I don't act anymore," Charlotte said diplomatically. "*Christmas, Truly* was a sort of . . . one-off for me."

"You could have made it a two-off," the woman said dejectedly; she seemed to be lapsing into sadness rather than anger, which made Charlotte possibly even more uncomfortable. She didn't handle feelings well—hers or anyone else's. The woman's expression brightened after a moment. "But wait a second—what are you doing here? Revisiting it for old times' sake? Any chance we can change your mind?" She moved toward Charlotte eagerly, and Charlotte continued to resolutely inch backward, praying that she didn't accidentally topple a priceless vase in the process.

"I don't think so," she said, smiling as politely as she could manage under the circumstances. "I need to go find my family, though, so it's been nice—"

"Oi! What are you doing here?!" Ordinarily, this interruption would have been alarming, but at the moment, to Charlotte's desperate ears, it sounded like a chorus of angels. She whirled around to see one of the trumpeters eyeing them suspiciously.

"Just leaving, actually," she said breezily, flashing him a winning smile; he looked to be about seventy, and appeared momentarily dazzled, which was why she deployed her brightest smile only on carefully selected occasions. Charlie Rose Lane had smiled a *lot*, and Charlotte had lost her taste for it.

"They told us no one was supposed to come up here except staff while the event was on," the trumpeter continued, recovering enough from her smile to look suspicious.

"Well," Charlotte said, a bit shortly, "perhaps they should have put up a *sign* or roped it off or something, rather than just assuming that I would miraculously divine that I wasn't supposed to be here."

The trumpeter frowned. The foulmouthed blonde woman frowned.

"I don't think Tallulah would have ever said anything like that," she said reproachfully.

"Because Tallulah wasn't real," Charlotte said curtly, and then turned and made her exit, ignoring the muffled profanity and unimpressed tutting behind her.

Once she made it downstairs, she paused to take a breath before plunging back into the madness; the crowds appeared to have split into various groups, with a lengthy, very noisy queue heavily dominated by young families stretching along the wall away from the fireplace, waiting to take photos with the costumed character of their choosing. Charlotte squinted and saw that Ava and Kit were standing in this line, Alice strapped to Ava's chest and scowling heavily at everyone around her. The brass band seemed to be preparing to launch into another set, and there were a number of people lined up for mince pies and mulled wine. John and Simone were nowhere in sight, but Charlotte gathered from the snippets of conversation she overheard that there were different activities in some of the rooms branching off from the main hall, and she assumed that was where they'd vanished to.

She hovered uneasily at the base of the staircase, finding the idea of plunging back into the crowds before her extremely unappealing; she also felt strangely visible after her encounter with the woman upstairs, though she knew that the internet was a strange, fragmented place, and that the viral article that had caused so much recent havoc in her life had probably gone entirely unnoticed by the vast majority of the population.

However, knowing that on a logical, academic level and making her body believe it were two different things entirely, and she thought she'd feel more at ease if she could just squirrel herself away in a corner until it was time to go home. She wound her way through the throngs of people, many of whom were looking distinctly rosy-cheeked (presumably from the mulled wine; it wasn't actually that cold outside), aside from the parents of young children, who looked distinctly harried (as so often seemed to be the case).

She turned, scanning the room in search of somewhere a bit more private, before realizing that there was an alcove hidden away, almost out of sight, beneath the staircase she'd just descended. She darted across the room, and a quick glimpse within showed that it contained nothing except a single bench; a hallway led in one direction and vanished around a corner, and Charlotte presumed this had been designed as some sort of shortcut to be used by servants in the house's earlier years. She sank down onto the bench gratefully.

Glancing through the doorway she'd just passed through, she realized that this angle afforded her a good view of the room beyond, and particularly the Christmas tree. Without fully realizing what she was doing, she reached into her bag for the sketchbook and pouch of drawing pencils she always carried with her, just in case.

Her eyes fixed on the Christmas tree, Charlotte began to sketch. She drew quickly, in broad, loose strokes; she could feel her shoulders relaxing as she did so, and she slipped into the almost trancelike state that always seemed to descend upon her the second she put a pencil to paper. She wasn't thinking about the weeks of forced Christmas cheer that awaited her; she wasn't thinking about the fact that her parents hadn't even thought to tell her that they had (once again) reconciled; she wasn't thinking about the hordes of angry DMs that glared at her from her inbox every time she opened Instagram. She thought about nothing except the scrape of her pencil against paper, the weight of it in her hand, and the vision slowly forming on the page in front of her. She was so immersed that it took several seconds for the chanting to creep into her consciousness; by the time she registered what was happening, they were down to ". . . four, three, two, one!" and then, instantly, the tree she was staring at was ablaze with light.

And it was . . .

It was just a *Christmas tree*, for god's sake, she thought irritably, listening to first the dramatic, collective indrawn breath, then the chorus of "oooooh," and then the thunderous round of applause. You would think that none of these people had ever seen a Christmas tree before. It was one thing for the children, who hadn't yet been jaded by too many years of bad Christmas movies and alarming January credit card bills. But for fully grown adults to stand there gaping at a fir tree bedecked with string lights, orange slices, and some admittedly lovely, vintage-looking glass ornaments—well, it was honestly ridiculous.

And yet, here she was, sketching it. And in spite of herself, she was already picturing how it would look in watercolors, with the white lights shining like stars against the darker green paint of the fir needles. The dark blue of the wallpaper would be a perfect backdrop; indeed, the moody hues of the room overall gave the tree and its surroundings a sort of classic, secular wintry vibe, one that she appreciated considerably more than multicolored lights and ornaments featuring Baby's First Handprint. (Better, however, than the ones her mom had had made, featuring Ava's and Charlotte's first teeth!)

She worked herself into enough of a huff that she very nearly poked a hole through the page in her sketchbook, when—quite suddenly—there was a man standing in front of her. And he had the audacity to look *irritated*, of all things.

He was also, she registered after a moment . . . part reindeer? He had a reindeer body with a human head?

"What the hell?" she wondered, not convinced she wasn't hallucinating, and also wondering if the mulled wine had been spiked with something stronger. And then, mercifully, her brain caught up to her eyes, and she realized he was the person inside the reindeer costume she'd seen earlier—he'd just removed the headpiece, which he was currently carrying under his arm, like some sort of weird hunting trophy.

"What the hell?" he echoed, sounding extremely English and vaguely annoyed.

"Can I help you?" she asked, a bit coolly.

The man raised an eyebrow at her. "Good afternoon to you too." The combination of an English accent, a deep voice, and the vaguely old-fashioned greeting made her fairly certain that, were Padma here in her place, she would actually combust on the spot.

Not to mention, Charlotte noted entirely unwillingly, the fact that he was dark-haired and wearing horn-rimmed glasses. (Charlotte had an extremely unfortunate weakness for bespectacled men.) And now, suddenly, he appeared to be . . . stripping?

"Um, hello?" She dropped her pencil and waved a hand. "I'm sitting here? Maybe find a bathroom?"

"I promise there will be no inappropriate nudity that might offend your delicate eyes," he said shortly, which did nothing to convince Charlotte that he *wasn't* a time traveler from the nineteenth century.

"Is there not anywhere else you can do this?" she asked. "I'm trying to hide."

He laughed under his breath as he wriggled out of his reindeer suit; it was basically impossible to look dignified while doing this, but he somehow managed it, particularly once it was revealed that he was wearing an oxford shirt and plaid trousers underneath.

"I *wish* that I could hide right now," he muttered, not entirely to her, and it was her turn to raise a brow.

"Did someone force you into that reindeer suit at gunpoint?" she asked. "Is this a hostage situation?"

"Pretty much," he confirmed, doing his best to fold the reindeer suit neatly, though it was definitely not a garment that lent itself to retail-quality folding. He set it down next to Charlotte on the bench and then, disturbingly, rested the head atop it. He stepped back and looked at Charlotte somewhat expectantly.

"Can I help you with something?" she asked, glancing down at her half-finished sketch longingly.

"I wonder if I should be asking you that question," he said slowly, something like amusement hinted at in the corners of his mouth. This, naturally, did not endear him to her. "You seem a bit . . . distressed."

"I'm not *distressed*," she objected, then paused to consider. "Actually, if I decided to channel a BBC drama and tell you that I *was* distressed, would you leave me alone?"

"Have we met before?"

"That seems highly unlikely."

"It's just that usually I make a decent enough first impression that people wait until our second meeting before being this annoyed by me." He adopted a wounded look. "Are you biased against reindeer?"

"You caught me," she said, deadpan. "I took one of those implicit bias tests, and my reindeer prejudice was off the charts." She sighed. "Sorry. I was avoiding the crowds, and you crashed my hiding spot."

"*Your* hiding spot," he repeated, his mouth doing that maybe-amused curving at the corners again, though she didn't understand *why* at the moment.

"I was here first. I think that makes it mine."

"Does it?" He was glancing back over his shoulder, distracted, as he spoke; the brass band, which had struck up another rousing round of Christmas carols upon the lighting of the tree, seemed to at last be winding down, and she wondered vaguely how much time had passed since she'd secreted herself into this nook—she tended to lose track of time when she was working. "I was looking for somewhere to catch my breath for a few minutes, but since you're already here, I suppose I'll go elsewhere."

"Don't bother," she said with a sigh, standing up and sliding her sketchbook into her bag. The clamor of voices beyond the room began to be the sort that signaled the end of an event. "I need to go find my family—somehow," she added wryly, watching a large crowd cluster at the door, trying to exit. She pulled her phone from her dress pocket, thinking it might be easier to text Ava to find out where she was at the moment, but her hideout-crasher waved a dismissive hand.

"Don't bother. Mobile signal is abysmal in the house. Old buildings, you know?"

"I'm from America, where our idea of 'old' is about thirty years ago, so no, I don't know. Doesn't the family still live here? How do they get by without cell signal?"

"A landline, and very good Wi-Fi."

"Have you met them?" she asked curiously, wondering what it

would be like to live in a historic house that had been passed through the same family for generations.

He nodded. "I grew up around here."

"Don't tell me," she said, pressing her finger to her chin in thought. "You were the alleged son of the vicar, but in actuality the natural son of the gentleman of the house—he paid for you to go to Oxford so that you might make something of yourself, even though he couldn't acknowledge you as his own."

"I didn't go to Oxford."

"But the rest is true?"

"Er. No. Do you read a lot of novels?"

"No," Charlotte said frankly; she listened to a lot of nonfiction audiobooks when she was working, but read novels far more sparingly. "But my best friend does. She has raised my expectations for what sort of characters I might run into in an English stately home."

"Fascinating," he murmured, extracting his own phone from his pocket. Before Charlotte could ask precisely how well he knew the family—well enough to have been entrusted with the Wi-Fi password, clearly, as he was tapping away with a furrowed brow—he glanced up at her, his brown eyes clearing at the sight of her. "Sorry, that was rude," he said, "but I unfortunately need to go find someone."

"I'm leaving anyway," she repeated, rather than think about any of this too hard. She gave a shallow, extremely wobbly curtsey. "Good evening, my lord."

And then, feeling quite pleased with herself, she swept past him.

Once she emerged from her nook, however, a quick scan of the room didn't reveal her family anywhere in sight. She weaved through the gradually dispersing crowd, searching for them, but they were nowhere to be found, and after a few minutes she found herself standing in the same spot again, puzzled, as the last trickle of visitors made their way out the front door. Maybe they were waiting for her at the car? She glanced down at her phone but saw that the handsome reindeer man had been correct: she had no signal. She slipped on her coat and made for the enormous oak front door, neatly sidestepping Cindy-Lou Who, who was carrying an enormous bucket full of dirty dishes.

Surely they'd be waiting for her at the car. Because it wasn't like her entire family would abandon her at a manor house in the English countryside . . . right?

CHAPTER THREE

This was, Charlotte decided fifteen minutes later, the most absurd thing that had happened in a day that had already involved being accosted by a *Christmas, Truly* fan *and* witnessing a man stripping out of a reindeer suit in front of her.

"...certain they didn't *really* leave you," the erstwhile Mrs. Cratchit was saying, after having rattled off the Wi-Fi password to Charlotte, who had returned to the house after confirming that both Ava and Kit's car *and* the one belonging to the Adeoyes were nowhere in sight; she'd gone on one last desperate loop around the ground floor of the house before conceding that she'd been abandoned. Now able to communicate with the outside world again, she pulled up WhatsApp and called her sister.

Ava answered on the second ring. "Hi, Charlotte. What's up?"

Charlotte inhaled slowly. "Is that all you have to say to me right now?"

"Um," Ava said slowly, sounding wary. "Yes? Is there something else I should be saying?"

"Did you forget something before leaving?" Charlotte asked, barely keeping a leash on her temper.

A lengthy pause. "I have Alice's diaper bag—"

"Ava!" Charlotte snapped. "Why am I still standing at Eden Priory while the rest of you are nowhere in sight?"

There was a muffled curse, then a slight pause. Ava's voice came back now, a bit tinny, and Charlotte was fairly certain she'd been put on speaker. "Oh no, my text never went through. Simone and I were going to change Alice's diaper and find you and head out, but Alice had a complete meltdown, so I texted Kit asking if he could find you instead and you could ride home with him—"

"And the text didn't send, because the cell service at this house is absolute shit," Charlotte said with a sigh. Just as the handsome, bespectacled reindeer man had said.

"Let me call Kit now, and he and John can turn around and come get you—"

"Or I can just get a cab to the station and catch the next train back to London," Charlotte said, not relishing the prospect. Hampshire wasn't that far, but she doubted there was a direct train from a village this small, and it was dark and growing cold and she was tired. A flicker at the corner of her eye caught her attention. The costumed brunette was waving her hand to catch Charlotte's attention.

"Hold on a sec, Ava," Charlotte said into the phone, and then lowered it.

"Sorry to interrupt," the brunette said, in the sort of refined, BBC English accent that most Americans thought all inhabitants of the British Isles possessed. "I couldn't help overhearing—you don't need a lift back to London by any chance, do you? My brother and I are headed in that direction in just a bit, and we could take you."

"I do," Charlotte said, not particularly relishing a drive back to the city in the company of complete strangers, but practical enough to realize it was a tidy solution. The harried brunette didn't seem like a serial killer—though the best serial killers probably didn't seem like serial killers, either, she reflected. "It might be out of your way, though," she hedged, wondering if she should take Ava up on her offer to call Kit instead. "I'm heading to Chiswick."

The brunette waved a hand. "Graham's in Chiswick, too, so it's no trouble! I'm sure he'd be more than happy to help—Graham! *Graham!*"

She waved her hand wildly in the direction of someone past Charlotte's shoulder, and she turned slowly, only to be faced with the handsome, bespectacled reindeer man. Who was the harried brunette's brother. And neither of them seemed to be costumed performers, hired for the night; rather, they knew the Wi-Fi password, spoke with some authority about the house—the harried brunette was even now murmuring instructions to the mulled-wine vendor. It was almost as if . . .

Almost as if this was *their* event. And, therefore, their house.

And now Charlotte was even more certain that these people weren't serial killers—because, clearly, they were Calloways.

"Ava," Charlotte said slowly, "I think I've got it figured out—no need for anyone to come get me."

"Great!" Ava said, half-cheerful, half-distracted, and the line abruptly went dead.

"Hello," the former reindeer said warily, approaching them slowly. He had his phone in one hand again, and was frowning down at it.

"Graham!" the brunette said brightly, turning back to Charlotte. "This is—oh, I'm so sorry, I don't think I got your name."

"Charlotte."

"Charlotte," she repeated, eyeing her with a bit more interest, which made Charlotte uneasy. Surely this woman didn't recognize her, too? "I'm Eloise!" she introduced, before adding, "Eloise Calloway," as an afterthought, confirming Charlotte's suspicion.

"Calloway," she repeated. "Meaning that this house . . . belongs to you?"

Eloise laughed. "My parents, really, but yes." She paused, and something dark flickered across her face, but quickly vanished. "Anyway!" she continued. "Graham—we can give Charlotte a lift back to Chiswick, can't we? She's been left behind."

"Has she?" he asked his sister, but keeping his eyes locked on Charlotte. He raised a single eyebrow at her, looking some cross between smug and amused, and she frowned at him.

"You weren't kidding about the cell signal here," she informed him, and a dimple had the audacity to appear in one cheek as he suppressed a smile.

"Where's Mum?" Eloise asked her brother now, hopping out of the way when a man carrying a large tuba came barreling past.

"In the red drawing room. The roof's leaking," Graham said to his sister, the set of his mouth grim. "Again."

Eloise sighed. "Does she need any help?"

"I've set up the usual buckets," he said, with the weary air of someone who had lots of experience with the travails of owning a very old house. "I'll ring the roofers tomorrow." He rubbed at the bridge of his nose, slightly dislodging his glasses in the process. There was a red mark on his skin where they rested, almost as if he'd been pressing his hands to them at some point that day.

"All right," Eloise said, biting her lip. "Does she know we're leaving?"

"I'll let her know," he said, a bit shortly, and turned and began weaving his way through the dispersing musicians and mulled-wine sellers.

"We'll meet you at the car!" Eloise called brightly after his retreating back. "Come along, Charlotte!"

And Charlotte, feeling as though she'd just been taken captive by the world's most charming and determined kidnapper, felt that she had little option but to follow.

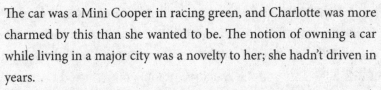

The car was a Mini Cooper in racing green, and Charlotte was more charmed by this than she wanted to be. The notion of owning a car while living in a major city was a novelty to her; she hadn't driven in years.

The car itself looked as though it had seen better days; there was a dent in one door, and it had the mud crawling up its tires and sides that was the hallmark of any vehicle that had driven down a country lane.

"This car," Eloise muttered, kicking it in an affectionate sort of way. "Do you know it already had the dent when he bought it used? He thinks it gives it character."

"Have you considered punching him in the nose to see if he thinks it gives his face character?" Charlotte asked, and Eloise cackled. Just then, there was the sound of rapidly approaching footsteps crunching on gravel; Graham was jogging toward them, a wool coat flung over one arm and a messenger bag over the opposite shoulder.

"Sorry," he said, slightly breathless. "I should have given you the keys."

"I was contemplating breaking a window," Eloise informed him. "It might have improved the looks of this car."

"For that, you can sit in the back seat," he said lightly. He turned to Charlotte and opened the passenger door. "After you."

Within ten minutes, they'd made their way down the winding gravel drive, up the narrow country lane that led to the house (Charlotte closing her eyes and hoping fervently, as she had on the journey down that afternoon, that they did not meet any oncoming traffic, because in no universe was this road wide enough for two cars), and onto the A road that would lead them north. Eloise had been largely responsible for maintaining the flow of conversation thus far, chattering away about her job doing educational outreach at Kew Gardens, their younger sister Lizzie, who was a fashion design student at Central Saint Martins, and the full program of Christmas festivities that would be on offer at Eden Priory that season. Charlotte had mostly directed her attention out the window, though it did her little good— it was fully dark, and she could see nothing other than dark lumps that she thought were hedges, and the occasional welcoming lights of farmhouses or far-off villages.

Eventually, however, Eloise fell silent, and then, belatedly seeming to think that she had been remiss in her hostess duties, she asked, "Charlotte, what do you do?"

"I'm an artist," Charlotte said absently, still staring out the window. Out of the corner of her eye, she saw Graham's head turn in her direction, lightning-fast, before turning back to the road ahead.

"Oh! What kind of art?" Eloise asked, sounding genuinely curious.

"Watercolors, mainly," Charlotte said, shifting in her seat. "I do some acrylics, too, depending on the project. I run a shop through my website where I sell prints—lots of florals and citrus fruits and patterns like that—and then I also accept commissions, and have done some brand collaborations—limited-edition stationery lines, that sort of thing. People often commission me to paint their vacation cottage, or childhood home, or something—they'll send me a photo to work off."

"And the occasional interior?" Graham asked casually, and Charlotte's head turned slowly toward his. In profile, his attention still fixed on the road, she could see the fine cut of his jaw—*not helpful, brain, thank you*—but also the amused curve of his mouth.

"Occasionally," she agreed.

"Am I missing something?" Eloise asked, leaning forward.

Graham's eyes flicked up to the rearview mirror to look at his sister. "We met earlier this evening—she was hiding in the nook behind the stairs."

"Ha! Graham's spot!" Eloise said, laughing gleefully. "Was he absolutely awful to you?" she asked Charlotte. "He's so possessive of that goddamn bench."

"No, he just started stripping."

"Graham, what the hell?" Eloise braced her arms on the back of his seat. "Do you want to get arrested?"

"My *reindeer* costume," he clarified.

"Well, you should be arrested for that, too," Eloise said darkly, leaning back against her seat. "You did not appreciate my creative vision."

"Were the costumes your idea?" Charlotte asked warily.

"They were!" Eloise said brightly, looking extremely pleased with herself. She dusted at the apron she was still wearing. "Graham's planned most of the events at the house lately, but I thought a Christmas lights switch-on is a bit *dull*, you know?"

Charlotte remained diplomatically silent, which was fine since Eloise didn't seem to actually be looking for a response.

"—so if the whole family channeled the spirit of beloved Christmas characters of the past, it would liven things up a bit! I wanted to write us an entire skit, but Graham said we should just let people take photos with us instead."

Charlotte turned to Graham inquiringly. "Do tell. Which specific reindeer were you? I assume you fully studied the character's background so that you could properly channel its spirit."

"Dasher," he said, not missing a beat, his eyes still on the road. "I like to run. Seems like the deer and I could relate to each other."

"Does Dasher refer to his running speed or his flying speed, though?" Charlotte asked thoughtfully.

"I promise you, I do not give a fuck."

"*This* is why you always ruin things," Eloise said, pouting. "You need to give more fucks, Graham. I wanted those people to believe that you *were* Dasher."

"Seems like a big ask from a bunch of felt," he said, but he flashed a grin at his sister in the rearview mirror, quick and fleeting.

"*Anyway*," Eloise said. "There was still no reason to strip out of your deer suit in front of a guest!"

"Don't worry, she made her feelings on the matter very clear to me," he said dryly, and Charlotte smiled smugly.

"I might have told him to go find a bathroom," Charlotte admitted, not feeling terribly repentant. "I was trying to sketch the Christmas tree and the fireplace, and wasn't thrilled when a guy showed up and randomly started removing a reindeer suit."

"Which is how you know that she draws interiors, too," Eloise said to her brother. She punched him in the shoulder.

"Have you lost your mind?" Graham inquired mildly. "Last I checked, physically assaulting the person driving the vehicle you're riding in was a bad idea." Despite his complaint, his hands hadn't budged from their spot on the steering wheel, and the Mini Cooper remained firmly in its lane.

"Sorry, sorry," Eloise said, making a show of remorse. "It's a famous Christmas tree and fireplace, you know!"

Charlotte stilled. "Is it?" she asked coolly.

"It was in that Christmas film," Eloise said cheerfully, apparently not noticing anything strange about Charlotte's tone. "*Christmas, Truly*—have you seen it? I'm sure you have."

"I'm not a big Christmas movie fan," Charlotte said carefully, which was both truthful and not really an answer to Eloise's question. "Not a big Christmas fan, period."

"Ha! You wouldn't last long around Eden Priory!" Eloise said, laughing as she took her phone out of her apron pocket. "We get loads of visitors because of the film—we're going to host a screening of it on Christmas Eve. 'Watch *Christmas, Truly* in the room where it was filmed'—that sort of thing. And Graham's decided that capitalizing on Christmas in general is how we're going to make enough money to get a new roof and not have to live like tragic Dickens characters surrounded by buckets and eating porridge."

"At least you'll already have an outfit ready, if it comes to that," Charlotte pointed out innocently, and next to her, Graham laughed quietly under his breath.

"You know," Eloise said, sounding thoughtful now as she tapped away at her phone, "if you're open to commissions, Charlotte, that might actually be a brilliant idea—a print we could sell in the gift shop, showing that scene from the film."

Charlotte's unease grew. "I don't know—"

"I'm sure you're busy," Eloise said, still texting away on her phone, only half paying attention; next to Charlotte, however, she could somehow sense that Graham was listening carefully. "That isn't a bad idea, though—Graham, maybe we should look into having someone else do it? If we can find an artist who's local? Maybe we'd expand it to other Christmas films, too—not just *Christmas, Truly*."

"Maybe," he agreed neutrally, his eyes still on the road, and Charlotte snuck a glance at him.

"Has your house ever been used to film anything else?" she asked curiously. "It's got great vibes—that turret alone . . ."

"No," Graham said—not curt exactly, but not in a tone that invited any future questions. "Just the one."

"It's a shame, too," Eloise said blithely, "since god knows we could use a nice fat check right about now—"

"We have a plan," Graham said, his tone firm. "We don't need a film crew overrunning the house—we've plenty of Christmas activities planned to keep us busy."

"Mmm," Eloise said, with a slight twist of her mouth, which Charlotte didn't think was quite meant to express her agreement. "Well," she said, more briskly, "Charlotte, now that you've visited the house, you should watch *Christmas, Truly* sometime—just to catch a glimpse of the spot you were drawing!"

"I'll . . . consider it," Charlotte said diplomatically.

"Liar," Graham muttered under his breath, quiet enough that Eloise, in the back seat, couldn't hear, and Charlotte flipped him off without missing a beat.

And tried not to notice how much she liked it when, once again, he let out that low, dark laugh.

*

By the time she was deposited at the flat, fussed over tearfully by Ava, apologized profusely to by Kit, subjected to a lengthy lecture by Simone on the tragedy of modern society's overreliance on technology in order to communicate, and fed exceedingly large quantities of soup by John, Charlotte was ready for nothing more than a glass of wine and a long bath. Both of these things were arranged, although the relaxing, wine-fueled soak was somewhat less zen of an experience than she'd anticipated, interrupted as it was by what she genuinely, momentarily thought was the sound of someone being murdered. (It was actually just Alice staging a protest about being put to bed.)

She eventually crawled out of the tub, happily pruny and a bit lightheaded from the hot water, put on her favorite pin-striped pajama set, and retreated to bed with a hot water bottle, a thick nonfiction book she'd stolen from Kit's bookshelf, and a vague plan for the work she planned to get done that week, and how she might use it as an excuse to avoid any further planned holiday outings, considering how this one had gone.

She hadn't checked Instagram all day, and she reached for her phone on the nightstand, opening the app and publishing one of her draft posts—this one a carefully staged photo that her assistant had taken of a framed set of her prints decorating a wall to the left of a tabletop Christmas tree, with a reminder about deadlines for holiday shipping. A quick scroll through her DMs confirmed that, while the hysterical *Christmas, Truly* messages were still rolling in—a number of them from burner accounts that seemed to have been created solely for this purpose, which was honestly insane—they were at least starting to decrease slightly in number. Her last thought as she fired off a few quick replies to messages of the non–*Christmas, Truly* variety, set her phone aside, and reached for her book was that, if this trend continued, then before too long things would die down entirely, and she wouldn't have to think about *Christmas, Truly* at all.

CHAPTER FOUR

It took less than forty-eight hours for Charlotte to be proven wrong.

It was Monday morning, and she'd escaped from the flat to a coffee shop down the street, where she was attempting to make sense of her inbox—which she'd been ignoring with increasing guilt since her arrival the week before—and create some sort of work schedule for herself for the week, to ensure she didn't fall behind on any of the remaining commissions on her calendar for the month. This time of year was busy; her online shop made five times as much in December as it did in January, and while she'd drastically scaled back the number of commissions she offered in the past year or so, given the increasingly lucrative business she was doing with various brands, she still liked to accept a limited number each month, usually booked months in advance. It was a lot to keep track of—hence the inbox hell she currently found herself in—but, fortunately, two years earlier she'd finally accepted the inevitable and hired an assistant to help with customer emails, maintenance of her website, and general admin, which was an absolute godsend.

She opened her inbox that morning to find an email awaiting her from the creative director of Perfect Paper, a luxury wallpaper company, which had reached out several weeks earlier, interested in a potential collaboration. Charlotte had sent over some sample sketches, but hadn't yet heard anything back; now, however, there was an email sitting there, inviting her to a meeting with the team in New York the first week after New Year's, at which they could discuss Charlotte's vision for the line and she could present more detailed samples. Her heart pounding, she replied, looping in her assistant, Sarah, to work out the details, and then clicked out of her inbox, reaching for her phone to text Padma.

> **Charlotte:** Got invited to meet with perfect paper after new year's
>
> **Padma:** !!!
>
> **Padma:** Omg. Definitely telling Andrew we have to hold off on redoing our bathroom, then, so that we can use MY BEST FRIEND'S WALLPAPER LINE to decorate it!
>
> **Charlotte:** Nothing confirmed yet!
>
> **Padma:** Crossing all my fingers!! And toes!!!

Charlotte set down her phone, smiling. Padma had gotten married that spring, and she and her new husband (a fellow lawyer; thoughts and prayers to their hypothetical future children) had bought a house in the suburbs that they were in the process of renovating. They were still an easy train ride from the city, but Charlotte had undeniably seen them less, these past few months, and she liked the thought of a pattern of hers on their walls, a reminder of her place in their lives. Not that she'd ever voice that thought aloud, of course—she never, ever wanted to seem like she needed attention, extra care. She'd spent her childhood trying to ignore the drama of the family that surrounded her, and maintained her status as the most low-maintenance friend to everyone she knew. No temperamental, needy artist type *here*. If her life felt a bit smaller and quieter, now that her very closest friend lived in New Jersey and spent a lot of time discussing the struggle to find a reliable plumber, this was nothing she'd ever mention to anyone. Shaking her head at this thought, she returned her attention to her inbox, opening her planner to the page for a new week, uncapping her pen, and beginning a to-do list.

A couple of hours later, she shut her laptop, her eyes beginning to cross, and tugged her now-cold coffee toward her, draining the dregs of it and contemplating ordering another. She glanced over her shoulder, registered the queue at the counter, and instead opened her sketchbook to pass a few minutes while she waited for the line to shrink. She glanced out the window and began a rough sketch of the scene before her: a row of terraced houses, most featuring winter greenery wrapped around the wrought-iron railings on their front steps, each door sporting an enormous wreath. Charlotte had never had an exterior-facing door, thanks to an entire adult life spent in various apartments in Manhattan and Brooklyn, but having caught a glimpse of the prices of the wreaths on offer at the Christmas tree vendor at the end of Ava's street, she decided that if she ever *did* possess an exterior door, she would not be spending a week's grocery money on a circle of shrubbery.

These cheerful thoughts distracted her enough that she didn't notice that she was no longer alone until she heard the faint thunk of a ceramic mug set down on the counter, and she turned, startled, to see Graham Calloway settling onto the stool next to her.

"Hello?" she said. The *what are you doing here?* was, she thought, clearly implied.

"Good morning," he said, then nodded at the mug he'd set down before her. "That's for you."

She lifted it and sniffed suspiciously.

"I didn't poison it," he added.

"Ha," she said darkly, taking another sniff. It seemed to be plain black coffee—in other words, exactly what she would have ordered for herself. "How did you know what to order?"

"I've been watching you for the past three hours," he said matter-of-factly.

"I'm calling the police. It's nine-nine-nine over here, isn't it?"

"I asked the man at the till what you'd ordered," he said, lifting his own cup to his lips. She could see from the tea bag dangling from the small teapot he'd set down before him that it was peppermint tea. This seemed irritatingly virtuous compared to her own possibly problematic caffeine habits.

"I've been told never to accept drinks from strange men," she said primly, unable to resist taking a sip anyway. It had been a particularly early morning, after Alice awoke the entire flat at four and then refused to go to sleep again.

"You were probably told not to get into cars with them, either," he said, raising that eyebrow at her again. She was pretty sure that he found himself very charming, and she was therefore determined not to.

"You don't have any brothers, do you?" she asked.

His brow furrowed slightly. "Er, no."

"I figured," she said triumphantly. "You're pleased with yourself the way only a straight man raised in a household full of women could be."

"Thank you."

"Wasn't a compliment."

"Are you certain?"

She looked at him stonily. "Very."

He sighed, then rubbed at the back of his head in a way that left his dark hair slightly rumpled. He was dressed casually in jeans and a cashmere sweater, a wool coat carefully hanging from the back of his stool. She wondered what he did for a living—everything about his clothing screamed money, despite what he and his sister had mentioned about the family finances on Saturday.

"I didn't actually seek you out merely to buy you a coffee and irritate you," he said, taking another sip of tea and then setting down his cup.

It was her turn to raise a brow. "Oh?"

"No. I wanted to speak to you because I've been thinking about Eloise's idea of commissioning artwork for the shop at Eden Priory after she mentioned it in the car the other night."

Charlotte frowned. "I don't—"

He raised a hand. "Let me make my proposal, all right?"

Charlotte was not generally a fan of men interrupting her, but she bit back her impatience and instead nodded, taking a sip of coffee. "Okay."

"I looked up your website yesterday," he said matter-of-factly. "I thought it was extremely impressive."

Charlotte knew this already—she didn't tend to suffer from impostor syndrome—but said, "Thank you."

"I understand that you have plenty of work to occupy you, but I was curious how many customers you have in the UK, given that you ship from America."

"I have some," she said carefully. "The shipping is expensive, but especially if you're ordering more than one print, it's not prohibitive, I don't think."

"But I'm guessing most of your customers are still based in America?"

She nodded. She had stats on it, and tended to devote a day every six months or so to looking at all the data on where her business was coming from geographically, as well as the portion that found her from Instagram compared to web searches.

"I'm wondering if you'd be interested in having your work stocked in our shop at Eden Priory. It's not much to speak of at the moment, but I'm trying to get in a new line of products—works from local artisans, honey from a chap in the village who has his own hives, that sort of thing—*and* to focus the shop a bit more specifically on art, given my great-great-grandfather's career. I don't know what your rates are for wholesale, and we could work out all the details later, but if you'd be willing to do us a series of prints on a holiday film theme, then in return I'll stock your other art year-round."

Charlotte's mind raced; her prints were sold in some brick-and-mortar shops in New York, Boston, and a handful of touristy towns elsewhere in the Northeast. Graham's proposal, however, would open her art up to a new consumer market—because while she *did* have British customers, she knew that the cost of international shipping definitely limited the number of them. But if her artwork was sold in a gift shop, year-round, at a famous house once owned by a famous artist, full of art-loving visitors passing though looking for something to take home with them from their visit . . .

It was a really tempting offer. Except . . .

"How many of these Christmas prints do you want?" she asked, resisting the urge to grimace on the word "Christmas." It wouldn't be the first time she'd done a holiday-themed commission, of course, but the *Christmas, Truly* connection made her even less enthusiastic about the idea than usual.

"Five," he said. "I've written up a list—well, Eloise has," he amended with a wry twist to his mouth, and reached into his back pocket for his phone, pulling up his notes app. He passed it to her.

"I don't think I've seen any of these movies," she said, scanning the list with a frown. Except *Christmas, Truly*, of course—but the less said about that, the better.

"I, unfortunately, have seen most of them," he said, a bit wearily. "Sisters," he added darkly, seeing her raised eyebrows. "I can't believe you haven't seen any."

"I wasn't kidding about hating Christmas," she said, equally darkly, and his mouth curved up a bit. "Are all of these in London?" she asked; she recognized the neighborhoods listed for a couple of them, but the others were unfamiliar.

"No, a couple of them are in villages—none too far, but it would probably be easiest to drive." He paused, clearly weighing his words, and then added, "I could take you—if you wanted."

She glanced up from studying the list on his phone. "Don't you have to work? I'd probably want to go on weekdays, just to avoid crowds."

Another, briefer pause. "Not at the moment. Eden Priory's my sole focus right now, so I'm already driving to and from Hampshire a few days a week—I don't mind adding another few outings into the mix. I'd like to take a look at them, anyway—see if they've done anything to capitalize on their film connections in a way that we could replicate."

She was curious about the circumstances that led to this mysterious abundance of free time, but since it was none of her business, she instead asked, "How soon would you need these? I have some deadlines while I'm here."

He looked unconcerned. "There's not enough time to stock them in the shop for this Christmas, so I'm looking ahead to next year—if you did the art while you were in the country this holiday season, that would give us plenty of time to get them printed and advertise it in advance of next Christmas."

"*If* I agree," Charlotte reminded him, feeling a bit contrary, and he leaned back on his stool, crossing his arms over his chest as he studied her.

"Is there something I could tell you that would convince you?" he asked bluntly. "Or we can start haggling over the money, if that's what will do the trick?"

At that moment, the door to the coffee shop burst open, and Ava and

Simone materialized, bundled up in coats and clutching baby Alice, who was wearing some sort of hooded onesie that made her look even more like a marshmallow than usual. "There you are!" Ava said brightly, and then her gaze slid to Graham, and her smile widened. "Well, *hello*."

"Dear god," Charlotte muttered. "Graham, this is my sister, Ava, and my niece, Alice, and Ava's mother-in-law, Simone. This is Graham—the one who gave me a ride home the other evening."

"We've met," Ava said, beaming. "He stopped by the flat to see you, and I told him where you were."

Charlotte hadn't even paused to wonder how Graham had found her at this specific coffee shop. She frowned at her sister. "Should you be giving out my whereabouts to strange men?"

Ava's eyes widened innocently. "He seemed *so* trustworthy," she said, passing her chubby offspring off to Simone without a second glance so that she could dedicate her full attention to Charlotte and Graham. "Besides, we know where he lives. If you went missing, I'd make Kit drive us to Hampshire and batter down the door until you were handed back to us unharmed."

"I don't think that would have been much use if I'd already been murdered and left in a ditch," Charlotte said severely.

"Charlotte, I don't think such a handsome man would possibly murder you," Simone said, batting her eyelashes at Graham, who smiled back at her.

"Have you heard of Ted Bundy, Simone?" Charlotte asked, crossing her arms. "I think we might need to study serial killers, just so you don't find yourself stuffed in someone's trunk."

"I feel I should note that I've no intention of murdering anyone, and my car boot isn't big enough for a body," Graham said calmly, taking another sip of his virtuous tea.

"Of course you aren't a murderer," Ava said with a dismissive wave of the hand. "Your family's house is so nice!"

"I appreciate the vote of confidence, but I do think your reasoning is a bit flawed," Graham said dryly. "Have you studied much English history?"

"It was never my strongest subject," Ava said, offering him a down-right flirtatious smile. Alice gave a squawk in Simone's arms, recalling Ava to the fact that she was not alone, but in fact married; in the company of her child and mother-in-law; and on a mission. "You'll forgive us for stealing Charlotte away, won't you? We're going ice skating and then to tea at Fortnum's."

"Of course," Graham said gravely, as though Ava had just informed him that they were headed to a state funeral. He glanced at Charlotte, his eyes alight with unholy glee, and mouthed, *Tea at Fortnum's?*

Charlotte stared grimly back.

"I've never been at Christmas before!" Ava said brightly. "I've heard the crowds are awful, but I want to see their window displays."

Charlotte contemplated drowning herself in the dregs of her coffee.

"Ready?" Ava asked, and Charlotte nodded like someone about to head to the gallows, took one last sip of her coffee, and—envisioning the lineup of other Christmas horrors that awaited her in the next few weeks, and weighing how desperately she wanted to escape them—tore the corner of a page out of her sketchbook and scribbled her number on it. This she handed to Graham.

"I need to finish up another commission I'm almost done with tomorrow," she told him, "but I'd be free to get started on this on Wednesday, if you were able to take me to one of the villages that day."

He glanced down at the number scribbled on the paper. "So that's a 'yes'?"

Charlotte glanced over her shoulder at Ava and Simone, distracted by Alice. "If I go on an excursion with you, I'll have an excuse not to go to the Christmas market in Hyde Park with Ava and her in-laws that day."

He pocketed the slip of paper, and leaned toward her, speaking in an undertone that only she could hear. "I feel as though I'm being used."

"That's because you are," she told him briskly, then shoved her sketchbook into her shoulder bag, pulled on her coat, and Ava swept her from the coffee shop and into an afternoon of Christmas hell.

She didn't allow herself to look back.

FOUR WEEKS
TO CHRISTMAS

CHAPTER FIVE

So, let me get this straight," Ava said on Wednesday morning, wearing a bathrobe and a sheet mask, sipping a cup of herbal tea. "You're going to Berkshire to draw people in corsets?"

"No," Charlotte said patiently from her spot at the kitchen table, nursing an enormous mug of coffee and responding to Instagram DMs on her laptop. There were an annoying number of message requests from people tagging her in memes from the movie; if she never again had to see her nine-year-old self in a red beret, eyes filled with tears, clutching a rabbit, it would be too soon. "I'm going to Berkshire to draw a *house* that was once used for a movie featuring people in corsets."

"And you're doing this for Sexy Reasons?" Ava pressed.

Charlotte frowned at a message request from someone offering a poorly spelled accusation that she was part of an evil plot to destroy Christianity by ruining Christmas culture, and hit the delete button with some satisfaction. "No," she said, glancing up at her sister. "I'm doing this for business reasons—Graham is going to stock my art in his gift shop year-round if I do this print series he's commissioned, so I can build a customer base in the UK."

"But," Ava pressed, scrutinizing a bowl of oranges before carefully selecting one, "your business relationship will just happen to involve an extremely handsome Englishman who *wears glasses*?"

Charlotte took a sip of coffee to hide her grimace. "I regret ever telling you about my glasses weakness."

"I would have known anyway," Ava said, reaching for a knife. "There's no other reason you would have dated that douchey start-up bro for so long otherwise."

Charlotte blinked, lowering her mug. "Craig?" she asked, naming the ex-boyfriend of her early to midtwenties—and, not at all coincidentally, her last long-term relationship. "He didn't wear glasses."

Ava lowered her knife. "Yes, he did."

Charlotte bit back an impatient reply, and instead said simply, "I promise you, he didn't. I dated him for three years—I think I would have noticed."

Ava began slicing her orange into quarters. "Maybe I was thinking of *my* ex-boyfriend," she said thoughtfully.

Charlotte rolled her eyes. This was not the first time Ava had made such a mistake. "You *are* right that he was a douche, though."

Ava frowned. "But if he didn't wear glasses, what was your excuse for dating him?"

That was territory that Charlotte didn't feel like getting into this morning, or possibly ever. "No comment."

"At least *this* one has a nice accent *and* a nice house in addition to the glasses," Ava noted as she placed her oranges on a plate and waltzed out of the room.

Informing Ava that she had no lascivious intentions where Graham Calloway was concerned would be pointless, so Charlotte saved her energy; her sister was an extremely bizarre combination of self-absorbed and nosy, which meant that she tried to sniff out any potential intrigue while also getting only about half the details right.

Plus, the fact was that Graham *did* look like he'd been designed in a lab, specifically to appeal to Charlotte: tall, dark-haired, interesting accent. But she wasn't enough of an idiot to mess up a promising business relationship just because of a handsome man in glasses, so she'd limit herself to an occasional appreciative glance.

An hour later, she was in the passenger seat of said handsome man's Mini Cooper, en route to a small village some distance outside Windsor. Charlotte spent the last few minutes of the drive googling their destination: the house they were visiting had once belonged to a Regency-era aristocrat—a second son who had bought a country house for his young family that was close enough to London to allow him to return frequently to the theater he owned in town—but had been donated to the National Trust a few decades earlier by one of his descendants, and was now open to public tours.

"Okay," she said as they climbed out of the car in the car park. "What is this movie, exactly?"

"*A Very Byron Christmas*," he said, for at least the third time since they'd left Chiswick, because the mere title sent Charlotte off into a fit of uncontrollable laughter. "It's a loose retelling of *A Christmas Carol* in which our hero—a selfish young Victorian duke—is visited by the ghosts of famous figures in English history to help him see the error of his ways and woo his lady love on Christmas Eve."

"And Lord Byron is one of those ghosts?"

Graham nodded solemnly as they approached a hut where a smiling woman emerged to accept the twenty-pound note Graham handed her for their entrance fee. "Henry VIII too. Shakespeare. Jane Austen. You know, the usual suspects."

"Ah yes. I've always thought that Henry VIII seems like a calm, reasonable sort of man who would give good advice."

"The only thing I can say in this film's favor is that Lizzie claims the various period costumes are accurate."

"Yes, I appreciate it when my unhinged Dickens retellings strive for historical accuracy," Charlotte quipped. Truthfully, she was astonished she hadn't seen this movie before—this 100 percent sounded like something Padma would have made her watch.

"I think what the average viewer appreciated about it is the scene in which the duke realizes the error of his ways and runs around the manor in the middle of the night, shirtless, with glistening abs."

Charlotte nearly tripped over her own two feet at this revelation, and Graham reached out easily to steady her with a hand on her elbow, which he removed a moment later. "Why were his abs glistening?"

"Because he awoke from his ghostly visitations in a cold sweat," Graham said, with the pained tone of a man who had been forced to sit through this movie multiple times. "A cold sweat that seemed to concentrate on one specific, extremely toned part of his body."

"Historical dukes really hit the gym, huh?" Charlotte said, before adding, "That was rhetorical, obviously: I know they did. My best friend reads a lot of romance novels. I know all about the heroes' abs."

"Glad to hear it," Graham said dryly, but there was a hint of a smile curving at his mouth, even as he kept his eyes on the path before them.

After another moment, they rounded a corner to find the Gothic Revival house, featuring some fanciful architectural details including casement windows and a porte cochere, and an extensive garden that must have been gorgeous in the summer. There were, conveniently, several wooden benches scattered around, and Charlotte claimed one of these now, opening her bag to retrieve her pouch of pencils and her sketchbook. She had decided to do a couple of detailed sketches on-site and take extensive photographs she could reference later as she worked on the final piece.

Graham watched in silence as she flipped to a blank page in her sketchbook and carefully selected a pencil, then glanced back at the house before her.

"Is this angle all right?" she asked, and he stepped closer to her, close enough that she could smell the pine scent of his soap as the edge of his coat brushed against her arm. She sketched a quick thumbnail, just to nail the placement of the house, and he glanced down at her work, then looked ahead, squinting slightly in the weak November sunlight.

"I think that's fine—the house will be clearly identifiable to anyone who's seen the film." He stepped back, and there was a whisper of cold air where the warmth of his body had been a moment before. "I'm going to take a look around indoors while you work," he said, reaching into the messenger bag he had slung over one shoulder and extracting a leather-bound notebook and an honest-to-god fountain pen. "My sisters want to incorporate *Christmas, Truly* more into the programming and tours at Eden Priory, and I want to see how they've capitalized on the fame of *A Very Byron Christmas* here."

"Okay, I'll be here," Charlotte said, turning her attention to the blank page before her. A faint niggle of guilt was starting to work at her, owing to the fact that she hadn't told him yet who she was—or, rather, who she once had been. While she didn't tend to announce her brief childhood fame to people upon meeting them, the connection between the movie and Graham's family home was starting to make this omission feel a bit . . . dishonest.

He set off, and she returned her attention to her work; soon enough, her focus narrowed to the page before her, the sketch taking shape, and the thoughts, the guilt, the worry slipped away—as they always did when she was working, when she wondered how she could ever do anything but this. She had never once, for the entire duration of filming *Christmas, Truly*, felt that way in front of a camera, or when rehearsing lines, but for as long as she could remember, the moment a pencil or paintbrush was set in her hand, all her other worries had fled.

Her parents hadn't understood this, of course; even Ava, much as Charlotte loved her, had gotten the acting bug, and couldn't understand how a role in a successful film hadn't led her to want to do more, more, more. But Charlotte had known, deep down, even as a kid, that it wasn't right for her—and had spent the twenty years since proving to herself, and to her family, that *this* was.

She didn't know how much time had passed when she felt someone next to her on the bench, and she glanced up to see that Graham had returned.

"Hello," he said, glancing down at her sketchbook and then quickly away again, as if he'd caught sight of her in her underwear. She didn't know why she found this small bit of understanding that she might want to keep her art private so touching, but she did—especially considering that *he* was the one who was commissioning her to make it, and therefore had every right to look at it. "Almost done?"

"Yes, actually," she said, finishing up some shading of one of the gables on the roof and setting down her pencil. She reached for her phone. "I'll take some photos of the house to make sure I have enough to work with later, and then we can go." He nodded, and she rose from the bench to begin taking photos; at one point, she glanced over her shoulder to see that he was studying the house before him with a faint frown. She took one last photo, then turned back to him. "Did you find what you needed inside?"

He hesitated ever-so-slightly, fiddling with the cap of his pen; there was a small smudge of black ink on his middle finger, the hallmark of any fountain pen user. "It wasn't that helpful—since it's the National Trust that owns it now, they're more focused on the actual history of the house and its owners than on the film. There's a single sign in one of the bedrooms about it, but that's about it." He sighed, frustration writ in the faint lines at the corners of his eyes.

Charlotte walked back to the bench and slipped her phone into her bag, then began packing her pencils and sketchbook away. "Will lunch make you feel better?" she asked. "Because I'm hungry."

He glanced up at her, his expression clearing. "Always."

Ten minutes later, they were settled into the small café that had been built in the former stables on the property, bowls of soup before them.

"So," Charlotte said, breaking off the end of the slice of thick, brown bread that had come with her soup, "you're trying to convert your family home into some sort of shrine to a Christmas movie?" She avoided mentioning *Christmas, Truly* by name, for reasons that were probably weird and illogical, telling herself that if she didn't name it directly, it wouldn't seem strange if (when) he eventually found out her personal connection to the movie.

Across the table from her, Graham sighed, then ate a spoonful of soup before setting his spoon down with a clatter and saying, very bluntly, "No." Seeing Charlotte's confused look, he added, "My mum and sisters want to, though."

"But you don't?"

He rubbed at his nose, dislodging his glasses slightly. "The house survived for decades before that goddamn film came out, so I don't think we need to go all in on *Christmas, Truly* now."

"But you want to see how other houses are dealing with their connection to Christmas movies . . ." she prompted, still a bit confused.

"To see if there's a way to work it in without turning the whole house into some sort of nightmarish tourist trap," he said, lifting his spoon to his mouth again. "The print series for the gift shop is fine—it's a nice way to capitalize on the film, I think, but not over-the-top—but this screening of *Christmas, Truly* that Eloise has planned is the least of her ideas for the house, and I don't want us to get too far away from focusing on my great-great-grandfather's legacy."

Charlotte ate her soup in silence for a moment, contemplating. "Is it only recently that there have been money issues?" she asked, realizing that this was probably a rude question only after the words had already slipped out.

His mouth was set in a grim line. "Owning an old house is expensive, and always has been—my dad worked in corporate law, nearly killed himself with long hours for as long as I can remember, in part so that we could afford the upkeep on the house, since we've never made enough from tours and events to entirely pay for the maintenance. Turns out, even that wasn't enough—but I didn't realize it until recently." There was a closed-off note to his voice as he relayed this information that told her that this was a sensitive subject for him; considering this was the third time they'd ever met, she didn't feel comfortable prying, but the way he spoke of his dad made her wonder, so . . .

"Your dad," she said carefully. "Is he—"

"Dead." His tone was short. Final. "Two years ago."

She swallowed. "I'm so sorry."

He nodded, and returned his attention to his soup, leaving Charlotte to slowly tear a piece of bread into smaller and smaller pieces while trying to figure out how to make this a bit less uncomfortable a conversation. Her usual bluntness didn't seem like quite the right fit for a delicate moment like this, and she definitely didn't think that any further questions on this topic would be welcomed.

"You said you live in New York?" he asked, glancing up at her after another couple of moments, and she latched onto this question gratefully. She had a higher tolerance than most for an awkward silence, but something about Graham made her feel uncomfortable in her own skin.

"Yes," she said. "Born and raised. I moved away for school, and then moved back as soon as I graduated."

"Seems like an expensive place to live, as an artist."

"It is," she confirmed with a grimace. "But my best friend moved there after college, and my parents were there for a long time—not anymore, though—and it's just . . . home. There's nowhere else that I like as much, so I never really considered leaving." Even if some of the things—the people—who had made it feel like home were no longer there. She didn't voice this thought, instead asking, "Do you like living in London?"

He shrugged. "I didn't think too much about it—it was always a given, you know? I wasn't going to stay in Hampshire—there was no way I could find a job in the village, not the sort I'd need, if I was going to support Eden Priory someday. So I moved to London for uni and studied accounting, and I've been there ever since."

His phone buzzed on the table and he glanced down at the screen, a frown creasing his forehead. He set down his spoon and quickly began to type. Charlotte ate her soup in a thoughtful silence, casting surreptitious glances at him between spoonfuls. "Sorry," he said, glancing back up at her after a couple of minutes, "but I need to get back into town—I've a call I need to take."

"Sure thing," she said, scraping her spoon along the bottom of her bowl. She crumbled up her paper napkin and tossed it into her empty bowl, then rose to her feet. And then—maybe because of the frown that had left deep lines in his forehead, or the tense note in his voice when he spoke of his dad, or maybe just because something ineffable about him made her want to talk to him, made her care what he had to say in return—she said, "I'll probably go to the next filming location later this week—it's in Primrose Hill, right?" He nodded; she paused, and then added, "You could join me, if you wanted."

He looked at her for a long moment, then raised that goddamn eyebrow and said, "All right."

And she tried not to be too happy about his answer.

CHAPTER SIX

Two days later, Charlotte was trying her very hardest not to be charmed.

"Why is this so cute?" she demanded as they walked up Regent's Park Road and into the neighborhood of Primrose Hill; the street was dotted with small shops and restaurants, there were terraced houses painted in various shades of pastels, and the entire vibe was like what an American's dream of a charming London street would look like. There were Christmas decorations everywhere—sparkling lights, greenery, cheerful wreaths, even windows with snowflakes painted on them. Charlotte sternly reminded herself that she was not the sort of idiot that would be taken in by a bit of festive cheer.

"Because it's where posh people live," Graham replied.

"Says the man whose family owns a house with a *name*."

"Touché." She glanced sideways at him in time to catch a fleeting dimple in his cheek as he bit back a smile. She personally thought men shouldn't be allowed to have dimples. He was wearing a navy-blue wool coat over a pair of jeans, and a plaid scarf was knotted around his neck. His dark hair was mussed slightly by the wind, and there was a day's worth of stubble on his face. None of this was at all interesting to her, obviously.

"Where is this square, exactly?" she asked.

He nodded at a street up ahead. "We'll turn right there, and it's just round the corner."

Their destination was Chalcot Square, in which a Christmas party in an early aughts rom-com had taken place. Charlotte had never seen the movie in question—it wasn't, strictly speaking, a Christmas movie, rather a movie with an iconic Christmas scene—but from what she gathered from being a human on the internet, its heroine was a magazine editor (like the heroines of approximately 50 percent of the rom-coms in existence) who lived in an improbably fabulous flat and had many romantic travails while trying to plan her best friend's New Year's Eve bachelorette party. (Why on earth anyone in their right mind would have a bachelorette party on New Year's Eve was not ever addressed, as far as Charlotte could tell.) Charlotte had taken a quick YouTube journey through some of its highlights the night before, and had found it extremely annoying, with two potential love interests who had the charisma of a bowl of oatmeal.

However: the Christmas party scene—culminating with the rival love interests having a fistfight in the snow outside the posh flat where the party took place—was iconic, and so here Charlotte was.

In a few minutes, they found themselves outside the building in question; it was around three, so it would be dark in less than an hour, and the windows glowed invitingly. She surveyed the scene before her and pulled out her phone, where she'd saved a screenshot from the scene in the movie. She, obviously, could probably have done all the sketches for this project based on screenshots, but there was something to be said for seeing a location in person—and, more important, there was something to be said for not spending every waking hour of the next month trapped in family Christmas hell. (This afternoon's outing coincided with a day trip to a Christmas event at the LEGOLAND in Windsor that sounded a) like a completely wasted effort for a *baby* and b) objectively terrible.)

"You don't want me to actually include the characters, right?" she asked Graham, glancing up from her phone to find him watching her with an inscrutable expression on his face.

"Right," he confirmed, leaning back against the wrought-iron fence that encircled the garden behind them. "Eloise likes the idea of it just being the architecture—people who recognize it will know what it is, but it will just look like a nice painting of a historic property to anyone who doesn't know."

"Got it." She glanced down at her phone screen again, clocking the angle of the shot in the movie, then slid it back into her pocket. She was wearing one of her favorite coats—green wool, with shiny brass buttons and a decorative bow at the neck—and had given her blonde bob a careful blowout. Where Ava swanned around in caftans with her hair in a messy bun, Charlotte wore lots of simple dresses in solid colors, her hair carefully styled. She sometimes felt like the artistic whimsy that gripped the rest of her family seemed to have run out of its supply by the time she was born. She pulled her sketchbook from her bag and, leaning against the fence next to Graham, began to sketch.

It was a rough sketch, just enough to get her initial impressions of the facade down; she'd refine it later, at home, based on photos she'd take before they left, but a photo couldn't compare to in-person impressions, which was why she didn't want to base her final piece on the photos alone. She was quiet as she worked, her eyes trained on the colorful Italianate terraced house before her, taking in the intricate corbels and overhanging eaves. It was a weekday, but not yet rush hour, so the streets around them were relatively quiet—or, rather, as quiet as streets in London could be—and she could hear the scrape of her pencil against paper.

When Charlotte had pulled out her sketchbook, Graham had pulled out his phone and proceeded to frown down at it, and she couldn't help wondering what caused the frown that the contents of his phone seemed to often provoke. Perhaps he had an extremely demanding girlfriend who bombarded him with messages at all hours of the day.

Her next pencil stroke was particularly vicious.

"So you're not working right now?" she asked, keeping her gaze firmly fixed on her work.

"Not at the moment," he confirmed. "Lots to do at the house, so I decided to focus on that full-time for a year."

There was a barely concealed note of strain underlying the words, and Charlotte frowned down at her sketch. Given what he'd said about the expenses of maintaining Eden Priory, she wondered how bad things were, if he'd felt the need to take a break from work to focus on this. She got the impression that this was a man who would go to great lengths to convince everyone around him that there was nothing wrong, which was why she was not expecting much in the way of a candid answer when she asked, "What happened with your roof?"

There was a pause, and she glanced up in time to see him lock his phone screen and slide the phone back in his pocket in a smooth motion that didn't distract her from the slight tightening of his mouth. "The house needs a new roof, because of course it does." There was barely leashed frustration in his voice.

"And I'm guessing that's expensive?"

He snorted. "Think how much a normal roof costs to replace, then triple the size of the roof, and add in the fact that the house is listed, so there are all sorts of historical requirements for any repairs we do—it's a goddamn mess."

"Have you considered making a pinup calendar of you dressed as various reindeer?" she asked, still sketching busily. "You can sell copies as a fundraiser."

"If I'd known my stripping out of that reindeer suit would have this effect on you, I'd have been more careful not to inflame your lust."

This time, it was Charlotte's turn to suppress a smile. And then, belatedly, something occurred to her—something that she might have realized earlier, if she'd thought about it for half a second, or done a bit more research. "This house isn't open to the public." She nodded at the building she was drawing.

"No," Graham agreed, sounding slightly startled.

"It's just a private home," she clarified. "No tours—so they're not doing anything to capitalize on their connection to *Ninety Days of Bessie Black*."

"Right," he agreed, more slowly this time, clearly beginning to understand her meaning.

"And," Charlotte persisted, "I didn't need a ride to get here."

There was a slight pause. "No," he said.

"Meaning," she finished, "that you don't need to be here with me at all." She kept her eyes on her work as she spoke; she didn't know what, precisely, she was afraid that she would—or wouldn't—see on his face, if she looked at him, but it felt safer, somehow, to look at the page before her instead.

"No," he said, after another, longer pause. "I guess I didn't." There was nothing sheepish or embarrassed in his tone; it was clear to her that she was not pointing out anything that he didn't already know. She did glance up now, unable to resist, and found him looking at her, that arrogant eyebrow slightly raised. "Shall I leave you to it, then?"

She felt suddenly off-balance, like this was some sort of test—like her answer would reveal more than she wanted it to.

"You're already here," she said, as lightly as possible. "You may as well stay, I suppose."

"I suppose," he echoed, and she saw the hint of a dimple again, and returned her attention to her sketchbook.

Silence fell once more as she continued to work, finishing a series of thumbnails, then a couple of full-page rough sketches, before flipping to a fresh page to draw some of the architectural features in greater detail. After a while, she sensed that his eyes were on her.

"This isn't a spectator sport, you know," she murmured, not removing her eyes from her sketchpad as she shaded a bit of the lamp blazing next to the door.

"I promise you don't want my assistance," came his reply. "I'm rubbish at art."

"I *meant*," she said, with what she considered to be infinite patience, "that you could go do . . . something else. While I'm working."

There was a long pause, during which his gaze did not leave the side of her face, and hers did not leave her sketchpad. "You don't try to make people like you, do you?"

She shrugged. "I've never seen much point—some people like me, some people don't. Just like everyone else—I just angst about it less." She had realized this at a young age; one thing that was to be said for having a brief period of being a child star and general movie darling was that it had taught her how little other people's adoration really mattered, overall. There had been an awful lot of people, all those years ago, telling her how *cute* she was and how *sweet* and how *absolutely darling* she was in the movie, but it hadn't mattered to her—not when she, at the age of ten, had realized that acting wasn't something that made her happy, even if it *had* made people like her. For a little while, at least. She narrowed her eyes at Graham. "*You* care about being liked, though." She barely knew him—and yet, somehow, she knew this.

He immediately looked defensive. "Why do you think that?"

"Because," she said, on a sudden, uncanny hunch, "you always *have* been, and so you don't know what to do when someone doesn't immediately fall under your spell."

He crossed his arms and tilted his weight slightly sideways so that he was leaning toward her, which she should have found annoying but didn't, because apparently she enjoyed attractive men leaning against things, which was infuriating.

"Let's say you were correct," he said, a wry, amused edge to his voice that she hadn't expected. It made her like him a bit more; she realized, in a sudden flash, that each thing she'd learned about him had had that effect so far. "That would still do nothing to explain why you, specifically, seem to not want to like me."

"I don't not like you," she protested, which was the truth.

"I know," he agreed, a bit smug. "But you don't *want* to like me. It's against your will."

"You surprised me, when you found me at Eden Priory," she admitted, realizing that he was right; this was quite perceptive of him, and it made her wonder, for a brief, uncomfortable moment, if he was paying more attention to her than she realized.

He lifted an eyebrow. "You were at a Christmas lights switch-on attended by hundreds of people. You can't possibly have expected to be alone."

This was fair, and she hesitated. She avoided explaining anything about her past to people she didn't know well; she wasn't constantly recognized, but it did happen from time to time, and so she avoided making the connection for people who didn't make it themselves, to spare herself more conversations about both a holiday and a movie that she disliked.

However, she was beginning to think that it was inevitable that Graham—or, more likely, one of his sisters—was going to figure out who she was, and that the longer she went without telling him, the weirder it would be.

"Okay, so," she said, taking a deep breath, and bracing herself as if she were about to jump into a freezing lake. "I may have had a brief moment of fame as a child star."

To his credit, Graham didn't blink. "May have?" he repeated slowly.

She sighed. "My dad's a director, and a friend of his was directing a—a Christmas rom-com." She paused. "*Christmas, Truly*, to be specific."

"Ah," he said, his expression unreadable, and Charlotte suddenly felt the pressing urge to explain this better.

"I had no idea that Eden Priory had been used in the movie until we got there on Saturday and I recognized it," she said in a rush, suddenly concerned that—what? That he'd think she was so obsessed with her elementary school glory days that she'd deliberately seek out the filming locations of the one movie she'd ever acted in?

"Anyway," she said, "I ended up in the movie—I was the kid in New York that was getting letters from the poor little rich English kid."

"Pip."

"Yes, Pip. And I was Tallulah." She allowed herself an eloquent eye roll. "Anyway, I didn't actually *like* acting, turns out—I'd never done it before, so when they had me do a screen test I thought it seemed like fun—an excuse to get out of school, at least. And filming the movie was . . . fine, I guess. But it's a lot of people, a lot of waiting around—I had no desire to ever do it again. My parents were disappointed—Ava, my sister, she's a stage actress and has played a lot of prestigious roles, and was already really into acting even when we were kids—and my dad directs art-house films, and my mom's a playwright. They assumed after *Christmas, Truly* that I'd get the acting bug, too, and I'd have a career in the movies. They were genuinely confused when I decided to go to art school, and they could not give less of a shit about my art. They don't think it's *bad*, I don't think, but it just . . . doesn't interest them. And they don't understand why I'm interested in something that the rest of the family isn't."

She broke off, realizing that she had detoured a bit from what she'd actually intended to tell him, but he hadn't interrupted—was instead watching her intently, a faint frown wrinkling the skin between his eyebrows.

"That's ridiculous," he said, so simply and without any elaboration that Charlotte, who had opened her mouth to continue speaking, snapped it shut again.

It was ridiculous, of course. But something about the way he said it—without trying to flatter her by telling her how worthwhile her work was, how talented she was—made this feel unlike any other time she'd had this exact conversation with someone. Usually, people were indignant on her behalf—one weekend in college when Padma and Charlotte had gotten drunk on cheap wine, Padma had spent an entertaining twenty minutes coming up with increasingly crea-tive, though decreasingly logical, insults to describe her parents—but something about his calm, quiet rejection of the very premise was even more reassuring.

"Right," she said slowly. "I mean, yes—thank you." She waved a hand. "It doesn't really matter, except that earlier this year, I was approached—through my dad, of course; I don't even have a film agent or anything—about doing a reboot."

"A reboot."

"Of *Christmas, Truly*," Charlotte confirmed. "Set twenty years later."

"Dear god," he muttered. "Is anyone asking for this?"

"Apparently, yes," she said darkly. "At the time, I told them that it would be a cold day in hell before I ever got in front of a movie cam-era again."

He choked on a laugh. "In those exact terms, I hope."

"I'm guessing my dad softened the blow a bit when he passed it on. I kind of forgot about it, until there was a *Variety* article a couple of weeks ago full of quotes from an 'anonymous source' about how the entire cast was on board for the reboot . . . except me."

"For fuck's sake."

"My thoughts exactly," she agreed. "The reporter did some digging—it's not hard to figure out who I am; I've done some interviews in the past to promote my work that mentioned that I'm *the* Charlie Rose Lane, which is . . . I mean, it's fine. It's whatever. If it helps my art sell, I'm not above cashing in on this incredibly dumb and specific bit of fame. But whoever this 'source' was claimed that I thought my art was more important than *Christmas, Truly*—which I can't even be mad about, because, uh, I do?"

By this point, Graham was laughing—actually laughing, not just chuckling—and she felt something unclench within her at the sound.

"As you might expect, since it's the internet, a bunch of rabid *Christmas, Truly* fans—"

"I was unaware such a thing existed."

"Come on!" Charlotte protested, laughing now as well. "It's on TV *every year*. It's a modern Christmas classic!"

"I've never seen it," he admitted with a smug smile, and she rolled her eyes.

"Of course you haven't," she said. "A gentleman with his own manor house would never deign to do something as low as watch a *holiday rom-com*, even if it *was* filmed there."

"Coming from the woman who is, by her own admission, a holiday-romance-hater? Who has seen none of the films Eloise wants her to paint scenes from?"

"Because," she said, leaning toward him conspiratorially, "they're all *really bad*."

He huffed out another laugh at that, low and intimate this time, entirely different from the way he'd been laughing a moment before.

"What I was *saying* was," she said, determined to actually finish this godforsaken story, "the deranged *Christmas, Truly* corner of the internet found me—apparently it's really taken off with Gen Z, god only knows why—and my DMs have been full of a mix of death threats and genuinely funny burns. Someone told me that my art looked like the paint by numbers their grandmother worked on in the nursing home. I figured it would all die down, but then this, um, extremely passionate teenager accosted me when I was running in Central Park, and I thought it might be time to get out of New York for a bit."

"So, just to be clear, you were scared out of town by a child who can't even drive?"

"It's New York City—*I* can barely drive," Charlotte said, in the interest of fairness. "But essentially, yes. I always come to see Ava for the holidays—or I have, ever since she and Kit got married, because my parents are exhausting and usually in the stages of either separating or reconciling, and I just want somewhere quiet I can sleep for a week after the holiday rush—so after I was verbally assaulted by a sixteen-year-old, I decided to come earlier this year. But when we were at Eden Priory on Saturday, someone there recognized me— a big fan of the movie."

"I wish *I'd* run into this person," he muttered. "Could've asked them how to lure them and their fellow *Christmas, Truly* enthusiasts to the house without staging a reenactment of the entire film." Catching sight of Charlotte's raised eyebrows, he added dryly, "A genuine suggestion of Eloise's."

"I am *not* reprising my role," she warned, and he grinned at her. "But anyway—given recent events, running into this fan of the movie was a bit much for me, which is why I went and hid."

"And then I interrupted you," he said, comprehension dawning.

"And started *removing clothing*," she reminded him.

"A reindeer suit! A *felt* reindeer suit."

"How was I supposed to know what you had on underneath? I thought it might be like Scottish people and their kilts. I will admit that I might have been a *bit* short with you, though."

A smile curved at his lips. "A bit. I'm not overly vain, but abject horror is not *usually* the reaction women have to my arrival."

At this, Charlotte snapped shut her sketchbook—long abandoned, in any case—and, without the slightest hesitation, used it to whack him in the head.

"Jesus Christ! I knew Americans were blood-crazed lunatics, but I hadn't heard that they were so creative in their choice of weapons."

"Shut up, you're fine," Charlotte said, slipping the sketchbook in her bag and pulling her phone out of her coat pocket. She glanced down to see a couple of texts from Ava, including photos of a furious-looking Alice in front of a series of elaborate holiday-themed LEGO creations, and said a prayer of thanks to the heavens that she was not going to be present for what she suspected would be an absolutely epic meltdown.

"My ears are ringing," he said.

"You're just angry because I messed up your hair," she said, snapping several photos of the house. This, combined with her sketch, would be sufficient for her final painting. She returned her phone to her bag, eyed him speculatively, and said, on a whim, "Where can we get a drink around here?"

❄

"I don't understand how it is that you're the one who assaulted me, yet I'm the one who paid for the drinks," Graham said twenty minutes later, sliding into the booth opposite her and slipping a glass mug of mulled wine across the table toward her.

"*You're* the one who said you'd get the drinks," Charlotte said, exasperated. "What's your Venmo handle? PoshTwat07?"

He waved her off. "Nice use of the native dialect, though." He took a sip of mulled wine, surveying her thoughtfully. "Why do you dislike Christmas so much? Beyond the film, I mean?"

Charlotte cupped her own mug in her hands, savoring the warmth. The pub Graham had chosen was a Victorian-era hole in the wall, all antique mirrors and worn velvet booths and cozy lighting. She hated to admit it, but she loved it.

"My family has never been terribly . . . good at Christmas."

"How can you be bad at Christmas? It's not an exam."

She rolled her eyes. "I'm sure your family is *great* at Christmas," she said. "Historic family home, lots of vibes, zero time spent listening to your parents arguing in the other room or, god forbid, being asked to fly off to some remote location to meet your mother's latest paramour."

"They sound like a treat, your parents," he said, frowning down into his mug of wine.

"That's one word for it. It's what you get when two capital-*A* Artists marry each other."

"You know that being an artist doesn't automatically make you an ass, don't you?" he asked conversationally.

"I've got a lot of evidence to the contrary," she said shortly, before reluctantly amending, "Myself excluded, obviously. And Ava's fine—selfish at times, but I love her, and she's a good sister. Mostly."

"My sister's an artist, you know," he said slowly. "Not Eloise—Lizzie, our little sister. She's in her final year at Central Saint Martins, studying fashion design. She's incredibly talented," he added, with an unmistakable note of pride. He loved his sisters—she could hear it in his voice, every time he spoke of them. "And she's one of the least selfish people I've ever met. She's very weird, don't get me wrong, and slightly terrifying to strangers, I think—but she's not selfish at all." He shook his head. "I just think . . . if your family has convinced you that it's acceptable, or understandable, for your parents to be shit parents, just because they're devoted to their *craft* or whatever . . . well, it's bullshit. And you deserve better parents than that."

She stared at him, a bit astonished. "Are you secretly *kind*?" she asked, leaning forward conspiratorially.

He spluttered. "I don't think I'm *secretly* kind. There are plenty of people who would call me kind."

She crossed her arms across her chest, leaning back against the soft, upholstered booth. "Name them."

"My mother."

"Doesn't count. Mothers can't see their children objectively."

"My sisters."

"Would they, though?" she asked shrewdly. "I'll bet you were a nightmare of an older brother. You probably gave them absolute hell."

He grinned suddenly—a wolfish, fierce grin unlike any of the smiles she had yet seen cross his face. "I hid Eloise's hairbrush every evening after she went to bed."

Charlotte blinked. "Her . . . hairbrush?"

"Yes. She read an article in a magazine telling her how many strokes she needed to brush her hair every morning and every night and became fixated on it. It was extremely annoying—she kept making us late for school, because she wouldn't stop brushing her hair."

Charlotte could imagine, in a sudden flash, child Graham, in his school uniform, tapping his foot impatiently, checking his watch, absolutely *horrified* by the notion of being late.

"So one night I hid it in a closet. She had an absolute fit the next morning, wouldn't stop shrieking about her hair—we were late for school anyway, but it was worth it just to get to watch it all. So the next night I hid it again, in a different spot. She worked out it was me pretty quickly, but instead of telling our mum, she started creating elaborate traps inside her room to catch me when I tried to sneak in to steal it."

"Please tell me it involved chocolate syrup being dumped on your head and a fan spraying feathers on you," said Charlotte, who had watched *The Parent Trap* a possibly worrying number of times.

"Nothing quite that elaborate, but she did once manage to rig up one of those contraptions where the door opens and tips flour down on the head of whoever is walking through the doorway."

"Why didn't she just lock her door?"

Graham snorted. "Because it's a three-hundred-year-old house with old-fashioned locks and my mother hid the keys from us because she didn't trust us—probably a good call," he added thoughtfully.

"Probably," Charlotte agreed, and they lapsed into a comfortable silence for a moment, each sipping at their wine.

"So," she said slowly, lowering her mug of wine. "Where's our next stop on this holiday movie tour?"

"Our," he repeated, and looked at her over his mug, a smile playing at the corners of his mouth.

"If you wanted," she said. "To do more research, of course." She took a breath. "My point is, I . . . wouldn't mind."

"Neither would I," he said quietly. He pulled out his phone and glanced down at his list from Eloise. "We need to go to Sloane Square, so that's easy enough. I've plans this weekend, though, and I have to go down to Hampshire for a couple of nights starting on Monday."

"That's fine—I do have other work to do, you know," she added, a bit acerbically. "I should just wait and see what nightmarish Christmas activity my family has planned for next week and choose the best day to escape."

"I would hate to interrupt any family bonding experiences," he said solemnly. "Shall we invite them along? Go on a little artistic outing, then a trip to see Father Christmas afterward? A photo shoot in matching Christmas jumpers, perhaps? I am here to make your holiday dreams come true, Charlie Rose Lane."

He ducked in time to avoid the coaster she tossed at him.

"Ugh. Do *not* call me that—I don't know what my parents were thinking. *Charlie Rose?* Horrifying."

"Fair enough," he said, and then added, "Lane it is." He grinned at her again, and she liked it, too much. Liked the sound of her last name in his voice.

And, in retrospect, that should have been the moment that she first realized that she was in trouble.

CHAPTER SEVEN

W hy, precisely, do we have to spend the evening freezing and damp just to see Christmas lights?" Charlotte asked for at least the third time the following day as they jostled their way onto a crowded Tube car and a harried-looking Ava handed a scowling Alice off to Kit.

"Because it's *festive*, Charlotte, Jesus Christ," Ava said, sticking a pacifier unceremoniously into Alice's mouth before she could unleash hell on the innocent commuters on the train. "Are you a robot?"

"No," Charlotte said patiently, taking a seat opposite Kit and his parents and giving Alice a wave. The baby stared unsmilingly back. "Merely someone who is being forced to engage in more Christmas merriment in a week than she has in her entire life."

Charlotte truly didn't think this was much of an exaggeration; so far this week, in addition to her outings with Graham, she had baked and decorated Christmas cookies, been forced to watch the Christmas episode of every season of *Friends*, and stage-managed a photo shoot in front of the Christmas tree in which Alice had been forced into a baby-sized Santa hat, which had ended with predictably disastrous results. (Namely: Alice had cried so hard she vomited; Ava, with nothing more useful to hand, had shown admirably quick reflexes and caught said vomit in the Santa hat.) After skipping the family outings on both Wednesday and Friday, Charlotte had felt that it might be nice to put in an appearance this evening, but she was already thinking longingly of the empty flat that she could have had to herself for a few hours.

"It's going to be *fun*," Ava said through gritted teeth. "Also, there's a bar."

Charlotte's ears perked up at this intriguing tidbit of information, and she spent the rest of the brief Tube ride to Kew scrolling through photos on her phone and trying not to laugh hysterically at the series she had featuring Ava cradling the vomit-filled Santa hat in her hand while a horrified Kit looked on, a screaming Alice in his arms. Kit and Ava had been wearing matching Christmas sweaters that John had knitted them. It was, honestly, spectacular. Charlotte was considering framing one of them.

By the time they had arrived at Kew Gardens station and walked the ten minutes to the gardens themselves, Charlotte's good mood was fading once again; it was cold, her socks weren't warm enough, and it was pitch-black at five p.m., which made her want to cry. Once they entered through the gates and scanned their tickets, however, she had to admit that this was not the worst Christmas activity she'd ever experienced—and, indeed, compared to the rest of the week, it was probably a high.

"What a ringing endorsement," Ava said, when Charlotte made an observation to this effect. "I'm so glad we've salvaged at least a fraction of your week from complete torture."

"Ava," Charlotte said, startled; had she been complaining *that* often? She decided that she was going to stop bitching about Christmas so much. Ava knew perfectly well how she felt about it and had enough on her plate at the moment without a ceaseless litany of complaints from Charlotte. Besides, Charlotte had managed to escape a lot of it—she'd been returning to that same coffee shop where she'd run into Graham to work, and as a result spent all of the morning and much of the afternoon each day away from Ava's flat.

Half an hour into their visit—they were progressing slowly along a trail that wound through the gardens, thousands of lights illuminating the plants, shrubbery, and trees surrounding them—they paused to visit one of the food and drink vendors that had been set up along the path. Charlotte volunteered to stand in line, and she was so busy scrutinizing the menu that it took ninety seconds before she realized that Eloise Calloway was directly ahead of her in the queue.

No sooner had she made this realization than Eloise glanced behind her, then did a double take. "Charlotte!" The woman standing next to her turned curiously as Charlotte waved hello, and Eloise added, "This is Jess, my girlfriend. Jess, this is Charlotte—the woman we gave a lift back from the switch-on."

"Hello," Jess said, eyeing Charlotte in an interested sort of way that made Charlotte vaguely nervous. Jess was as short and curvy as Eloise was lanky, with curly brown hair and glasses.

"Hi," Charlotte said, a bit warily; she didn't miss the glance that Eloise and Jess briefly exchanged, and the slight frown on Jess's face as she looked at her girlfriend.

"I'm so pleased Graham was able to convince you to do the Christmas commission for our shop," Eloise said. A delicate pause. "And it was awfully *friendly* of him to offer to show you the houses himself." She didn't even attempt to disguise the intrigued gleam in her eyes.

"I needed a ride to Berkshire," Charlotte explained, which was true enough, at least as an excuse for Wednesday's trip. Friday's outing to Primrose Hill—and the one planned for next week—were a bit more difficult to explain, so she didn't try.

They had reached the front of the line, and after placing their orders, Eloise and Jess lingered nearby, offering Charlotte a hand with her unruly collection of cups.

"Thanks," Charlotte said gratefully as they made their way back to where her family awaited. She quickly rattled off names as cups of wine were handed around, and then said, "This is Eloise and Jess." She paused for a longer-than-socially-acceptable amount of time before adding reluctantly, "Eloise is Graham's brother."

"*Is* she?" Ava asked, gleeful.

"I *am*," Eloise agreed.

"I'm Eloise's *girlfriend*," Jess said, then shrugged when multiple brows were furrowed in her general direction. "I thought we were all talking in italics now. It seemed fun."

"This is fascinating," Ava said. "Is your brother here?"

"He is," Eloise said, and Charlotte, who was about to take a sip of mulled wine, stilled for a moment, hoping no one noticed. "With his best friend, Leo. I'm sure they're around here somewhere . . ." She turned, surveying the surrounding crowds—not a terribly easy task, given the darkness, as well as the fact that everyone was bundled up against the chilly night air, giving them a sort of uniform, lumpy appearance.

"I think we were just about to get going, actually," Charlotte said hastily, but Simone—curse the inconveniently polite woman—frowned.

"Charlotte, dear, we wouldn't want to leave without saying hello to your young man."

"Oh my god," Charlotte said, wishing that quicksand was as omnipresent as the media of her youth had led her to believe. She would pay someone to cause a sinkhole to spontaneously appear beneath her right this second. "He's not my *young man*."

"Not all that young, really," Eloise said cheerfully. "Just turned thirty-three, in fact. One foot in the grave."

Ava gave her a scathing look. "*I* just turned thirty-three."

"You wear it much better than my brother," Eloise assured her.

This seemed to mollify Ava. "It's the Botox."

This, at least, was sufficient to distract Charlotte from her current woes. "Since when do you get Botox?" she asked her sister.

Ava sniffed. "Since I spent my twenties acting with my eyebrows." She paused, considering. "And since I had a baby. I may have gray hairs and spit-up on every single sweater, but at least my forehead is smooth."

Before Charlotte could respond, Ava brightened, and waved at someone over Charlotte's shoulder. "Graham! Hello!"

Charlotte turned slowly to find that Graham was, indeed, standing a few feet behind her, holding a paper cup of his own and watching her with an entirely inscrutable expression. "Hello," she said, pleased to note that she sounded cool and collected, despite the presence of her insane family, which felt like a victory.

"Lane," he said, nodding at her. He tilted his head sideways toward the lanky redhead standing directly next to him, who was wearing possibly the most well-tailored coat Charlotte had ever seen on a man. "This is Leo."

"Charlotte," she said, extending a hand toward him. He shook it firmly with a smile, eyeing her with frank curiosity. His eyes shot over her shoulder, however, and all his interest in Charlotte immediately faded. "Ava Lane?"

Ava blinked. "Yes?"

"Holy shit. I saw you as Lady Macbeth three years ago, and it was one of the most terrifying experiences of my life," he said, reaching over to shake her hand reverently. "You were *incredible*."

Ava, who loved nothing more than meeting a fan—something that happened a surprising amount, considering she acted exclusively on the stage, and had never once appeared on television or in a film—

beamed at him. "Thank you," she said, tossing her hair. "It was one of my favorite roles."

Graham snapped his fingers. "I knew you looked familiar!" He shook his head. "Leo dragged me to that show."

Leo regarded his friend with disgust. "You mean to say you've met *Ava Lane* multiple times and not recognized her? You are useless."

Graham shrugged, unrepentant. "It's hard to see their faces onstage, you know? We were sitting quite far back."

"I *told* you that we needed to book tickets early to get good seats—"

"Yes, yes," Graham said wearily; this was clearly an argument they'd had a number of times—it had the worn, slightly affectionate quality of well-trod conversational territory.

"Shall we keep walking?" Kit asked now, stamping his feet. "Bit cold out, and all."

There was a general murmur of agreement, and the group split into pairs and groups of three, introductions being made and chitchat being commenced as they continued their progress down the trail. Charlotte, somehow—through circumstances that she very much doubted were coincidental—ended up walking alongside Graham, slightly behind the rest of the group. She drained her mulled wine, and Graham neatly plucked her empty cup from her hand, stacking his inside it.

"You're here under duress, I assume?" he said conversationally.

"There are only so many family outings I can skip without seeming like an asshole," she agreed gloomily. "What about you?" she added, curious. "Did your sister bully you into coming?"

"No." Was it her imagination, or had his cheeks gone slightly pinker? "I genuinely love Christmas at Kew. We used to come every year as a family."

"That's . . ." "Adorable" was the first word that sprang to mind, but she certainly wasn't going to tell him *that*.

"Nice," she finished weakly, and he shot her a sideways glance, as if he thought she was being sarcastic. "I mean it!" she protested, raising her hands. "Not everything I say to you is an insult!"

"What a charming change," he murmured, pausing momentarily to toss their cups in a trash can. He turned back to her. "Anyway, my sisters and I still come every year—Lizzie's ill tonight, or she'd be here, too—and Leo tags along because we've been friends since we were at school and he's practically a member of the family at this point. For better or for worse," he added dryly.

"He could probably tell me absolutely *fascinating* stories about you," she mused. "And your sordid past."

"Hardly sordid."

"Oh, I bet there's some romantic history there that you'd rather he didn't shout in the village square."

"You do realize that we live in the twenty-first century and not the village in *Beauty and the Beast*, don't you?"

"Of all the references you could come up with, *that's* the one you choose?"

"I may have watched it a few times. Lizzie was obsessed with it when she was about four, and she was going through a phase at the time where she wanted me to sit with her whenever I was home."

"How old were you?"

"Fifteen."

"And how many times would you say you and Lizzie watched *Beauty and the Beast*?" she asked, already highly amused.

"Er. A few," he hedged.

"Give me a ballpark figure. Five?"

"More."

"Fifty?"

He looked a bit harried. "Possibly."

"Oh my god." She couldn't help it: the mental image of an

adolescent Graham sitting next to his preschool-aged sister, patiently watching *Beauty and the Beast* for the thirtieth time, was one of the most adorable things she'd ever contemplated. "You *are* nice."

Now he looked a bit indignant. "I *told* you."

She shrugged, unrepentant. "I think it's good for you, that I didn't immediately fall under your spell. Keeps you humble."

"Believe me, I'm feeling plenty humble these days," he said, and there was a wry, almost unhappy note to his voice as he said it.

"Does this have to do with your roof woes?" she asked, which was definitely a sentence she had never uttered in her life.

"Among other things," he said, sounding tired. There was a pause then, and they walked in silence for a few moments. "We need an injection of cash—just enough to ensure that every time the roof leaks it's not some mad scramble to figure out how to pay for it," he said at last. "My dad inherited some family money, made quite a large salary, but we've nearly spent through it, and we need to work out something else. I had a meeting this week with a potential investor—someone I worked with several years ago. His idea is to convert the house into some sort of *Christmas, Truly*–themed holiday let—allow people to come stay at the holidays, plan a whole itinerary around the film for them. My mum and sisters want to consider it, since it would only be for a few weeks a year, but I just . . . can't." His voice was heavy as he spoke, the distaste evident in each word. "I spent my entire career, up until now, helping people make calculated, logical business decisions, but it turns out it's much harder to be cool and logical when it's *your* family business you're trying to save. And with my mum and sisters and I not seeing eye to eye on things, it's . . . difficult."

"I can imagine," she said, and this was true; she considered herself something of an expert on not seeing eye to eye with one's family. Him speaking of his family, however, made her realize a conspicuous absence this evening. "Does your mom not come with you guys to this anymore?" She gestured around at the lit-up topiaries all around them to encompass the "this" that she meant.

He hesitated—only slightly, but just long enough that she noticed. "No. It makes her sad, I think, since . . . since my dad died." She noticed how soft his voice went, whenever he mentioned his dad's death. Wondered how often he spoke about it—and, if it was as rare as she suspected, why he'd spoken of it to *her*, of all people. "The holidays are difficult for her these days."

"Of course," she said softly, thinking about her own parents—imperfect, frustrating, not at all the sort of parents she would have designed for herself, had she been given the choice . . . and yet, still, two people who would leave an absolutely gaping hole in her life, if they were suddenly gone.

"That's why I quit my job," he said abruptly, and she glanced at him in surprise; she'd thought he'd clear his throat, change the subject, perhaps try to catch up to Leo or Eloise or someone else in their group, something that would allow him to change the subject. He didn't seem the sort to bare his soul to a virtual stranger—which, ultimately, was what Charlotte was. Even if, increasingly, it didn't feel that way.

"My dad didn't like to let any of the kids help out with the business side of things at Eden Priory—he always told me that he could handle it, whenever I offered to help, once I left uni and started working in financial accounting," he continued. Frustration laced his voice, faint but noticeable. "But when my dad died, I got a proper look at the books at Eden Priory and realized that the finances were a mess—my parents had been taking on debt for years, not enormous amounts, but enough each year that it was starting to accrue. I have some savings, so I left my job six months ago, and I've been trying to figure out what needs to be done—and of course, the damn roof is just another thing to add to the list."

Charlotte, who had watched every season of *Downton Abbey* with Padma, vaguely understood that owning a house as large and historic as Eden Priory was not quite as glamorous as it might seem these days. "Old houses like Eden Priory are expensive to maintain, right?"

His nod was grim. "Right. The heating costs alone are . . . exorbitant. When we're not hosting an event, we keep a lot of the public rooms closed off so we don't have to heat the entire house."

"This is like something out of a movie."

"Considerably less romantic, I promise." She glanced at him in time to see the wry twist of his mouth. "We generate income for the property by giving tours of the house a couple of days a week, and renting it out for events sometimes, but I think we could lean into the Christmas thing to earn more. We could do more events—give candlelit tours, get historical reenactors to illustrate how Calloway and his family would have celebrated the season, that sort of thing. We're not that far from London, so I think we could draw in people from the city, tourists . . . we've been doing the lights switch-on for years, but it's just one day, and if we could keep visitors coming all season long, we could eventually make enough money in December to provide a cushion for the rest of the year."

"And your family doesn't agree?" she asked curiously.

"Not entirely—they like the Christmas programming, but Eloise and Lizzie both think that we should try to market ourselves for *Christmas, Truly* tourism—center all the decorations, all the exhibits at the house, around the film. Ignore the fact that a world-famous artist once lived there, that that's what the house, our *family*, is known for, and just focus all our attention on a mediocre Christmas film, try to attract people who would be interested in *that*." He sighed heavily, a frustrated sound, and Charlotte, who was looking at the path ahead and the lights surrounding them, sneaked a glance at him, noted the lines at the corners of his eyes, the grim set of his mouth.

"At the end of the day, it's still our family home, and it has been for generations, and I don't want that to change. My dad had very specific ideas about how the house should be run, and *I* don't think that we should ignore those just because—" Here he broke off abruptly, and took a long, slow breath. "Just because he's gone," he finished quietly, and Charlotte turned away again, giving him a moment to collect himself. She didn't think she'd imagined the emphasis on the word "I," and guessed that this was where the disagreement with his family came in.

Much as she despised discussing her cinematic history, there seemed like an obvious solution to this problem. "Being used as a set for *Christmas, Truly*—that must have paid well?"

"I've not looked at the books that far back, but I believe so, yes." There was something almost expectant in his tone. He clearly knew where she was going with this. "But my father hated that film, and swore he'd never let the house be used as a filming location ever again."

Charlotte blinked. "I mean, I hate that movie, too, but that seems extreme."

He shrugged, tension radiating off his body, subtle but completely noticeable to Charlotte. "He thought it was embarrassing—that we were betraying his great-grandfather's legacy by allowing the house to be used for a Christmas film. I think money was particularly tight when he agreed to it, but he regretted it, later." He hesitated, then added, "Forever."

Charlotte glanced at him—at the careful way he looked directly ahead, not meeting her eyes; at the tightness of his jaw, the stiffness of his posture—and, despite the warning signs that were present, advising her otherwise, she said, reckless, "But your father isn't here anymore."

"No," he said sharply, not breaking his stride. "He's not. And the least I can do is ensure that we don't turn Eden Priory into something he would have hated, all in the name of saving it."

He increased his pace then, subtly but enough that Charlotte noticed, hurrying to keep up, and within a few moments they had rejoined Leo and Eloise, who seemed to be flirting cheerfully—merely to annoy Graham, Charlotte suspected, since Jess was walking nearby and looked entirely unconcerned. Graham made an effort to join the conversation, punching Leo in the shoulder when he made a particularly suggestive remark, and if anyone else noticed that his laughter had a slightly forced quality to it, they didn't mention it.

Neither did Charlotte. But she walked next to him, quiet, listening. And thinking.

CHAPTER EIGHT

On Sunday, Charlotte called her mom.

This was a task she generally avoided; the conversations often ended with her resisting the urge to tear her hair out, and she tended to put calls on her calendar monthly, treating them like dentist appointments—unavoidable obligations. At least, thanks to Ava's recent intel, she knew that the parental unit was currently on cordial terms, so she could get away with a single phone call and trust that her life updates would be shared, rather than having to call her father too.

"Charlotte, *darling*," her mother said dramatically as soon as she answered the phone. "I've been *so* worried."

Charlotte—sitting at the desk in the guest room at Ava and Kit's, scrutinizing the painting she'd just finished—frowned. "Why?"

"The *press*," her mother replied. "Have they been hounding you terribly? I told your father I wanted him to find whoever that 'anonymous source' is and ensure they never work again—"

"Mom, I don't want anyone to lose their job!" Charlotte interrupted, alarmed. Whoever the "anonymous source" was wouldn't be on her Christmas card list anytime soon (were she the type of person to send Christmas cards), but she didn't take it as far as destroying someone's career for, basically, sharing gossip. She also found her mom's histrionics a bit hard to swallow, given that her mom's concern at the time had extended only as far as a cursory text telling her not to leave her apartment looking schlubby, as there might be paparazzi around. "I'm fine—I'm at Ava's; it's been a nice excuse to have a longer-than-usual vacation for the holidays."

"Hmm," her mom said, sounding suspicious. "I thought you could never take time off for Christmas because your little shop is so busy." This was reliably how she referred to Charlotte's career—in a slightly dismissive way—and Charlotte inhaled slowly, trying to keep her temper.

"I can work from anywhere, you know," she said, forcing some semblance of cheerful patience into her voice. "Especially since I have an assistant now."

Her mother was quiet for a long moment, then said, "Sounds like business is booming." Charlotte didn't think she was imagining the begrudging tone of this, and she sighed, rubbing her temple and eyeing her glass of water, wishing it was whiskey instead, for all that it was—she glanced down at her phone—3:24 on a Sunday afternoon.

"It's always so great to catch up, Mom," she said, feeling very grateful that this was not a video call, because she had an inconveniently honest face. "We're having a great time here—Kit's parents are visiting, and we're taking Alice on all sorts of holiday outings."

"I don't think Alice needs holiday outings," her mother replied, sounding very skeptical about this program of events. "I think that baby needs a sedative."

Charlotte privately thought her mom had a point, but instead said, "No, she loves it! Ava's taking her to meet Santa next weekend."

"I hope she likes him better than Ava did at that age," her mother said dubiously. "We took her to some awful 'breakfast with Santa' event, and she screamed so loudly that we were asked to leave by one of the elves."

Charlotte suddenly had an alarming premonition of what Alice's visit to Santa would be like, and decided to start feigning a cough now, so that by the time the day rolled around, no one would question her need to sit this one out.

"Well, it's always good to chat, Mom," Charlotte said breezily, already wondering why on earth she'd initiated this call. "Is Dad there?"

"No, he's in LA at the moment," her mother said idly, sounding as though her husband's presence or absence was not of particular import to her. Typical.

Charlotte frowned. "Aren't *you* in LA?" Her parents now lived there most of the year, despite her mother's insistence that California was for heathens and that the only *real* culture was in New York.

"No, of course not, darling," her mother said, as if Charlotte should keep tabs on her whereabouts at all times. "I'm in Vermont."

Charlotte blinked. "Why are you in *Vermont*?" Did her mom even know anyone in Vermont?

"I'm on a writing retreat," her mom said impatiently, as though this should have been obvious. "Unlike some, my art cannot flourish with all the . . . *noise* around me, constantly, this time of year. I'm living in a converted barn on a local family's property, and one of the sons of the family has been bringing me meals in a little basket. It's very charming—you should see the flannels he wears!"

"Um," said Charlotte, saying a quick prayer for the virtue of this hearty New England farm boy. Her mother might be past sixty, but her feminine wiles were not to be underestimated.

"But I'll be home next week, and I'll be sure to tell your father that you say hello," her mom added. "By the way, are you open to commissions right now?"

"Not until after the holidays, and I have a long wait list," Charlotte said warily. "Why?"

"Jamie Dyer is looking for someone to do custom invitations for the launch party for his new show," her mom replied.

Charlotte suppressed a sigh. Dyer was one of her mom's friends— a fellow playwright who had written several successful shows that had involved a surprising amount of nudity. "He's welcome to get in touch, but I can't make any promises." It always felt a bit . . . icky when her mom made requests like this. They felt like a naked ploy to try to drag Charlotte back into the world of film and theater, where the rest of the family was comfortable and Charlotte was decidedly *not*.

"I'll let him know," her mom said, sounding a bit distracted. "I have to run, Charlotte—inspiration has struck and I must seize it!" Without a further word of farewell, the line went dead. Charlotte stared down at her phone.

"Love you, too," she muttered, tossing it onto the bed. Why had she even bothered? This was, more or less, what all her conversations with her parents were like—they were very eager to tell her about their lives, which were of course endlessly fascinating, and not remotely interested in whatever was happening with their younger, more disappointing daughter.

She knew why she'd bothered, though: it was Graham. Their conversation the night before, the pain that clearly still lingered from his dad's death, had made her feel . . . well, guilty. She still had both of her parents, and she spoke to them only once a month, if that. Why should she get to have two living parents when Graham and his sisters didn't?

She'd have to talk to them again in a few weeks, because Ava always called their parents on Christmas morning, and they were then subjected to five to ten minutes of guilt-tripping about their presence, together, on one side of the ocean, while their "poor, ailing, unappreciated" (Peter Lane, Christmas 2022) parents languished together at home.

It was exhausting.

Not, however, as exhausting as what John had in store for her the following day.

"But *why*?" Charlotte asked plaintively on Monday morning, staring at the kitchen chaos displayed before her.

"Because it's tradition!" John said brightly, handing Charlotte an apron that said *O Christmas Cheese!* and featured an illustration of a block of cheese bedecked with ornaments, topped with a star. "Nothing says Christmas like mince pie!" He was already wearing an apron of his own that said *Fizz the Season!* above an image of a champagne bottle and a Christmas tree holding hands.

"I think this is why I don't like Christmas," Charlotte muttered, tying the apron around her waist and sending Ava a helpless look. "Don't you need help with the baby?" she asked hopefully.

"No," Ava said cheerfully, a glass of prosecco in one hand while she spoon-fed Alice mashed-up banana with the other, despite the fact that it was not yet eleven a.m. ("Because it's Christmas.")

Drinking at inappropriate hours of the morning was one of the only things about Christmas that Charlotte actually liked, so she poured herself a glass as well, and prepared for the forced labor ahead.

"We need to get the mincemeat from the fridge," John instructed eagerly, and Charlotte spotted an opportunity.

"Actually, I'm a vegetarian," she said virtuously, adopting a look of reluctant apology. "So I'm afraid my morals won't permit me to help you with this."

"There's no meat in mincemeat!" John said brightly. "So you needn't worry!"

"She's not worried," Ava called from her spot by the kitchen island.

John patted Charlotte sympathetically on the arm, then paused, frowning, before asking, very gently, "Charlotte, love, you know that beef comes from a cow, don't you?" He asked this in the tone of someone afraid that they might be the one breaking the news to a child that Santa didn't exist. "Because you were eating an awful lot of that Sunday roast at the pub yesterday."

"It was a cheat day?" Charlotte suggested, but then a merciful god intervened and the doorbell rang.

"I've got it!" she screeched, bolting for the door; she'd forgotten that there was an easily alarmed baby in close range, and a moment later an indignant squawk could be heard, followed in rapid succession by an extremely creative bit of swearing from Ava.

"I don't think that's the sort of language you want to be teaching Alice!" Charlotte called over her shoulder as she raced into the hall, skidded to a halt in her socks, and opened the door. She hadn't paused to consider who it would be, but was expecting the UPS guy, or perhaps Ava's mail carrier, with whom she'd had several conversations since her arrival and who always called her "love," but she was decidedly *not* expecting it to be . . .

Graham.

"You!" she said, and realized as soon as she said it that she sounded like a character in a bad melodrama encountering an accused murderer.

"Hello," he said, lifting a brow. "I was going to text you, but I was walking by and thought I'd just stop by to see when you wanted to go to Sloane Square this week."

"You were walking by," she repeated suspiciously.

"Yes," he repeated, mimicking her tone. "I know that Americans don't understand the notion of using one's own two feet to get places and that you likely want to haul out one of your shotguns and take aim at anyone on your doorstep."

"Shut up," she said, laughing in spite of herself. "I live in New York—how do you think I get everywhere?"

"From what I've gathered from the time Eloise made me watch an entire season of *Sex and the City*, you wave down one of those absurd yellow taxis."

"Exactly how many pieces of media did your sisters force you to watch?" she asked, raising her eyebrows. "Were you ever allowed to leave the house, or did they keep you chained to the sofa?"

"Thank you for your concern—no one appreciates how I've suffered." He offered a mournful shake of his head, and Charlotte refused to reward him with a laugh, despite having to bite the inside of her cheek to prevent it.

Instead, she asked, "Would Wednesday work for Sloane Square? I have a meeting with my assistant tomorrow and I'm in mince pie hell today, but Wednesday is free."

"Mince pies?" She could practically *see* his ears perk up. This was mystifying. She was honestly beginning to think that there was something badly wrong with the entire population of this island.

"Yes," she said darkly. "John is insisting that we make them. I've taken to the bottle to cope."

"You're drinking at eleven in the morning because of mince pies?"

"They're disgusting."

He looked as outraged as if she'd just insulted a member of his family. "They're fucking not!"

She closed her eyes wearily. "Jesus. What is wrong with you people?"

"You've never had a proper one," he said confidently. "There's no chance you'd think they're disgusting if you'd had a good one."

"I do not believe that such a thing exists."

"I'm going to arrange to have you deported."

"Please don't tease me with false promises. I could be in the States in eight hours and have a decent taco for dinner." She sighed dreamily. "Maybe I'll call immigration on myself."

His mouth curved up then, his eyes gleaming as he looked at

her, and she felt something warm unfurling in her stomach, the odd sensation that the air between them had come alive. Perhaps this accounted for the fact that she then said the first thing that sprang to mind, without pausing to consider, and that thing was:

"Why don't you come in?"

Which is how, somehow, she ended up spending the rest of her morning drinking an entire bottle of prosecco and making mince pies with *Graham Calloway*.

"*Hello,*" Ava said, glancing up from her attempt to quiet her off-spring by shoving a spoon in her mouth, and then doing a legitimate double take when she realized who Charlotte had just led into the kitchen. "What a *delightful* surprise."

"I stopped by to ask your sister a question but feel obliged to step in and help defend the culinary reputation of my country," he said, leaning over to examine Alice's banana-covered, scowling face. (Charlotte personally thought he was quite brave to willingly come into such close contact with her, given her penchant for unexpected flailing fists.)

"Do you want to help?" John asked brightly, sounding delighted by the prospect, given the decided lack of enthusiasm of the other current occupants of the house—namely: outright disdain (Charlotte), mild disinterest (Ava), conspicuous absence (Simone, who was occupied by some sort of complicated nail-and-skin-care routine in their flat upstairs), and, of course, somewhat resentful ignorance (Alice).

"I'd love to," Graham said, with a smug smile at Charlotte.

"He's going to give you an appalling apron," Charlotte said, leaning her hip against the counter and trying not to enjoy the sight of Graham in this familiar domestic setting, surrounded by her family.

"The more appalling, the better," Graham said brazenly, though he did falter somewhat when John eagerly handed him an apron that said *Making Spirits Bright!* in horrifying mommy-blogger script, with an image of martini glasses clinking directly beneath the words.

"Famous last words," Charlotte said cheerfully, then reached for the prosecco bottle. "Bubbles?"

"No," Graham said somberly. "I need to focus on my craft."

"That's the spirit!" John said happily. "It's nice to have a man in the kitchen with me—these ladies, god love them, don't know their way around a rolling pin."

"Perhaps we should just wait for Kit to come home and have him help you instead," Ava offered, now trying to clean Alice's face with a wet wipe while Alice attempted to launch herself out of her high chair.

John grimaced, then hastily hitched his smile back into place. "Kit's a good lad, but he is a bit . . . overenthusiastic in the kitchen." No one could argue with this assessment.

Charlotte, resigned to the fact that she was not going to be able to escape this activity entirely now that Graham was here, busied herself setting out the ingredients John requested, so that nothing involving actual culinary skill was asked of her. This seemed a satisfactory arrangement for everyone—John and Graham were conferring in serious tones about the desired thickness of the pastry, and Ava was humming tunelessly to Alice while topping up her glass of prosecco. Charlotte drifted toward her sister.

"I talked to Mom yesterday," she said, reaching out to stroke a careful finger down Alice's impossibly soft, fuzzy head, then neatly dodging Alice's attempt to smear her with a bit of banana she'd secreted away in a tiny fist.

Ava raised an eyebrow at her, an expression that definitely had less range than it had pre-Botox. "Why?" Ava's relationship with their parents was less fraught than Charlotte's was, although in their adolescence, the situation had been reversed, Ava having been much more rebellious than Charlotte. They, obviously, were delighted by Ava's later career choices. Ava's teenage rebellion had always seemed to Charlotte some sort of desperate ploy for their parents' attention, whereas Charlotte simply didn't care. She'd learned at age nine what happened when her parents paid too much attention to her, and she had lurked quietly at the edges of various family dramas ever since.

"I was feeling guilty, I guess," Charlotte said, shifting uncomfortably from foot to foot and draining the last of her glass of prosecco. Against her will, she glanced over her shoulder at Graham, who was joking with John as he stirred the contents of a mixing bowl. He'd rolled his sleeves up, and she made a very conscious effort *not* to look at his forearms. He looked . . . relaxed, she realized. It was as though every time she'd seen him previously, even in the company of the sisters that he was clearly so fond of, he'd been carrying some unseen weight, and she realized it now only in its absence.

"You don't normally waste much time on feeling guilty," Ava said idly, her attention drifting down to Alice, who scowled up at her mother. "I've always admired that about you, you know."

Charlotte, mid-reach for the prosecco bottle, blinked at her sister. "What?"

"Mom and Dad are . . . what they are," Ava said, with a vague hand gesture that somehow perfectly encompassed the never-ending drama of their parents' lives. "They mean well, but they're, you know, pretty self-involved."

"Ha," Charlotte said. This was an understatement.

"But you're never bothered by it," Ava continued. "You don't let them guilt-trip you about the Christmas thing—if it weren't for you, I would have caved years ago and started flying to California for Christmas, no matter what my show schedule looked like. But you're just so . . . steady."

Charlotte topped up her glass and took a slow sip, considering. "I didn't realize you saw me that way." She'd never been sure how much attention her sister paid to her, period. She loved Ava dearly, but her elder sister was undeniably the more melodramatic of the two, the one comfortable with a spotlight, the one who never hesitated to make her own needs known. Charlotte, by comparison, had always felt like she bobbed along just below the surface, living her life as she pleased—which was itself definitely a luxury—but not attracting much in the way of notice from her family. She'd spent a large chunk of her life ensuring that she wasn't someone that *needed* much notice. But maybe Ava had been paying attention all along.

"Well, I do," Ava said, reaching out her own glass to clink against Charlotte's. "So now that I've flattered you, do I get to tell you that you need to let our erstwhile mince pie baker over there blow your back out?"

"We're just . . . business partners," Charlotte said, which did not sound convincing even to her own ears. Ava gave her a vaguely pitying look.

"If that's what the kids are calling it these days," Ava said doubtfully, and then laughed as she dodged the prosecco cork that Charlotte tossed at her head.

Charlotte cast another surreptitious glance over her shoulder at the forearms on display and sighed.

❄

"No," Charlotte said definitively a couple of hours later. It was nearly one; Ava was simultaneously trying to give Alice a bottle and also check on her phone to see what time the Thai restaurant around the corner opened for takeaway, because the kitchen was not in a state that was remotely conducive to preparing lunch.

"What do you mean, 'no'?" Graham demanded. He took a bite of the mince pie in his hand, and his eyes fluttered shut, a rapturous expression on his face. Charlotte, who was already somewhat in denial about the fact that she spent a disturbing amount of time trying not to imagine what having sex with this man might be like, did not find this to be helpful. "It's delicious."

"No," she repeated firmly, taking another small bite of her own mince pie and grimacing. "It's weird. The texture and the flavor combined."

"Don't listen to her," Graham told John solemnly. "And might I induce you to share your recipe?"

John beamed at him. "Of course! I've spent years developing it, but you seem trustworthy."

Graham placed a hand upon his heart. "I promise you, I will guard it carefully."

John smiled fondly at him; Charlotte was mildly outraged, merely on principle. Was there anyone this man couldn't charm? "John," she said wheedlingly, "don't you think that's a bit reckless? We barely *know* him," she added in a stage whisper, nodding in Graham's direction. "He could be a criminal. You can't entrust a criminal with your mince pie recipe."

John looked unmoved. "Charlotte, love, his family's lived in the same house for three hundred years. I think we'd know by now if he was a criminal—he wouldn't be hard to track down."

"Besides," added Simone, who had been waltzing in and out of the kitchen all morning, apparently as the mood took her, "I don't think John should allow *your* romantic entanglements to cloud *his* mince pie judgment."

"*Romantic—*"

"Thank you, John," Graham said loudly, cutting off Charlotte and leaving her to splutter incoherently in an outraged fashion. "If you'll just let me pop my number in your phone—"

John happily handed over his iPhone, Graham typed away, and

before Charlotte quite knew what was happening, he was being sent off with a Tupperware of mince pies, promises to text the recipe post-haste, and repeated inquiries from Ava about whether he was *sure* he had to leave before lunch.

"I've a meeting in the City this afternoon, unfortunately, and then I'm headed down to Eden Priory for the night," he said apologetically, shrugging back into his coat in a languid, elegant way that was extremely irritating, because it had never occurred to Charlotte until this moment that there was a sexy way to don a coat. Something dark crossed his face at this, like a thundercloud scuttling across the sky, but it was quickly erased. His glance flicked toward her and snagged on her face. "I'll see you Wednesday?" he asked, in a slightly lower tone.

"Yes. The afternoon?"

"I'll pick you up at two," he said, and then with a wave he was gone.

And Charlotte was left in his wake with a messy kitchen to clean, and forty-eight hours in which to try to convince herself that she wasn't counting the minutes until she'd see him again.

THREE WEEKS
TO CHRISTMAS

CHAPTER NINE

hate rich people."

"Doesn't your dad work in Hollywood? Feels a bit pot-kettle."

"I don't think you want to go down that road with me, Country Estate Man." Charlotte looked darkly at the Maserati idling directly opposite the bench she was settling onto in Sloane Square. "My point is more that they buy such stupid things with all their piles of money." She gestured at the car before her, which had probably cost an amount that would make her cry.

"Lane, that is an objectively beautiful car."

"And yet you're driving around in a banged-up Mini Cooper."

"In case you hadn't noticed, I currently can't afford a new roof, so I sure as hell can't afford a Maserati."

She eyed him skeptically; he looked a bit posher than usual today, wearing wool trousers and an oxford shirt underneath a crisp gray coat. She guessed this was what he looked like in his regular life, when he was going to his fancy job every day, and it was strange to think of him in that context, which felt very removed from worries about a leaky roof and escorting her on these outings around London and the surrounding countryside.

"But when you bought that Mini Cooper, you could have afforded something nicer," she said on a sudden hunch, and the slight reddening of the tips of his ears informed her that she'd guessed right.

"I will grant you that I'm not a spend-a-couple-of-years'-salary-on-a-car type of man," he admitted.

"Ha! Which returns us to my original point: rich people suck." She opened her sketchbook to a blank page. "Which my investigation into this particular movie already convinced me of, by the way."

Charlotte, having done some Wikipedia research that morning, was genuinely appalled by the fact that this movie—titled, ridiculously, *A London Home for Christmas*—even existed.

Graham shifted on the bench, looking a bit guilty. "I don't know much about it."

Charlotte, who had begun to sketch in rough strokes, glanced up at him, frowning. "You said you'd seen all of the movies with your sisters."

"*Most* of them," he corrected. "I fell asleep ten minutes into this one. I recognize the building, and Eloise has given me strict instructions on the angle you're supposed to capture, but otherwise I couldn't tell you a thing about it."

"How fortunate for you that *I* can enlighten you," Charlotte said smugly, her eyes on the mansard roof of the redbrick mansion block before her. Apparently the building had been converted into a hotel several years earlier, so she carefully omitted the hotel signs and ostentatiously waving flags from her sketch.

"You? Charlotte *I have never seen a Christmas film* Lane?"

"A fun fact about me is that I *do* know how to use the internet," she said. "And I went on an absolutely fascinating Wikipedia journey this morning. First of all, you didn't mention that this movie is basically the British equivalent of a Hallmark movie."

"A what?" He sounded genuinely confused, and Charlotte experienced a moment of overpowering envy. What she wouldn't give to be similarly unwise to the ways of the Hallmark Christmas universe.

She waved the hand holding her pencil. "You know. Big-city woman with an impressive career heads back to her charming, rural hometown for Christmas, where she falls in love with a Christmas tree farmer who makes her realize that professional success means nothing and that all she really needs is marriage and the bonds of community."

He stared at her, appalled. "That's nightmarish."

"You have no idea. There are also ones that involve strangers trying to travel in the middle of a snowstorm and being forced to string together a series of unconventional transportation options to reach their destination, and an entire subgenre involving royalty, and this series where Vanessa Hudgens plays, like, three different characters—"

"Please stop."

"Happily." She heaved a world-weary sigh. "I thought they were an American phenomenon, but it sounds like this one was a one-off hit that took the internet by storm about ten years ago. I don't know how I've never heard of it before."

"Too busy sitting in a cold cave wearing all black and blocking the word 'Christmas' in all of your social media settings," he said, and she could tell without looking at him that he was smiling.

She rolled her eyes, suppressing her own urge to smile. "Anyway. Would you like to know the plot?"

"I have a feeling you're going to tell me regardless."

"Correct." She flipped to a new page in her sketchbook and began working on a detailed sketch of one of the dormer windows. "Our tale begins with a plucky girl from bumblefuck nowhere—"

"Meaning?"

Charlotte paused, wracking her brain. "Wales, maybe? There was definitely some sort of attempt at a colorful accent in the one clip I watched."

"Noted. Please continue."

"Anyway, she was, like, a dairy maid—"

"I'm sorry—was this historical?"

"Nope. She was a *modern* dairy maid."

"I'm starting to regret having slept through this."

"Just wait. She found out that she was the only heiress to a distant relative, and she inherited his house on Sloane Square—"

"Was her distant relative a duke?"

"No. Just a humble man of mystery with some sort of wealth that was probably gained through investing in Russian oil companies or something. Wholesome stuff."

"So she inherited his house," Graham prompted, and Charlotte knew she had him.

"But there was a codicil in the will that meant that she *had* to spend the entire month of December in the house every year or she'd forfeit her inheritance, because the distant relative had had no family and desperately wanted his house to *experience the magic of the Christmas season* again."

"Please tell me that was a direct quote."

"It was. I googled it. Anyway," she said, as he choked on a laugh, "she moves into her mansion, charms the entire staff that works there, *Beauty and the Beast*-style—to put it in parlance that you'd understand—"

"Fuck off."

"And then she falls in love with the house's caretaker, who turns out to be a *European prince in disguise*—"

"From which country?" he asked, nonplussed.

She waved her hand. "One of the fake ones they make up for Hallmark movies, which always seem to be some sort of French/Swiss/

Austrian/Italian mash-up, and are named, like, Grimovia or something."

"Why is he in disguise as a caretaker in a square in Belgravia?"

"To escape his royal destiny."

"But how did he end up in this specific house?"

"Don't worry about it. The first rule of Hallmark movies is not to ask too many questions; the entire thing cracks like an egg under the slightest bit of scrutiny. *Anyway*, the climactic scene is when she realizes that he's a prince and not a humble caretaker, and she declares that she *cannot be with him*, not because he lied to her, but because of her unfailing loyalty to her own royal family—"

"And this girl's from *Wales*?" he asked with an incredulous snort. "Didn't realize there were so many ardent millennial royalists in Wales."

"Did you not *just* hear me? You don't question the internal logic of a Hallmark movie! So she flees from the mansion in tears, and he chases her through the streets of London—"

"On foot?"

"Yes. They're running the entire time. She's apparently half a block ahead at all times—I found an entire Reddit thread dedicated to discussion of her footwear in this scene—and they make it to Trafalgar Square—"

"From Belgravia? That's got to be two miles."

"Well, they're very fit, clearly, from all the stairs in the mansion. And he catches up to her in front of the Christmas tree, and he tells her that he's going to *renounce his claim to the throne* so that they can get married and stay in London. And eventually, he'll get British citizenship."

"Is this pro-Brexit propaganda?" he asked suspiciously.

"Unclear. If you squint, you could almost call it a heartwarming tale of immigration and assimilation."

"Christ almighty. I cannot believe Eloise wanted this film to be included in this series."

"From what I can tell, it was *wildly* popular." She reached into her pouch of drawing pencils for a fresh one; glancing up, she saw that Graham, sitting next to her on the bench they'd claimed, looked horrified. "It's nice to see that Americans don't have a monopoly on movies like this," she said, feeling suddenly quite cheerful.

"Can we please acknowledge how disturbing it is that you are describing this god-awful piece of media so gleefully? I *like* Christmas, but feel offended on behalf of the holiday just listening to this."

"It's part of my evil plan to make you realize that this holiday is a nightmare invented by capitalism."

"Might need to check with some religious scholars on that one, Lane," he said dryly, and as she turned her attention back to her sketch, she couldn't prevent the smile tugging at the corners of her mouth.

❄

"So this is what hell looks like."

"That's the spirit. Very charming. Have I mentioned what a radiant font of holiday joy you are?"

"I'm sorry that not all of us were born with some sort of deranged need to charm the pants off every person we meet."

"Have I charmed *your* pants off?"

"I do seem to be wearing them, if you hadn't noticed."

"I think you've forgotten that 'pants' means something different in Britain than it does in America."

"If you discuss my underwear again, I am going to shove you into that fountain."

"Noted."

They were in Trafalgar Square, which was a truly harrowing place this time of year, particularly for someone who had not the slightest desire to elbow her way through the teeming hordes of tourists solely to get a photo of a Christmas tree.

They'd wandered this way once she'd finished her sketches and taken enough photos of the mansion block that she felt confident she could re-create it in detail later on; Graham, meanwhile, had vanished into the hotel, pausing to chat with the doorman for a couple of minutes on the way in. He'd returned about ten minutes later, looking exceedingly grim, and reported that the hotel seemed to "have no concerns for their dignity," because there was a photo opportunity by one of the lobby Christmas trees, in which visitors could take photos with cardboard cutouts of the movie characters. This had made Charlotte laugh for about a minute straight, while Graham had sat next to her on the bench, looking pained.

"Do *not* mention this to Eloise; I don't want to give her any ideas," he said darkly.

"You *are* trying to figure out how to capitalize on your *Christmas, Truly* fame," she said, once she'd stopped laughing. "This could be the way!"

"I'm trying to work out how to do it in a *non-horrifying* way, if you recall," he said repressively. "And I don't think you'll be laughing if *you* end up as one of the cardboard cutouts," he added, which was enough to shut Charlotte up in a hurry.

By the time they'd arrived in Trafalgar Square after nearly forty-five minutes of walking, she had to admit that Graham was right, and the notion of running that route in heeled boots was, frankly, insane.

"Please remove me from this terrifying nightmare," she said, eyeing the ridiculous lines of people at the various food stalls at the Christmas market that had been erected in the square. Even Graham was looking a bit harried by this point, so they took refuge in the National Gallery. "At least it's warm in here," she said as they left their coats at coat check and set off at a slow, meandering pace. Compared to the crowds outside, taking selfies in front of the Christmas tree and browsing the stalls at the pop-up market, the museum, crowded as it was, felt like something of an oasis of calm.

"Do you have anything you wanted to see?" he asked.

She shook her head. "Not particularly—if you don't mind just wandering? I haven't been here in a few years."

"I don't think I have, either," he confessed as they set off. "When I was at my previous job, I never had time."

"Financial accounting," she said vaguely, recalling their previous conversation and trying not to sound too bored at the thought. Charlotte had never had a proper desk job—had left school and immediately used her savings (thank you, *Christmas, Truly*) to launch her business and keep herself afloat those first few years—but she was pretty confident that there were lots (and lots) of traditional nine-to-five jobs that would be more interesting than whatever Graham had done, until recently, for work.

"Yeah, with a consulting firm in the City. Long hours, late nights, pretty much what you'd expect. And on the weekends, my girlfriend never wanted to come back into central London—not when we spent so much time here during the week already." He paused, then cleared his throat. "My *ex*-girlfriend," he added quietly, and something within Charlotte loosened.

"Did you . . . like it?" she asked, in part because she didn't want to address the ex-girlfriend question head-on, in part because she was actually curious.

"It was fine." He sighed, running a hand through his neatly combed hair. There were dark smudges beneath his eyes, as if he'd had several late nights recently. She wondered precisely how serious the financial situation at Eden Priory was, for him to look like this.

Unless—the thought suddenly occurred to her—the late nights

that his face offered proof of were not from work or worry at all, but from something more fun. He might have spent a couple of days with Charlotte, but she had no idea how he was spending his nights—and his comment about his ex-girlfriend really hadn't done anything to clarify that question.

And it was definitely, definitely none of her business.

"I was always good at maths, so it wasn't as though I wasn't suited to the work—I wanted a career that would allow me to save enough to serve as a cushion for Eden Priory, like my dad did; we'd be in a lot worse trouble right now if he'd not worked in corporate law. And I—well. I didn't want my sisters to have to worry about that, when it came time for them to decide what to study. I wanted them to be able to do something they loved."

She hesitated, then asked, "If you could do any job, what would it be? If you didn't have the house—if you didn't need to worry."

He was silent for long enough that she wondered if he was going to reply at all; they passed a large group of French tourists and found themselves before a Turner painting of a ship listing in a turbulent sea. Turner had never been her favorite, personally—too many ships; too many ocean scenes in general—but pretty much anything seemed impressive when you slapped a large gilt frame on it and hung it in a setting as spectacular as this one.

"I'd like to work for . . . a nonprofit, some sort of charity," he said softly, at last. "I'm good at what I do, but it would be nice to use those skills for something that felt a bit more worthwhile." He hesitated, and Charlotte remained silent, hoping that, if she didn't say anything, he wouldn't realize she was there, gaining this rare insight into his head—his heart. "A friend of mine from uni works at a firm that specializes in nonprofit accounting," he said quietly. "He tried to recruit me, a couple of years ago—right around the time when my dad got sick. But it would have been a pretty big pay cut, and with my dad having to step back from his job around that time . . . it felt irresponsible."

She stared determinedly at the painting before her, the brushstrokes that created the foaming, angry sea. "You deserve to have a job that you love—or at least one that you care about," she said softly, and she felt his eyes slide away from the painting and toward her face, even as she didn't turn to meet his gaze. For the briefest moment, she considered reaching out to brush his hand—but just as quickly jerked her hand back. She didn't think he'd noticed.

She started to wander toward the next painting, and he walked quietly beside her, his hands in his pockets. She risked a glance at him, and saw that his brow was slightly furrowed. "Maybe, if we can somehow make the house turn a profit consistently . . ." He trailed off, gave a small shake of the head, as if to dismiss the thought. Charlotte bit her lip, but didn't say anything as they strolled into the next room, a bit quieter, full of Victorian art. Her gaze landed on a painting at random, and she approached it, her eyes widening when they snagged on the name. "Oh—this is a Christian Calloway piece!"

She turned to see him standing behind her, regarding the painting in question with the dispassionate eye of an expert. "I always forget that he has a few in here from the end of his career."

Charlotte vaguely knew—in the way she vaguely knew the history of a number of artists, but didn't actually have an art history degree, so couldn't speak with expertise on any of them—that Christian Calloway's work had started out incredibly commercial (book illustrations, textiles and wallpaper, home goods), and then, in later life, once he was financially secure, he'd turned to less sellable works that had earned him great critical acclaim. Eden Priory featured more examples of his early work, since there was much more of it, and also because the National Gallery, she recalled now, owned the most famous pieces from his late-career renaissance.

The one they were now standing before was a landscape; Charlotte wasn't familiar enough with the subtleties of the various English counties to tell if this was Hampshire, somewhere near Eden Priory, or somewhere else farther afield; the informational placard merely stated that it depicted a farmer at work, and that it was intended to be some sort of commentary on the class system in England. Calloway had, she recalled, been an early socialist, though she couldn't help but wonder precisely how deep his socialist tendencies had run, given, again, the *literal mansion* that he'd inherited from his father.

She considered it for a moment, tilting her head to the side. After several seconds had passed, she realized that Graham was not looking at the painting, but at her.

"What?" she asked, a bit defensively.

"What do you think of it?" he asked. There was nothing in his tone to indicate that this was intended to be a test, but it was undeniably a bit weird to be asked your opinion on a piece of artwork by a relative of the artist himself.

"I don't know," she said cautiously. She considered it again; it was dark in tone, and despite its rural setting, there were none of the rolling green hills that you might expect from an English pastoral painting. The sky was ominous, the fields golden and brown—clearly harvest time, as the depiction of the many laborers in the field implied. "It's a bit . . . grim. I think . . ." She hesitated, then decided that there was no point in starting to lie to him now. She'd hardly made an effort to charm him thus far. "I think I prefer his commercial art."

His mouth twitched. "So do I."

She glanced at him, startled. "You do?"

He nodded. "He's most famous for it for a reason."

"Because it was more available to an everyday person and not hidden away in a museum," she pointed out, for the sake of playing devil's advocate.

"Fair enough," he agreed. "But also . . . it's better."

"It is." She glanced at him, and saw that he was smiling faintly; she liked his smile. She liked when he smiled at *her*, as if they had a private joke.

"Have you ever thought about your art being in a museum some-day?" he asked a few minutes later; they were in a room full of Cézanne and Renoir, and Charlotte had paused for a moment upon entering, soaking in the sight of this many spectacular pieces of art in such a confined space.

"About what?" she asked, distracted by the sight of a child running in circles around his parents, cackling maniacally. She was extremely grateful that Alice couldn't walk yet, and also extremely disturbed by the prospect of what her future Christmases might look like.

"This." He waved his hand around, encompassing the entire room. "Your art. On display in a gallery."

Charlotte shook her head. "My art is really commercial—very clearly the sort of thing you'd sell in a shop, not hang in a gallery."

"Is that always what you envisioned making?"

Charlotte paused, considering; usually, when asked about how she became an artist, she merely mentioned her love of painting, of creating something from a blank page—which was true. But she rarely thought about—or discussed—why she made the specific type of art that she did, the memories that drove her. She said, after another few seconds, "When I was a kid, I loved picture books—all kids do, obviously. But even as I got older, I kept looking at them, kept looking at all the illustrations. The way they made me feel—the world they depicted . . . it felt so warm and safe. I started making art that made me feel the same way. When I go to fancy gallery openings, or museum exhibits about . . . I don't know, Important Art, I can appreciate the skill of the artist, I can even feel the emotions they're trying to invoke, but it doesn't make me feel the way that I want my art to make people feel."

She broke off, a bit startled; she hadn't meant to lecture him about her artistic vision—hadn't meant to share this much of something that felt so personal to her, for all that it was how she made a living.

Graham, however, was smiling faintly. "That seems like as good a reason as I've ever heard, for anyone to do anything."

She sighed, her mouth flattening. "I wish my parents had been that easily convinced."

"You're doing something you love, that you're incredibly good at," he objected, frowning slightly.

She shrugged. "But it's not the thing that *they're* good at, so they don't understand it. Sometimes I wonder . . ." She trailed off, hesitating.

"What?" He sounded genuinely curious—he always did, when he spoke to her. In all their conversations, it felt as though her answers really mattered to him, no matter how trivial the topic. It made her feel seen in a way that she hadn't realized she'd been craving.

She sighed. "Sometimes I wonder, if I *did* make highbrow art that made it to museums, or was exhibited in fancy galleries, if they'd be more impressed. If they'd *care* more."

Graham's frown deepened, his lips pressed into a thin line. "If they don't care, that says nothing about you, Lane—and everything about them. Because your art is brilliant." He said it casually, as if he'd not said anything important at all—anything that mattered. But it mattered to her—and this felt dangerous, for reasons that she couldn't quite explain.

But it occupied her thoughts as they continued their slow progress through the museum, paying a visit to one of Charlotte's favorite rooms, full of Dutch flower paintings. She'd spent the past four years turning herself into someone no one needed to be concerned about, after the disastrous end of her last relationship. Padma, her friends from college, her friends in the city—they'd been worried about her, then, but once the dust had settled and she felt like herself again, she was determined to never let herself feel that way again. Never cause anyone to *worry* over her again. She was just Charlotte—steady, unemotional, unneedy. Not someone who required any concern, any reassurance.

But she'd allowed Graham this peek at her—at the touchy, vulnerable side of herself that she kept carefully hidden—and he'd not even hesitated for a moment before coming to her defense. Before making it clear that what her parents—or anyone else—thought about her was irrelevant to what *he* did.

And Charlotte, who had tried her hardest not to care what anyone thought of her for a very, very long time, was beginning to wonder, as they made their way back to the entrance to retrieve their coats and then step into the December chill, if she might care, just a tiny bit, about Graham Calloway's opinion.

CHAPTER TEN

Two days later, she was working in the coffee shop down the street from Ava's when Graham sat down in the chair opposite her without so much as a word in greeting, clutching a cup of tea and wearing a Christmas sweater so ugly that she honestly wondered if he'd lost a bet.

"Why in god's name are you wearing that?" she asked, deciding that they were past any need for niceties in their relationship.

He glanced down, his expression softening slightly at the sight of the giant, glowing-nosed Rudolph that had been carefully knitted onto the green sweater. "It's my Christmas jumper."

"It's the most horrifying thing I've ever seen. Where did you get it—dumpster diving in the dead of night?"

He took a sip of tea, then set down his cup on the table. "It belonged to my father," he said evenly.

His *dead* father, he didn't bother to clarify.

"Oh." Charlotte scrambled to salvage this. "It's . . . whimsical."

"Is it?" he asked dryly, running a finger idly around the rim of his cup. "I'm so glad to hear it. You can't imagine how desperately I strive for whimsy."

"I mean, it has a sort of . . . vintage charm," she offered this time, trying a different tack. "You know—so ugly it's good, that sort of thing?"

"I think you were best off calling it horrifying and leaving it at that," he advised.

"Noted." She paused, wishing that her coffee cup wasn't empty, so that she'd have something to bury her face in. "Did you have a reason for stopping by, other than to have me unknowingly insult cherished family heirlooms?"

This, at least, prompted a smile—or the small curve of the lips that came when he was trying *not* to smile, but couldn't quite manage it. She preferred it to many of the proper smiles she'd ever seen. "I actually came to ask if you had plans this evening. I do not don the Rudolph sweater lightly, and it's time for my annual drunk Christmas night with my sisters and Leo."

"Your . . . what?" Was this some quaint English custom that she should be aware of? It didn't *sound* terribly quaint, but lots of things here sounded nothing like what they actually were, so maybe it was just a continuation of that noble tradition.

He waved a hand. "We started it when I was at uni, and it's continued ever since then. Lizzie is a more recent addition to the guest list," he added hastily, as though concerned she'd think he'd been leading his adolescent sister into vice and sin. "We compete to make the best Christmas cocktails and do a blind taste test."

"How blind can the taste test really be, if there are only four of you?" she asked skeptically.

"Five, now, because Jess comes too. And it used to be six—Leo broke up with his longtime girlfriend a few months ago."

Charlotte hesitated; she knew that Ava and Kit didn't have plans tonight, other than a delivery pizza and watching some of the old *Bake Off* Christmas specials (further proof that Christmas was bad:

the fact that they sprinkled a bunch of fake snow in a random field in Berkshire, had the bakers don Christmas ensembles, and expected people to ignore the fact that there were green leaves on all the trees outside; this holiday was *so stupid*).

She should say no. Should resist this strange pull, which made her feel nervous and exhilarated and worried, all at once. If it had just been simple attraction, she'd have known what to do with it—it was maybe not the world's *best* decision to sleep with the guy she'd just entered into a business arrangement with, but she was pretty sure they'd be able to handle it like adults, if that was all it was.

The problem, however, was that she was growing increasingly worried that this was something else entirely—something more. Something that she'd find it harder to walk away from.

But when he looked at her the way he was now—the arrogant smile gone, something close to naked hope in his eyes—and the air still felt charged between them, and every sentence they exchanged somehow felt full of possibility . . .

She didn't want to say no.

The ugly Christmas sweater seemed to be a family thing. "Charlotte!" Eloise said, flinging open the door and looking thrilled—*too* thrilled—to see her. "Graham didn't tell us that he'd invited you." She turned and called over her shoulder, "What an interesting omission." She was wearing a sweater that looked as though 1993 had vomited all over it; there was a terrifying polar bear wearing a Christmas sweater of its own, and whoever had stitched on the eyes hadn't filled them in with a different color thread, so they were the same red as the sweater, giving the polar bear a slightly demonic look.

Charlotte smiled a bit uncertainly, and then lifted the bottle of bourbon she carried. "I brought cocktail provisions?"

Eloise flung a dramatic hand before her eyes. "Don't show me! We're not meant to see any of the ingredients anyone's bringing!"

"How on earth can you possibly do a blind taste test if you all need to assemble the cocktails?" Charlotte asked as Eloise stepped back to let her into Graham's flat, on the first floor of a terraced house on a quiet, tree-lined street a couple of blocks from the Chiswick high street. She noted the sleek shoe rack just inside the door, and toed off her own boots, feeling very pleased that she was wearing her *Fuck off, I'm reading* socks, which she'd bought matching pairs of for herself and Padma a few years back.

"You can't," came Graham's voice from another room, in answer to her question. "The notion of the blind taste test is a complete fiction that Eloise insists on clinging to."

"Let me have my illusions!" Eloise smiled cheerfully at Charlotte, then led her into what turned out to be the kitchen.

"Wow," she said, as soon as she walked in. "This looks like a kitchen in a magazine." It really did: there were cabinets painted a gorgeous navy blue, fitted with brass hardware; a black-and-white tiled floor; beautiful, retro-looking appliances; a copper light fixture casting a warm glow above the marble-topped kitchen island, which currently featured an assortment of liquors, liqueurs, and mixers.

"It's because he *sold his soul to work for the capitalist pigs*," Eloise said dramatically. Charlotte thought about Graham's coldly logical decision to pursue a specific line of work in order to support Eden Priory, partly to ensure that his sisters didn't have to, and had to bite her lip to hold back a retort. This wasn't her family—wasn't her fight. And Graham wasn't hers to protect.

"Says the woman whose greatest dream is to open a florist's shop and sell flowers to posh people in Richmond," Jess said dryly from where she was sitting at the kitchen table, cross-legged in her chair, a half-full coupe of champagne in her hand.

"Rude," Eloise said.

"It's because I love to cook," Graham said patiently to Charlotte. "So I spent my entire renovation budget on a single room."

"Mystifying," Charlotte said, and he flashed a grin at her. "All I need in my kitchen is an air fryer so that my leftover take-out fries can be reheated properly."

Eloise brandished a bottle of champagne in Charlotte's direction. "Bubbly?"

"Why not?" Charlotte said. She turned to face Graham, who was peeling a lemon to create lemon twists. "This is fancy."

He glanced up at her, his hands still busy. He was still wearing his appalling Christmas sweater—of course—but the sleeves were rolled up, revealing his forearms. There was a battered watch on one wrist that looked as though it had seen a few generations of use. "I told you, we take drunk Christmas seriously."

"Hence starting with champagne, despite the fact that we're all about to be drinking large quantities of liquor?"

"Precisely." He set down the peeler, reached for a knife, and began slicing an orange. There was something oddly mesmerizing about watching the movement of his hands, which was so assured. Oh no— she had a competence kink. She knew this about herself. Did slicing citrus fruits count for this kink? She wouldn't have thought so, but the fact that she couldn't tear her eyes from him indicated otherwise.

Eloise handed her a champagne coupe.

"Where's Leo?" Charlotte asked, leaning back against the counter.

"Picking up the curries," he replied, eyes on the task before him. "And Lizzie's on her way."

"Correction!" came a voice from the other room. "Lizzie is here!"

Charlotte turned to see the erstwhile Cindy-Lou Who from the Christmas lights switch-on entering the kitchen; Graham dropped his knife and crossed the kitchen to take the reusable Waitrose bag she clutched in her arms. She was wearing an oversized Christmas sweater featuring—Charlotte did a double take to confirm—a bunch of dancing skeletons in Santa hats and an elf emerging from a coffin.

"Lizzie, this is Charlotte—Charlotte, Lizzie's my youngest sister."

"Hello," Charlotte said, a bit wary in light of the expression of undisguised curiosity on Lizzie's face.

"Nice to meet you," Lizzie said simply, and Charlotte—who had been halfway expecting some sort of interrogation—breathed a sigh of relief. "You're the one who's an artist, right? Graham mentioned it. I'd love to buy you a coffee sometime and pick your brain about making a living in the arts."

"Of course," Charlotte said, flattered; it was always a strange, novel pleasure whenever someone was impressed by her art career, rather than vaguely amused by it, as had always been the case in her family. "Nice sweater."

Lizzie glanced down at it. "It's my protest sweater, because Halloween is clearly superior to Christmas, and I want this party moved to October."

"Halloween doesn't have the right *flavors* for festive cocktails," Eloise protested, and Jess rolled her eyes; this was clearly a long-standing family debate.

"It does," Lizzie insisted with a frown. "You're just unimaginative."

"Your feedback has been taken into consideration, as always," Graham said, ruffling his sister's hair. She directed her scowl at him.

There was more commotion from the other room, and in another moment Leo entered the kitchen, his arms full of takeaway containers and in the midst of some sort of monologue about the environmental impact of takeaway.

"I'll reuse the containers," Graham said, "so long as you stop whingeing now and actually let us eat in peace."

"I'll agree," Leo said, nodding seriously as though they were taking some sort of solemn oath together, "only because I want us to eat before it gets cold, because based on previous years' experience with this event, it's best not done on an empty stomach." He looked at Charlotte, assessing. "I hope you're up to this. You're a bit small."

Charlotte drained her glass of champagne. "I once drank my college boyfriend under the table, and he was ten inches taller than me."

Leo considered her for a long moment, then turned to look at Graham, who was now plating the food.

"What are you doing?" Graham asked, not looking up from the container in his hands.

"Considering your height difference with Charlotte here. I believe it's about ten inches as well." Leo turned back to Charlotte. "Would you say that's your preferred height difference with a romantic partner?"

"Leo?" Graham asked, his tone pleasant.

"Yes, oldest friend in the universe?"

"Please shut up."

In the fuss that followed, as everyone was occupied with retrieving plates and dishing up heaping servings, Charlotte was able to busy herself pouring another glass of champagne, claiming a plate of her own, and fighting the blush creeping up her throat, carefully avoiding looking at Graham for even a second.

❋

Three hours later, Charlotte had decided that the drunk Christmas party was the best idea *ever*.

"Seriously," she said to Eloise, definitely not for the first time, "I think I should have come up with this."

"I know!" Eloise squealed; it was a relief to note that however much Charlotte had had to drink so far that evening, it was still not as much as Eloise, who had been going back for seconds of some of the contest entries.

Graham, of course, had been right: the notion of it being a blind taste test was insane, and the entire evening had almost immediately devolved into chaos, with each of them advocating loudly for their personal creation. Graham, annoyingly, had won; he'd made some sort of delicious mulled whiskey with clementines—Charlotte had already had two glasses of it, and was very tempted to go back for a third. (The knowledge of how badly her head was already likely to hurt tomorrow morning was the only thing causing her to exercise a small degree of restraint.)

Eloise turned to face Leo, who was in the process of explaining to a very tolerant Jess why his pomegranate martini had been better than Eloise's rosemary gin fizz. "There's not a prize for second place," Jess said patiently; she alone among them had limited herself to a few sips of each cocktail, and was therefore something of the parent in the room at the moment.

"There's not a prize for *first* place," Graham put in, sounding annoyed. He was sprawled in an armchair opposite Charlotte across the coffee table, one leg slung over one of the arms. His glasses were a bit askew, his cheeks flushed from the drink. Every time his dark eyes landed on her, she felt a wave of goose bumps rising on her arms.

"Your prize is the satisfaction of a job well done," Lizzie told him, leaning over to offer him a poke in the side. He gave her a look of tolerant affection that softened something within Charlotte.

"Then why," he asked his sister, "did you make me buy you the world's most expensive notebook the year you won?"

"I just wanted to see if you'd do it," Lizzie said frankly. She turned to Charlotte. "If I ever win again, though, I'm demanding a holiday change as my prize."

"Does this mean that I can ask *you* for some overpriced bit of rub- bish this year, then?"

Lizzie considered. "No." She reached up to ruffle her brother's hair.

"When I start working for an evil consulting firm making heaps of money, we can revisit this conversation."

"Need I remind you that I am not, at the moment, making any money at all?"

"Well, then it's good you won the cocktail contest this year, so you can save your pounds instead of buying me nice stationery."

"Why," Graham wondered to the room at large, "do I feel as though I've been taken advantage of?" He looked at Charlotte, and her skin prickled again, despite the fact that there wasn't—*shouldn't* have been—anything at all suggestive in what he'd said.

"At least Francesca's not around anymore, making that same elder-flower cocktail *every single year*," Eloise said, draining her glass.

"I liked that cocktail," Leo said with a frown. He turned to Graham. "You should've got the recipe off her before breaking up."

"Noted," Graham said, extremely dryly. "Next time I'm ending a yearslong relationship, I'll be certain to write down any important recipes ahead of time."

Eloise yawned and reached for her phone on the coffee table, checking the time. "God, we need to go. Jess and I both have to work tomorrow, no matter how hungover."

"*Some* of us considered this fact at the beginning of the evening," Jess said, a bit smugly. Eloise flipped two fingers at her.

"I should go, too," Lizzie said. "I signed up for a yoga class at eight."

"Since when do you do yoga?" Eloise asked her sister, looking astonished. "You hate all forms of exercise."

"Since my back started hurting when I get up in the morning. Aging is terrible," Lizzie informed them solemnly, with predictable, profanity-ridden results.

"I'm taking a cab home," Leo told Lizzie, once he'd stopped telling her that twenty-two-year-olds should be legally banned from complaining about aging. "Want to split it?"

"Yes, please!" Lizzie said, visibly brightening with the promise of a warm cab rather than a chilly walk to the Tube. She turned to Charlotte. "Are you headed far? Do you need a lift, too—or we can walk you to the bus?"

"I'll walk her," Graham said easily, before any other offers could come in, and Charlotte slid a glance at him. This, apparently, sounded exactly as suggestive to the others as it did to her, which meant that no one questioned it for even a second, since—as she was slowly beginning to realize—she and Graham were the subject of an intense, extremely avid bit of collective matchmaking. She hadn't been on the receiving end of an effort this strong since college. And then, within a matter of minutes, they were alone, and the silence suddenly felt heavy.

She stood, rubbing her hands on her leggings. "I'll help you clean up," she said, and Graham rose, too, collecting glasses from seemingly every flat surface in the room. She was glad he didn't tell her to leave it for later; she didn't know what to do with herself, despite the fact that this was hardly the first time they'd been alone together.

She set the dishes down on the counter, and turned to the kitchen table, gathering up the plates they'd eaten on to hand to Graham, who was standing at the sink, rinsing the dishes in cursory fashion before loading them into the dishwasher. He carefully rinsed each of the reusable plastic takeaway containers, true to his word to Leo.

All too soon, however, the dishwasher was loaded and quietly humming away, the paper bags the takeaway had come in tossed in the trash, and Graham was wiping down the counter. He was very neat, she'd noticed; after a party like this, under ordinary circumstances—circumstances in which she wasn't trying to avoid having a conversation with the man standing next to her, because she had no idea what to say, no idea how to alleviate the pressure that seemed to be growing around them—she'd have dumped the dishes in the sink and gone to bed, worrying about the mess the following morning. (A strategy that she always regretted the next day, of course, but she never learned her lesson.) But his kitchen was once again spotless; the living room, too, had the sort of cozy-and-lived-in-but-tidy look to it that Charlotte had dreamed of achieving but never quite managed, given her propensity for leaving art supplies and books and empty coffee mugs scattered around all the common areas of whatever apartment she happened to live in. And compared to the new-baby disorder of Ava and Kit's flat, this felt like something out of a catalog.

Graham tossed the rag in the sink and turned to look at her. Despite the ill-advised number of cocktails she'd consumed that evening, Charlotte felt suddenly wide awake, alert to every movement of his body. He looked at her for a long moment, and then reached out slowly—so slowly that she could have stepped easily out of his reach, if she wanted.

But she didn't want.

Instead, she let him hook his thumb and forefinger around her wrist, tugging her closer.

She felt her heart thumping in her chest.

She looked down at his hand, the fingers tanned a shade darker than the fair skin of her wrist, and felt the tap of her pulse against his thumb.

She looked up and met his eyes.

He swallowed.

"I'll walk you home," he said softly, after a long moment in which they stood in silence, linked by his fingers on her skin, neither of them speaking.

"What if I wanted to stay?" she replied, equally softly, and she saw him exhale slowly—*felt* it, somehow, in her chest.

"If we'd not just drunk our body weights in liquor, I'd want you to," he said. He hesitated. Reached out. And very, very slowly tucked a loose strand of hair behind her ear. His eyes were dark on her; a curl had broken ranks and tumbled onto his forehead, and she didn't trust herself to reach up and push it back. Didn't trust herself to touch him at all. She, apparently, had less self-control than he did.

And then, at last, his eyes slid from hers. "I'll get your coat," he said, his voice low.

And while she waited for him to hand it to her—while he walked her home, along the streets of Chiswick, aglow with Christmas lights, passing the occasional throng of Friday-night revelers—and when he left her on Ava's front steps with a last, lingering glance—she knew that something, somehow, had changed.

And that she was in very deep trouble.

CHAPTER ELEVEN

Y ou look awful."

This helpful greeting was Ava's way of saying good morning on Saturday, when Charlotte staggered into the kitchen at a little past nine, which, all things considered, she thought was a completely reasonable time to awaken. It had not been an entirely peaceful lie-in— Alice had woken up at five, resisted all of Kit's murmured attempts to soothe her, screeched fitfully for some time, and finally been removed to the living room, allowing Charlotte to drift back into a doze, which had involved a very weird dream in which she and Graham were in costume as Santa and Mrs. Claus, serving cocktails to the Grinch.

"I'm too old for drunk Christmas, I think," she muttered, sinking down at the kitchen table and gratefully accepting the mug of coffee that Ava set down in front of her.

"I miss hangovers," Ava said wistfully; now that Charlotte got a proper look at her, she could see that Ava was tired, too, with dark circles under her eyes and the bleary look that seemed to be common to all new parents. Charlotte wondered if Ava would be offended if she bought her an eye cream for Christmas, before immediately deciding that yes, she would.

Right on cue, there was a howl from the living room.

"But you've traded hangovers for the knowledge that you have contributed to the continuation of life on earth," Charlotte informed her sister with a saccharine smile; Ava responded by flipping her off, then rose to see if Kit needed an assist.

Left alone in the relative peace of the kitchen, Charlotte pulled her phone out of the pocket of her joggers, mildly surprised to see that she had a text. Normally her phone was quiet in the mornings here, since everyone back home was still asleep.

> **Graham Calloway:** Good morning. Was wondering if you had plans tomorrow?

She stared down at the message, her heart tapping a strange beat in her chest, warring with an urge to laugh. Of course he used completely proper punctuation in his texting.

> **Charlotte:** Hello, sir. I do not have plans tomorrow, after careful consultation of my calendar.
>
> **Graham:** . . . . .
>
> **Graham:** Are you taking the piss?
>
> **Charlotte:** Yes re: the weirdly formal texting manners
>
> **Charlotte:** No re: not having plans
>
> **Charlotte:** Why
>
> **Graham:** I was wondering if you'd been to Borough Market yet—the food market? By London Bridge.
>
> **Charlotte:** No!
>
> **Charlotte:** I've heard it's delicious
>
> **Graham:** I thought we could go for lunch tomorrow?

Charlotte paused, staring down at her screen. She'd assumed some sort of invitation was forthcoming—why else would he be asking her about her plans?—and yet she still wavered for a moment. She had wondered, upon waking up this morning and remembering that she'd more or less propositioned him the night before, how he would respond—if things would be weird between them. If they'd try to ignore it, chalk it up to too many cocktails, and pretend it hadn't happened.

Clearly, Graham wasn't interested in doing so. But was she?

She sat still for a moment, staring unseeingly down at the screen of her phone, her mind racing—and then, without allowing time to second-guess herself, she simply replied, Noon? and hit send.

And couldn't help smiling when the reply came back:

Perfect.

Borough Market was a madhouse.

"How are there this many people here?" she asked Graham over her shoulder as they bumped and jostled their way through the crowds.

He leaned forward so that she could hear him, his mouth tilted over her shoulder toward her ear. "It's central London in December. It's always horrific."

This was uttered with such distaste that she nearly laughed. "This was *your idea*," she reminded him as they joined the line at some sort of Middle Eastern food stall. "If you hate crowds so much, why on earth did you insist that we come here on a weekend?"

She turned around to face him, just in time to see something unreadable flicker across his face. "You mentioned that the food was one of the things you liked. About Christmas," he clarified unnecessarily. "So I thought you might enjoy a food market."

She stared at him for a long moment. He'd brought her here because of an offhand comment she made over a week ago?

A bit of pink crept into his cheeks. "If you'd rather go elsewhere—"

"No," she said quickly. And then, more softly, "This is perfect." She turned to order a falafel salad before he could reply.

Once they'd claimed their food, they staked out seats, turfing out a couple who were lingering over empty plates, staring adoringly at each other at a table in the shadow of Southwark Cathedral.

"Do you reckon that was a bit rude?" Graham asked as they sat, the couple finally having quailed under Charlotte's unrelenting stare.

"Probably." She shrugged. "But fortune favors the bold—or those not afraid to make it clear that they don't want to eat standing up."

"Yes. I do believe I recall studying that exact quote in my history books at school."

"Where did you go to school?" she asked him curiously.

"LSE for uni. What about you?" he asked, taking a bite of his wrap. "You went to art school, right?"

She nodded. "RISD—the Rhode Island School of Design. I think that's when my mom started despairing—I think she thought that she'd still be able to convince me to stick with acting, but that was a pretty clear signal that it wasn't going to happen." She shrugged. "The good news is, my parents moved to LA a few years ago, so I don't see them nearly as often anymore, which I think is best for all of us. And, of course, they spend a lot more time thinking about themselves than they ever have about me, and the distance keeps them off my back."

He frowned. "Doesn't that bother you, though? They're your parents."

She sighed. It was hard to explain her parents to someone who had never met them. "I think Ava and I have both got used to it over the years." She speared a piece of falafel with her fork. "The problem is, my parents love us, and even love each other—in their weird, extremely dramatic way—but they love themselves the most. They love their own careers, their own reputations, and I think they view everyone around them through that lens. Which probably explains why they've spent most of my life having dramatic arguments and fleeing to remote, glamorous corners of the globe to nurse their wounds, and then coming back together again."

"I can't imagine growing up with parents with a relationship like that," he said slowly, shaking his head. "My parents got married quite young, and they were always sickeningly in love, right up until—"

He broke off sharply, his gaze dropping to the paper plate on the table before him.

"It must have been hard," she said carefully. "Losing your dad so young."

"I got to spent thirty years with him, so I suppose I shouldn't complain," he said, offering an attempt at a smile that didn't remotely pass muster. "If I'd known he'd get sick, though, I might not have spent so much time arguing with him."

"Did you not get along?"

He grimaced. "He . . . had a lot of ideas. About how things should be done. And he wasn't always good about listening to *other* people's ideas—and if he did, and he didn't like the idea, or something went wrong, he'd remind you about it forever. Like the damn Christmas film," he added ruefully, shaking his head. "The house brought out the worst in him sometimes."

He paused, his brow furrowing, and then glanced up to meet her eyes. "But also the best. He loved that house—he loved his family—he was so proud to be a Calloway, so glad to be raising his kids in the same house he'd grown up in. So even though we often disagreed, especially as I got older, I always knew he only got so worked up because he cared so much."

"Which is why you're so afraid to let him down," she said.

He'd lifted his wrap to his mouth to take another bite, but froze now, his hand suspended halfway to his mouth. "I'm not afraid of letting him down," he said mildly.

"Yes, you are," Charlotte said definitively.

"He's dead," he said, an edge creeping into his voice. "There's no way to let him down anymore." He inhaled sharply through his nose, set the wrap down again on his plate. The breath he exhaled was ever-so-slightly shaky. On an impulse, Charlotte dropped her fork, reached across the table, and rested her hand atop his.

"I know," she said softly. "I just meant—you want to do him proud. You don't want to do anything that he would have disapproved of, since he's not here to do things himself."

Her hand was still resting on his; after a moment, he turned his hand to face palm-up, then squeezed her hand in his before drawing his away. "No, you're right—I just—I don't speak of him often."

Then why, Charlotte wanted to ask, was he speaking of his father to her?

But she didn't ask—because she already knew the answer, sort of. It was the same reason she had told him about her parents' complicated relationship with each other, with her, their thoughts on her career. It was the same reason she'd told him in his living room on Friday night that she wanted to stay. And the same reason that she had still, hours later, been able to feel the phantom touch of his fingers on her cheek when he'd brushed her hair behind her ear.

She couldn't put a name to it, whatever this was between them—but it was there, and she felt it, and she knew that he did too.

He glanced down at his watch. "I have good news."

She cleared her throat, trying to dispel the heaviness of her thoughts. "Oh?"

"It's after one, which means it's officially a socially acceptable time to drink on a Sunday. Can I shout you a pint?"

"Here?" she asked, raising her eyebrow at the surrounding crowds.

He shook his head. "No. I know a spot not far from here where we should be able to get a seat—and hear ourselves think."

But thinking, Charlotte thought, was precisely what she didn't want to do at the moment—because if she started thinking, she'd think about all the reasons it was a very, very bad idea to let him take her by the hand, lead her out of the teeming crowds and down the nearby streets, never once dropping her hand.

And she didn't want to think about that—instead, she just wanted to enjoy the weight of his palm against hers.

So she did.

They were nearly at the pub when she felt her phone buzz in her pocket, then buzz again—a call, not a text. She fished it out and glanced at the screen. Ava.

"Sorry, it's my sister," she said, and then pressed the green button on her screen. "Hi. What's up?"

"Charlotte?" Ava sounded breathless.

"Yes? You called me?"

"Right, right," Ava said, now sounding flustered. Good Christ, Charlotte hoped this hadn't been a pocket dial in the middle of some salacious moment with Kit—she'd never be able to look either of them in the face again. "Um, when were you planning on coming home again?"

"I'm not sure," Charlotte said, frowning. "We're in Southwark right now."

"Well, if there's any chance it's going to be in the next hour and a half or so, I was hoping you could do me a *massive* favor." Ava injected a winsome, slightly wheedling note into her voice that Charlotte instantly distrusted.

"Possibly," Charlotte said cautiously, having had too many years of experience with her sister to agree to anything without a bit more information.

"Do you think you could buy Alice a new Christmas dress?" Ava asked. "It's just, we have a bit of a . . . situation here . . ."

"What sort of a situation?" Charlotte asked suspiciously.

"Well, we've been trying to introduce different solid foods, you know, and I gave her sweet potato today and I don't think it agreed with her because—"

"Please do not finish that sentence," Charlotte interrupted.

"Well, the long and short of it is, all six of her Christmas dresses are currently . . . nonoperational. And we're supposed to meet John and Simone at the zoo to meet Santa—"

"Where are they now?" Charlotte asked.

"Kit took them to an exhibit at the Tate to get them out of my hair, so I could have five seconds to myself while Alice was napping, but now none of them are answering their phones—probably left them at coat check—and I am holding a baby that is *covered in shit*. Charlotte, I cannot express to you how much—"

"Please don't." Charlotte heaved a great sigh. "Does this replacement Christmas dress need to come from any shop in particular?"

"Just . . . somewhere nice?" Ava asked, a bit pleadingly. "And make sure it *looks Christmassy,* but not in a tacky way, you know? In a *classic* way. Plaid, wool, that sort of thing. No sequins, for god's sake, she's a *baby* and could *choke on one*—"

"Ava," Charlotte said, realizing that when her sister began to approach this level of theatrics it was best to cut her short, "I promise not to attempt to kill Alice via a Christmas dress. And I'll see you at home in . . . well, as soon as I can get there."

"Thankyouthankyou," Ava said, before there was an ominous howl in the background. "Sorry, I need to go. Hurry, please—"

The line went dead before Charlotte could offer some sort of comforting reply.

She looked at Graham, who was regarding her inquisitively. She thought longingly of a happy hour or two whiled away over pints in some cozy, darkened pub, rather than amid the teeming crowds of Christmas shoppers flooding the city, and sighed.

"How would you feel about going shopping?"

An hour later, Charlotte had to confront a fact that probably should have been obvious: she knew nothing about babies.

Reasoning that it made the most sense to return to Ava's neck of the woods, rather than brave the horrors of central London on a Sunday at Christmas, she and Graham had quickly hopped on the Tube and headed back to Chiswick, getting off the train at Turnham Green and striking out for the high street, where there would be plenty of bougie shops to choose from.

"She's how old?"

"Six months," Charlotte said helplessly. "Do you think she needs a three-to-six months dress, or a six-to-nine months one?"

"Well, is she a particularly large six-month-old?"

"How should I know?"

"Because she's your niece? And you've been living with her for weeks? I thought that at some point during that time you might have taken in her general . . . proportions," Graham said, gesturing bizarrely with his hands, the way you might size up a particularly nice watermelon at the grocery store.

"Have I ever done anything to give you the slightest impression that I know what I'm doing right now?" Charlotte protested.

"You do seem to have used me as an excuse to escape spending time with this baby on multiple occasions," he conceded.

"Well, *that's* because of all the Christmas . . . things," she said, waving her hands vaguely. "Not because of the baby. But the baby encourages the Christmas things—I mean, she doesn't, personally, she's only six months old, she doesn't know what Christmas is or why everyone around her has suddenly lost their minds—"

"Blaming a baby. Some might consider that underhanded, Lane."

"Be quiet. My point is, I don't object to Alice. She's fine." She shrugged. "Once she's older, I'm going to teach her how to sneak out of the house, just to annoy Ava. But she's not very interesting right now, is she?"

"I find her delightful," he said, a trace smugly. "And since you seem incapable of making any sort of decision around which of those little ruffled monstrosities to buy her"—the dress Charlotte had spotted was, admittedly, a bit ruffly—"then I suppose I'll have to take this situation in hand."

"Right," Charlotte scoffed, "because you're some sort of expert on babies and—"

"She's six months old, but she's large for her age—a bit tall, I think, though it's difficult to tell when she spends so much time in a carrier or a pram, but definitely chubby. I think the six-to-nine month will fit her fine," he said definitively. "And if she's already had a shit-related catastrophe this afternoon, then I think you'll want to buy her the matching bloomers, just in case—it might protect the dress long enough to salvage the situation for a photo with Father Christmas, should disaster strike again." He reached around her for the bloomers in question, checking the tag on the ones he pulled from the pile to ensure they were the right size. He then plucked the correct dress from Charlotte's hand, replaced the other one on the rack, and tilted his head. "Shall we?"

"I—what—you—what the fuck?" Charlotte asked, eloquent as ever.

He leaned closer to her. "I have a younger sister," he reminded her. "An eleven-years-younger sister." He led her toward the cash register. "I know my way around some baby clothes, let us just say."

Charlotte gaped at him mutely, so distracted that she didn't even protest when he paid for the outfit before she could fish her wallet out of her purse. She seemed to have been temporarily deprived of the power of speech, in fact, her mind racing at a feverish pace as he steered her down the crowded Chiswick high street and around a corner, until they arrived outside Ava's flat.

Charlotte found her footsteps slowing as they approached the door, reluctant for the afternoon—despite its unexpected detour—to conclude. She came to a halt at the foot of the front steps, and turned to face him.

"Thank you for your help," she said, nodding at the paper bag in his hand. "I'm impressed by your secret baby knowledge."

"I've a large and diverse skill set, Lane," he said, taking a step toward her and giving her a small, private smile that made that *dimple* appear in one cheek again, and that made her regret the fact that they were not alone, but instead standing on a public street at two thirty in the afternoon.

As if summoned by this thought, the door to Ava's flat opened and she poked her head out. "Thank god. Please tell me you have something for my offspring to wear."

"Hello, Ava," Graham said, reaching out to hand her the bag from the—extremely overpriced—boutique. "We thought Alice seemed somewhat round for her age and purchased accordingly. Hopefully that wasn't a mistake."

"*Graham* thought," Charlotte clarified. "I'm not qualified to make size assessments of babies."

"You don't need to tell me," Ava said, peering into the bag. "I've seen how you flee the room whenever anyone mentions a diaper change." She offered Graham a grateful smile. "This is perfect, thank you."

He waved her off. "Anything for a baby's first visit to Father Christmas," he said, bowing his head slightly, as solemn as if he were in church. Charlotte was torn between wanting to laugh and wanting to whack him in the back of the head.

He turned to face her now. "I'll text you?" he said, a slightly inquisitive note turning it into a question. "We still need to choose a day to go to Buckinghamshire."

"Right," Charlotte said; that was the location of the final village she needed to visit—one whose lack of a train station meant Graham's escort in the Mini Cooper was more or less necessary. "We can work out the details later, I guess."

He smiled crookedly at her, hesitated, and then—despite the fact that Ava was watching with breathless interest from the front steps— reached out with a hand to touch Charlotte's cheek, his hand warm against her skin. She took a step toward him, and his free hand brushed hers, his fingers curving around hers with fleeting tenderness, gone again a moment later.

He stepped away first—and then, with a wave, he was gone.

"You're swooning," Ava said smugly from the front steps, as Charlotte watched Graham's back retreating down the street, his shoulders broad in his wool coat.

Charlotte opened her mouth to retort, but before she could speak, her phone buzzed.

Graham Calloway: To be continued.

And she couldn't help herself: she smiled.

TWO WEEKS
TO CHRISTMAS

CHAPTER TWELVE

S o, let me be sure I understand this: this is your *favorite Christmas movie?*"

It was Wednesday afternoon, and Charlotte and Graham were en route to Buckinghamshire; their day had gotten off to a delayed start when Graham had to deal with some sort of Eden Priory emergency involving missing supplies for a gingerbread-making workshop. Charlotte had briefly considered rescheduling, but she thought that they'd still have time to get to their destination, make a sketch and take some photos, perhaps have an early dinner, and be back in London before too late. They were now weaving their way through the traffic on an A road north of London on their way to a bucolic English paradise. (Or, at least, that's what Charlotte *thought* awaited them, based on a lot of internet memes and a weird phenomenon whereby everyone posted the same clip from the movie every December 13, for reasons that she didn't understand, since she'd never seen the movie in question.)

"Correct," he said, his eyes on the road. He braked suddenly as a car ahead of them turned on their blinker and slammed on the brakes with no warning, then reached over to downshift. Men driving stick:

another weirdly specific kink she hadn't known she possessed until meeting Graham.

She tore her eyes from his forearms. "*The Christmas Cottage*? Of all the holiday movies on earth, *that's* your favorite?"

"Yes," he confirmed. "It's heartwarming! There's a sad couple from London who rent a cottage in the countryside and fall in love again. There's a lonely dog who adopts them, *and* a pig who becomes friends with the dog."

This, at least, was an aspect of the movie Charlotte was aware of, because people posted a lot of photos of the pig and dog curled up together every year at Christmas. It was almost enough to make her want to watch the movie.

"And," Graham added as an afterthought, "the actress in it is quite fit. I decided I was going to marry her when I was about ten."

"*Aha*." This was suddenly making more sense. "Which actress?"

"You know," he said vaguely. "The blonde one."

"Very specific."

"I've always had a thing for blondes," he said, with a sideways glance at her and a hint of a smile.

"How original. You and most of the men on earth."

"Ah, but the blonde in this film has a sharp tongue, too, and *that* really seems to be the irresistible combination for me." Now it was her turn to smile, and he flicked a glance at her long enough that she knew he saw it. "But no, I stand by this: it's a great film."

"Between this and the *Beauty and the Beast* references, you really could craft yourself into the man of the average millennial woman' dreams, you know. Do you have thoughts about how hot the fox i Robin Hood is?"

"I beg your pardon?" he asked incredulously, sounding a bit like duke from one of Padma's beloved historical romances. Honestly, was kind of hot.

"The fox," she repeated. "Everyone knows he's the hottest Disney character. There has been lengthy Twitter discourse about it."

"Are we talking about a metaphorical fox?"

"No, a literal one," she said, then paused. "Though he's extremely anthropomorphized, so I'm not really sure how to assign him a proper species category. It's one of those things you don't want to think about too hard."

"Just when I think I understand women, something new confounds me."

"I'm glad to do my part to keep you on your toes," she said, suppressing a smile and looking out the window at the passing scenery, which was extremely picturesque at the moment. Rolling green hills. Winding roads. They'd turned off the A road a couple of minutes earlier, and were now driving along the sorts of roads that, in America— well, they wouldn't exist, because people would not be able to squeeze two oversized SUVs down them. Even in Graham's Mini, it felt a bit dicey. But, slight fear for her safety aside, it was all very adorable. There were even sheep! A whole flock of sheep! A rather large flock of sheep, actually. And was it her imagination, or did they seem to be—

Graham slammed on the brakes. "For fuck's sake."

"There are *so* many of them," Charlotte said as she watched the spectacle unfolding before her. "Like, *so* many."

There were, truly, an astonishing number of sheep. It looked to her (entirely untrained and lacking in any shepherding knowledge whatsoever) eye to be an entire flock of sheep, all of whom needed to cross the road precisely where she and Graham were attempting to drive.

"This is the problem with going to the countryside," he muttered darkly, shifting into neutral and pulling up the hand brake. "Goddamn sheep everywhere."

"They're very fleecy," Charlotte said, impressed. She was not what you might call a nature girl, but she *was* an appreciator of a nice sweater. She wondered if she could find a friendly farmer and convince him to shear a sheep just for her.

"That's the idea, yes," Graham said. He glanced in the mirror. "I wonder if we're better off turning around—"

"*Baaaa!*" came an excited bleat from behind them. Very *close* behind them. Charlotte craned around in her seat as best she could manage.

"Hello, sir," she said, nodding coolly at the sheep who was now peering in through the rear window of the Mini. "Or ma'am, I suppose. You're not a ram. Don't want to misgender anyone."

"Very considerate. Do you think you could politely ask her to get the fuck out of the way so I can reverse the car?" Graham asked.

"Um," Charlotte said.

"*Baaa!*" "*Baaa!*" "*Baaa!*"

"I don't think so," she said, unclicking her seat belt so that she could fully rise up onto her knees, pushing down the headrest so that she could rest her chin atop it. "She seems to have a lot of friends, and it would appear they've chosen this spot to have a catch-up."

"Where's the bloody farmer?" Graham muttered irately, giving up and turning the car off. It was obvious they were going to be here for a while. "Can't he come herd them?"

"Why don't you give it a try?" Charlotte asked sweetly. "Wholesome country boy that you are?"

"Why don't *you*?" he shot back. "Since you seem to be on such good terms with them?"

"They have trouble understanding my accent," she said somberly. "A tragic tale of cross-cultural miscommunication."

"That would honestly make half of the conversations *I* have with you make more sense."

"Do they send out a book to all young English lads at a certain age? How to act like you've got an enormous stick up your ass?"

"*Baaaa!*" said a sheep outside her window, a bit severely.

"I don't think it liked your language," Graham said smugly.

Charlotte eyed the now-empty paper cup of takeaway coffee she'd bought before leaving London, wishing she'd rationed it better. She was fairly certain they were going to be here for a while.

❄

"A three-hour tour," she sang, two hours later. "A *threeeee-hourrrrrrr touuuuuuuuur.*"

"It was less than two hours, you psychopath," he said through gritted teeth as they—at long last—continued their journey down the country lane. It had taken a long—long—*long* time for a shepherd to materialize—one who had not seemed terribly contrite about the fact that his entire flock had made a break for it, and then congregated on a road, stopping all traffic in either direction. "And we'd have been better off abandoning the car and walking the rest of the way to the village."

"Not in these shoes," Charlotte said, nodding at the heeled leather booties she'd found in a vintage store in New York, which were not remotely suited to country walks down muddy lanes that must contain, at this point, a metric ton of sheep shit.

"Well, thank god your shoes were preserved. Perhaps I would have been wiser to fashion some sort of sedan chair for you out of branches from a tree, so that you might be carried to your destination?"

"When would you have had the time, though? You were very busy doing your little cell phone signal rain dance."

Said dance had primarily involved him circling the car several times, waving his phone in the air and muttering darkly to himself, and at one point growing so desperate as to climb atop a stone wall and come perilously close to toppling over the other side into the muddy field below. Charlotte had laughed herself sick when he'd stalked back to the car, jaw set, and had to rather forcefully shove a sheep aside to open the driver's-side door.

Charlotte, all in all, was growing rather fond of the English countryside.

All this meant, however, that it was nearly dark by the time they made their way into the charming village of Lower Hankering.

"Well, this is nauseating," she said, staring out the window as Graham somehow maneuvered the car into a parking space that barely looked large enough to fit a toy pedal car like the one she'd loved when she was four. The village high street, where they currently found themselves, was a narrow, winding road flanked on either side by an assortment of half-timbered buildings with steeply angled roofs. Now, at dusk, it was lit with a cozy glow from a number of the windows, and there were holiday lights strung along the eaves, greenery adorning the occasional lamppost. "How do places *look* like this? It's absurd. I feel like I'm about to get murdered in an Agatha Christie novel."

"A delightful prospect," Graham agreed. He turned the car off. "Shall we go draw your cottage?"

"Yes," she said. "If we hurry, we can get there before I lose the light entirely." They were already pushing it; the sun had just set, and the light of dusk was rapidly fading.

He looked skeptically out the window and sighed wearily, pushing his glasses up the bridge of his nose. "I think you should draw it in full daylight."

"Oh, okay, what a helpful suggestion, Apollo. If you could just bring the sun back at"—she checked her phone—"four o'clock in England in December, that would be great."

"We could stay the night," he said, nodding; following his gaze, she realized that they'd parked directly opposite an establishment that bore the sort of swinging sign she associated with Disney World (except considerably less terrifying and nightmarish), which read, THE DUKE OF YORK * INN AND PUB * FINE CASK ALES * EN SUITE ROOMS.

"What is it with this country's obsession with advertising the presence of bathrooms on all their hotel listings?" she wondered aloud.

"If you'd spent your childhood staying in Victorian-era bed-and-breakfasts with a single bathroom for every floor of the building, you'd understand," he said darkly. "Listen, I'm hungry, and tired of sitting in this goddamn car, and don't feel like facing the drive back to town tonight. Why don't we just stay? You can visit the cottage in the morning and make your sketch and then we'll be on the road back to London before lunch."

"Well," Charlotte said slowly, considering. She was starving, it had been a long, annoying afternoon, and the Duke of York looked extremely cozy, like something out of an Anglophile's fantasies of a countryside visit.

"Fine," she said shortly, opening the car door. "But if they only have one bed, all bets are off. I am not romance novel–ing this shit."

CHAPTER THIRTEEN

There were two beds, at least—but there was only one room.

"How is this even possible?" Charlotte asked incredulously as they unlocked the door and stared, unimpressed, at the two twin beds that beckoned them.

"It's Christmas in England—peak season for a bunch of tourists trying to live out their *Downton Abbey* fantasies," Graham said grimly, ushering her into the room with a hand at the small of her back so that he could close the door behind her. "We're lucky there's a room available at all."

She sighed dramatically, flinging her purse down onto one of the beds. There was nothing to unpack, of course—she hadn't packed anything, not having expected to be gone for more than an afternoon.

"I'm going to run to the shop down the street and get toiletries," Graham said, hands in his coat pockets. "Do you need anything else?"

She shook her head, already internally grimacing at the thought of how she'd look the following morning, in today's clothing, sans makeup. As soon as he had vanished out the door, she sank down onto the bed, pulled her phone from her bag, fired off a quick text to Ava, and then texted Padma.

Charlotte: tl;dr but there was a sheep traffic jam and now I'm spending the night with Graham, in a hotel room, in a quaint English village

Padma: . . . . .

Padma: With only one bed?????

Charlotte: No there are two

Charlotte: How did I know that would be your first question 🙄

Padma: Andrew wants to know if the power has gone out

Charlotte: . . . . . no?

Padma: Apparently he thinks that a power outage could cause the room to get cold enough that you and Graham have to cuddle for warmth

Charlotte: Have you been having him read your romance novels

Padma: Yeppppp

Padma: Please send me hourly updates, my life is very boring!!

Charlotte started to type, *That's what you get for moving to the suburbs*, then deleted it.

Charlotte: I'll do my best 😂

That sounded friendly! That sounded normal! That didn't sound bitter, or lonely, or like she resented her best friend for living her life and doing something perfectly normal like marrying a nice guy and buying a house and doing adult things, even if those adult things took place an hour away in New Jersey instead of a block away in Brooklyn.

She set her phone aside, and her stomach growled; she was suddenly acutely aware of the fact that "lunch" had consisted of an apple and a handful of almonds that she'd scrounged from the kitchen at Ava's. Fortunately, it was only another five minutes before she heard footsteps in the hallway, then a key in the lock.

"I think I could eat an entire cow," she informed Graham as soon as he entered the room.

"If we head back to that pasture where we were waylaid by sheep, we might be able to find you a particularly fresh one," he said, and she had to bite the inside of her cheek not to laugh.

Downstairs, the pub offered everything a cranky, hungry traveler could hope for: a roaring fire, cozy booths, a menu full of potatoes and cheese, and a wide selection of local beers. After they'd claimed a table and perused the menu, Graham ordered for them at the bar, accepting the credit card that Charlotte thrust in his face with possibly unnecessary aggression.

"I wasn't going to refuse, for Christ's sake," he said mildly, plucking the card from her fingers before she could accidentally maim him with it.

"You never know, with men," she said darkly, watching with satisfaction as he trotted off to procure them sustenance. He returned with a beer for him and a cider for her, and they sipped contentedly in silence for a minute, surveying their surroundings. There was a Christmas tree in one corner, strung with lights and tinsel, and bunting in red and green was hanging cheerfully above the bar. There were stockings above the fireplace, classic Christmas songs playing in the background, and paper snowflakes hung above every table. All of this should have made Charlotte extremely grumpy, but sitting there, after a day derailed by livestock, drinking her cider and awaiting the arrival of potato products, she mainly felt . . . cozy.

Was this why people liked Christmas?

She snuck a glance at Graham, and saw that he was leaning back in his seat, his index finger tracing an idle circle around the rim of his pint glass as his eyes scanned the room. He'd rolled back the sleeves of his green cable-knit sweater, and the same battered watch that she'd noted on previous occasions gleamed at his wrist. He wasn't glancing at it, though—she hadn't realized how often she'd noticed him doing this, on many of the afternoons they'd spent together, until he'd stopped. Despite the fact that they found themselves unexpectedly, if not quite *stranded*, then at the very least detained, in a small village with a single room to share, he looked remarkably relaxed, missing the invisible weight that he so often seemed to be carrying.

On the table, his phone buzzed, as if summoned by her thoughts; he glanced down at the screen, frowned, and flipped it over without unlocking it.

"Everything okay?" she asked, keeping her tone deliberately casual, taking another sip of her cider.

He looked across the table at her, his frown easing. "Fine. My mum's worried about ticket sales for our New Year's Eve masquerade at Eden Priory—I'll ring her tomorrow."

Charlotte raised an eyebrow. "A masquerade," she repeated. "That sounds elaborate."

Graham shrugged. "It's tradition. My grandparents started hosting one in the fifties, and we've been doing it ever since—it was initially for all of their posh friends, but eventually we opened it up to the public, started selling tickets. It's a nice way to cap off the season."

"Is it profitable?" she asked curiously; at some point, over the past few weeks, she realized that she'd gotten invested in the future of Eden Priory.

"Decently," he said, taking a sip of his beer. "I've been wondering if we should do more events at the house, ticketed things—not something as lavish as this, but more . . . workshops and the like. We've an ornament workshop that we run each year, but I think we should do more in that vein, maybe some arts and crafts classes—make the house somewhere people go for something more than simply tours of a historic property."

"What about the film screening?" Charlotte asked, remembering Eloise's mention of the *Christmas, Truly* screening they were hosting on Christmas Eve.

"That, sure," he said, suppressing a grimace, and Charlotte grinned at him.

"Oh my god, you can't even *pretend* to think it's a good idea," she said, trying not to laugh.

"I *do* think it's a good idea; it's why I agreed to it," he objected. "I just don't *like* it."

"Because it's not *artistic* enough," she said, in a god-awful attempt at some cross between an English accent and a Katharine Hepburn impression.

"I am going to refrain from pointing out the absurdity of *you* of all people objecting to my preference for hosting events focused on a *famous artist* rather than *Christmas, Truly*."

"Touché."

Their food arrived then—a meat pie and a side of chips for her, a salad (also with a side of chips, she noted approvingly) for him. She glanced at his plate as she raised her fork, and then paused, quickly mentally scanning through the other meals they'd eaten together.

"Are you a vegetarian?" she asked curiously, taking a bite of her pie.

He nodded, spearing a bit of halloumi and avocado on his fork. "Since I was at uni. Read a long-form article on factory farming and never ate another sausage again."

She reached for a chip and sighed at the sight of the woefully small ramekin of ketchup she'd been given. Without missing a beat, he pushed his own ketchup ramekin toward her, reaching for mayonnaise instead.

"Only heathens put mayo on fries," she said darkly.

"Tell that to the Dutch," he said, looking unbothered. "I spent some time in Amsterdam a few years back, when my firm was working with a Dutch client, and I cannot express to you how much mayonnaise I consumed."

"You shouldn't sound so proud of that fact," she advised him, and a grin crept across his face. "Have you thought about what you're going to do, when you go back to work?" she added, since he'd broached the topic first.

He took another bite of salad, shaking his head. "Not too much. I think they'd hire me back at my old firm, if I let them know I was interested—we parted on good terms, they offered to just let me take unpaid leave, but . . ." He trailed off, his expression darkening.

"But?" she prompted; at some point, she'd stopped worrying that if she reminded him of her presence, he'd clam up. Had started to believe that he was sharing these things *because* she was there, not in spite of it.

"I don't know if I can . . . do it. Anymore." His voice was quieter now, and he looked down at his plate, the corners of his mouth turning down. "I didn't realize how much pressure my dad was shouldering, worrying about the house while also working mad hours at a really intense job, and I just . . . don't know if I can do both. Once I realized that the house was really losing money, I started trying to go down there at weekends, or call my mum every evening to discuss things—I was having to leave work early so I could meet with my parents' solicitor, the accountant, and eventually it just got to be too much." There was a faint note of guilt lacing the words, and he was still staring down at his plate.

"Graham." Charlotte paused until he looked back up at her. "I think . . ." And here she hesitated, because she didn't know *what* she thought. She thought too many things at once. She thought too much—far too much—about him.

But despite that, she said something that was utterly, entirely true: "I think that what you're doing right now is enough." And then, against her better judgment—against every practical voice in her head, telling her why this was a bad idea—she reached across the table and rested her hand on his.

He turned his hand palm up and interlaced their fingers, then held her gaze, his eyes dark behind his glasses. The room around them—cozy and warm and softly lit, full of the pleasant murmur of conversation—faded. She couldn't look away—couldn't focus on anything other than his eyes, the strong lines of his face, the warmth of his hand against hers, the spot where his thumb rubbed a slow circle against her skin.

And the electric current that seemed to sizzle in the air between them, growing stronger with each second of silence.

"Do you know," he said softly, at last, "how often, lately, I've thought about kissing you?"

She swallowed, then said, just as softly, "How convenient, then. That we only have one room."

They didn't finish their dinner.

They were on the stairs, then walking down the hallway, and then her key was in her hand, fumbling with the lock—and still, still, it wasn't fast enough. He was, suddenly, quite close behind her, the heat of his body against her back, his breath on her neck as he murmured, "Have you never opened a door before?"

She laughed, a little breathless, as she tried again, and then—miracle—the key turned, the door swung open. "In America, we have keys that were designed this century," she said, turning to him as she entered the room, but she couldn't say anything more, because in a single, neat movement, he was shutting the door, turning her, pinning her against it.

He braced one arm above her on the door, looking down at her, his eyes dark. She reached up for his glasses, but he used his free hand to catch her wrist, stilling her hand. "Don't," he said softly, keeping her wrist trapped tight in his grip. "I want to see your face clearly." The heat of his body was a whisper away from her front. She tilted her chin up.

"Were you only interested in looking?" Her mouth curved into a smile—an invitation.

He took it.

He kissed her, she thought, like he knew her. There was no hesitation—none of the awkwardness that often characterized first kisses. There was simply his mouth on hers, his chest firm against her breasts. He dropped her wrist so that he could reach out to cup her chin, tilt her face to a slightly different angle, and she slid her fingers into the short hair at the base of his neck. She smiled against his mouth, and their teeth clicked.

"What," he murmured, pulling back enough to speak, pressing his forehead to hers.

"Nothing," she said, a bit breathless already. "Just . . ." She tightened her grip in his hair. "I stand corrected. We *are* romance novel–ing this shit."

"Lane?"

"Mmm?"

"Stop talking."

She opened her mouth to reply, but it was already covered by his again, his tongue tracing her lips, sliding into her mouth to tangle with her own. His stubble scraped against her cheek with a rasp, then against her throat as he moved lower. He was hard against her stomach, and she hooked a leg around his hip, angling her hips upward to try to relieve the pressure of the relentless pulse beating between her legs. The door was at her back, the doorknob an awkward, occasional bump against her hip, but she barely even noticed, all of her senses occupied by the warmth of his body, the feeling of his hair slipping through her fingers, the bare skin of his back where she slid a hand down to dip beneath his shirt. He pulled back, tugging his sweater and shirt over his head in one jerky motion, and Charlotte's mouth went dry at the sight of his bare chest, his taut stomach, the lean muscle in his arms. His glasses had been dislodged in the shirt removal, and he raised a hand to straighten them, swallowing as Charlotte pushed off the door, reached for the hem of her dress, and, in one smooth motion, tugged it over her head.

Only at this point did it occur to her that she should have removed her tights first. "Ugh," she said now, pushing off her boots, then hopping on one foot as she removed her tights, "this has to be the least sexy stripping in human history." She transferred her weight to the other foot, and tugged the other leg of her tights down and off.

"I beg to differ," he said, his voice a bit hoarse; Charlotte glanced down, pleased to be reminded that—in a fit of inspiration—she'd worn her favorite black lace bra this morning, and the bent-over hopping was definitely doing her breasts some favors, as Graham's riveted gaze was testament to.

She straightened, and then nodded at him. "Jeans off, please."

"Are you always this bossy?"

"I said please," she objected, hands on her hips, having to fight against the desire to reach out and rip his pants off herself, because the sight of him shirtless was causing some sort of horniness-induced short-circuiting in her brain, and she wasn't feeling very patient at the moment.

"Fair enough," he said, his mouth curving up into a half smile as he toed off his shoes, then unbuttoned his jeans and tugged them down to reveal . . .

"No." Charlotte shook her head. "You are *not* doing this to me right now."

Graham's smile had widened, his dimple putting in an appearance now. "In my defense, I didn't put these on thinking you'd see them."

"You did," she said definitively, crossing her arms. "You hired those sheep, all so that you could seduce me in a B and B—"

"No one is *seduced* in B and Bs, Lane."

Charlotte ignored him. "—and then wait until I was practically naked to reveal that *you have reindeer on your boxers.*"

Graham shrugged. "The Christmas spirit moved me this morning."

"You do not understand how deeply unsexy that sentence is to me," Charlotte said, frowning, but unable to prevent herself from taking another, extremely appreciative glance at the sight of Graham Calloway, in nothing but a pair of Christmas boxers, his cheeks a bit flushed, his hair mussed, eyeing her with naked hunger.

And suddenly, she was no longer thinking about reindeer boxers—or about anything at all, really, other than the *want* that coursed through her, and her need to feel his bare skin on hers.

She reached a hand toward him, and in a moment he was there, his hands in her hair, his mouth on hers—then on her throat—then on her breasts, the lace of her bra going damp beneath his tongue. She could feel his erection against her stomach as he reached behind her to unclasp her bra, his hands coming up to cup her breasts the moment she tossed it aside. She gasped against his throat, then bit down, her teeth gently grazing the spot where his neck met his shoulder, and he groaned, his hips rolling against her almost helplessly. Her hands came to rest on his hips, and she urged him backward, crossing the tiny room in a breathless stumble, laughing against each other's mouths, until he wrapped his arms around her waist and turned them in one smooth motion, easing her backward onto one of the beds. He settled over her, bracing his weight on his elbows as he gazed down at her, his expression softening. "This is why I kept my glasses on," he said, in a low, hoarse voice unlike any that she had yet heard from him. He reached out a hand and traced a slow line down her throat, between her breasts, down her stomach, her pulse jumping in each spot that he touched. At last, his fingers latched into the waistband of her underwear, and gently pulled them down her legs. She kicked them off, and he settled into the space between her thighs, leaning down to kiss her again, more urgently now. Her arms twined around his neck and her breasts were crushed against his chest and she hooked her leg over his hip, trying to generate enough friction to ease the growing ache at her core. He drew back enough to allow a hand to slip between them, his fingers assured as they slid through the wetness between her legs; she covered his hand with hers, helping him find a rhythm, and then her hand fell away again, her eyes fluttering shut as her breathing grew more ragged, his thumb rubbing increasingly tight circles until she came with a cry muffled against his shoulder.

The sound of her own breathing was loud in her ears, and she opened her eyes at the feel of his fingers at her temple, gently tucking a loose strand of hair behind her ears. He was breathing heavily, his cheeks even redder, his eyes slightly glazed as he took in the sight of her, and she thought she must look absolutely wrecked, legs splayed, unable to catch her breath, but she didn't care—she just wanted *more*. He leaned down to kiss her again, wet and messy and heated, and her hands went to the waistband of his boxers; he tore his mouth away from hers long enough to say, "One second," then turned to fish his wallet out of the pocket of his discarded jeans, producing a condom with a triumphant smile.

From there, things moved quickly—he yanked down his boxers and rolled on the condom with a sure hand, and then he was on his side next to her, pulling her leg back over his hip as he slid into her; he pulled back, a slow, agonizing movement leaving friction in his wake like sparks, and then thrust forward again—and again—and again— and she was conscious of nothing except the warm, sure feeling of his hand flat against her back, holding her to his chest as he moved within her, the slap of their hips meeting, the groans that worked their way from his chest to fill the space around them. At one point, he pulled out entirely, rolling her onto her stomach, and she braced herself on knees and elbows as he thrust into her once again, and again, a fast race to completion now, his hands a warm anchor at her hips, her own hand working between her legs, and she bit into the pillow as she cried out again, his cries muffled in her hair.

She didn't know how long they lay there, his weight a heavy, warm comfort above and around her, their breathing slowly evening out.

"Twin beds were not designed for this," she murmured at last, and his laugh was a warm huff of air against her neck.

"Better a twin bed than against a wall, or the floor," he said, his voice still in that hoarse, smoky register that was apparently his bed-room voice, which she didn't think she'd ever be able (or *want*) to unhear. "My back wouldn't have been able to take it."

"Very hot." He poked her in the side, and she smiled. "I need a shower," she added after another moment, and let it dangle there, an invitation to be picked up if he wanted to.

His mouth curved against her skin. "Shall we see how large it is?"

It turned out that it was large enough—though just barely— for Graham to prove to Charlotte that he had a very, *very* talented mouth. And when the water turned lukewarm, and then cold, and they yelped and swore and Graham hastily helped Charlotte rinse the shampoo out of her hair, she thought, ridiculously, that the sound of their laughter, echoing off the tile, was one of the best things she'd ever heard.

It was later—much later. The night outside their window was dark, the village streets quiet, their room full of shadows. They'd scrambled out of the shower, shivering and laughing, and dried off and tumbled onto her bed and picked up right where they'd left off, pausing only briefly for Graham to fumble for the box of condoms he'd apparently picked up on his toothpaste mission earlier that evening.

"Optimistic, were you?" Charlotte asked, arching a brow at him from her spot on the bed, resting on her elbows.

"Lane," he said, crawling back onto the bed and placing a lingering kiss at the base of her throat, "how could I not be? It's the most wonderful time of the year."

And then, laughing, dodged the pillow she aimed squarely at his head.

Now, hours later, they were still curled, spoonlike, in her tiny twin bed; she would have thought he'd fallen asleep, except for the occasional, slow stroke of his hand down the bare skin of her arm, leaving goose bumps in its wake.

"You can't sleep here," she mumbled, her voice slurring slightly from exhaustion—and quite possibly from some sort of postcoital drunken stupor, because *good god*—and he laughed silently, the only indication the warm huff of his breath against her neck.

"Not a cuddler?"

She wasn't, actually, but didn't want to tell him that, because she didn't want him to move—not yet, at least. "There's no way two of us can sleep in this tiny bed," she said instead. "So . . . just don't fall asleep here." This was, in her own way, an invitation—and perhaps he realized that, because he didn't move.

Silence fell, comfortable and sleepy, and Charlotte could feel her body growing heavy and warm. "This is nice," she said, so quiet that she wasn't sure she wanted him to hear.

"It is," he said, his arm tightening around her waist. "I'd . . . forgotten." He was silent for long enough that she didn't think he was going to speak again, but then, finally, quietly, he said, "Since I broke up with my ex—before that, even—I think I've been a bit . . . lonely. And no one I've slept with since then has changed that." She held her breath, waiting. "Until now."

His body was warm and comforting against hers, and she reached up slowly, not thinking about it too hard, and laced her fingers through his. Silence fell between them again, their slow breaths the only sound in the quiet of the room, and their interlaced fingers felt like a promise, though she didn't know what they were promising.

And, lying in the darkness with his arm around her—and even after he placed a last, lingering kiss on her neck and retreated to his own narrow bed—she realized that here, in this room with him, was the least lonely that she'd felt in a long, long time.

CHAPTER FOURTEEN

The next morning, Charlotte was awoken by the sound of . . . carolers?

"What the fuck?" she mumbled, summoning enough strength to tug the extra pillow that she'd apparently been spooning over her head.

"Good morning," said a deep, amused voice, and Charlotte suddenly went still. Nestled in her cozy little twin bed, she'd forgotten where she was and, more important, *who* she was with. She lifted the pillow to find Graham fully dressed in yesterday's clothes, sipping a mug of tea and reading a newspaper.

"How long have you been awake?" she asked indignantly, tossing aside her insufficiently noise-stifling pillow and sitting up. She tugged the duvet up to her chin, shivering slightly as the cooler air of the room hit her bare skin.

"A while," he said, glancing up at her and taking a sip of his tea. "I was going to wake you in a bit."

"What time is it?" she demanded, reaching for her phone on the bedside table. It was hard to gauge how much daylight there was with the thick curtains drawn. Had she overslept horribly? Had she slipped into some sort of sex coma?

It was . . . 7:22.

She groaned and slumped back against the pillows.

"You have got to be kidding me," she mumbled. "This is inhumane. It's still *dark* outside. Why on earth are people caroling before sunrise?"

"To be fair," he said, setting down his newspaper, " 'before sunrise' is a relative statement, this time of year."

"It's not!" she protested. "This isn't Iceland! The sun comes up at eight! I don't think asking people to hold off on caroling until at least *eight* is unreasonable!"

"Well, I met our intrepid carolers when I went downstairs to see about tea," he said. "And I don't think you would have much luck telling these people that there are appropriate times for caroling."

"Ideally never," she clarified. "*Never* would be my preferred time for caroling."

"I wouldn't recommend telling them that, either," he said, a devilish grin flickering across his face.

"Why do you look so happy?" she asked suspiciously. "I don't like it."

"Get dressed," he said cheerfully. "Breakfast starts at eight, and you'll find out for yourself."

"I liked you better before I learned you were a morning person," she informed him coldly as she pushed the covers back and prepared to race for the bathroom. Gratifyingly, his eyes went a bit glazed at the sight of all the bare skin she'd just revealed. She would have taken a moment to revel in this, but it was cold, and she didn't want to delay getting warm for even a second longer.

By the time she'd made it to the bathroom door, however, he'd recovered sufficiently to toss a would-be casual reply at her back:

"You seemed to like me fine last night."

Charlotte shut the bathroom door firmly behind her in lieu of a comeback—because honestly, it wasn't like she could argue with *that*.

There were so, so many carolers.

"No wonder there was only one room left," Charlotte hissed to Graham as they walked into the breakfast room downstairs half an hour later. Despite the fact that breakfast officially began being served at eight, and it was currently 8:03, the room was already buzzing, nearly every table filled. Admittedly, this was a bit relative—there were only six tables total—but each table had three to four carolers seated at it, all looking positively delighted to be sitting down to breakfast at a wholesome country inn on a chilly December morning.

But they weren't just carolers (which would be bad enough)—no, these were carolers in *period costumes*. There were shawls. There were top hats. There were *bonnets*.

Charlotte suddenly wished it were socially acceptable to drink this early.

"Good morning!" said a cheerful woman who looked to be in her early sixties. She seemed positively delighted to spot Graham and Charlotte, and was seated directly next to the one remaining empty table. Charlotte and Graham exchanged the world-weary looks of soldiers about to go into battle, and made their way across the room to their seats.

"Hello," Charlotte said politely as she settled herself at the table.

"Sleep well last night?" asked the improbably cheerful woman; she was wearing a *lot* of plaid, Charlotte realized now. A plaid shawl over a plaid floor-length dress, with the ribbons of a plaid bonnet tied securely beneath her chin. And none of it was the *same* plaid, despite all being in Christmassy colors—no doubt if she showed up in Scotland in this ensemble, she'd spark some sort of interclan warfare. She was clutching a cup of coffee eagerly, though Charlotte personally didn't think this woman needed any supplementary caffeine.

"We did," Graham said, in response to the woman's question. He smiled politely at her, and, predictably, Charlotte could see the woman melting at the sight. She couldn't be too judgmental about this, since it seemed that she, too, had a weakness for his smiles.

"Until the wake-up call, at least," Charlotte muttered under her breath. "Sounded strangely like carol singing." She frowned, as if deeply puzzled.

"Oh, goodness, that was us!" the woman said, cackling. "Did you hear that?" she asked, turning to her breakfast companions, who nodded eagerly. "I'm Nadine," she added, turning back to Charlotte and Graham. "And we're the Jingle Janglers."

"The what now?" Charlotte asked, pretty sure that she didn't actually want the amount of information that Nadine was going to provide, but curious nonetheless.

"The Jingle Janglers!" Nadine repeated brightly. "We travel around England providing carols in the most heartwarming settings."

"Wales, too, this year!" put in one of Nadine's tablemates. "Our first year branching out that far! Perhaps one day we'll make it to Scotland!"

"Go on! And the moon, too?" Nadine said, chortling, as the three immediately surrounding tables laughed heartily, as though this were a hilarious joke.

"English distance-based humor," Graham said in an undertone to Charlotte. "Doesn't tend to land with Americans."

"I think I am in hell," Charlotte muttered back to him, and he pressed his lips together, clearly trying not to smile.

"We're all amateurs, you see," Nadine said, leaning toward Graham and Charlotte confidingly. "We do it simply for the love of the carol."

"How noble," Graham said, nodding seriously. Charlotte cast him a narrow glance.

Nadine, meanwhile, was now frowning slightly at Charlotte in an intent way that made Charlotte vaguely nervous. She'd been on the receiving end of a frown like this before, and it usually meant . . .

"Tallulah!" Nadine snapped her fingers; Charlotte resisted the impulse to fling herself under the table. "Oh, good heavens! You look like Tallulah from *Christmas, Truly!*"

Graham—bless him—was a quick thinker. "Ha! What's that—the third time this week?" He elbowed Charlotte jovially, and she gave him a sharp look; he smiled at her in a sort of bossy way that managed to convey general *please play along so I can salvage this situation, you idiot* vibes, and she managed a belated chortle.

"Ha! Ha! Yes! Wow. What are the odds?"

The look Graham was giving her implied that he thought the filmmakers of *Christmas, Truly* must have been absolute lunatics to cast her, and she felt like reminding him that back then, no one had required her to improvise.

Graham gave an easy chuckle, and turned to Nadine, shaking his head ruefully. "It's so odd—she's been getting it constantly, lately. It's funnier because my Lucy has never even *seen* the film. Have you, Lucy?"

Charlotte, now Lucy, shook her head gravely. "I was raised by Jehovah's Witnesses. Never allowed to celebrate the holidays."

Graham seemed to be suppressing an eye roll with some effort. "Yes, well, she's escaped now, *clearly*," he added pointedly, "but her Christmas film education is a bit lacking."

"Oh, goodness!" Nadine clapped a hand to her mouth. "I could have sworn—but heavens, you simply *must* watch it. It's brilliant! It's about these two extended families—one in England, one in America, because there were two sisters, and one was sent to Canada during the war, while her older sister stayed in England to work with the Wrens—"

"I'll be sure to watch it, thank you," Charlotte said, before Nadine could recount the entire plot of *Christmas, Truly.*

"—and there's a series of interconnected romances with both the Americans and the Brits," Nadine continued, undeterred, "and it all ties together in the end, of course, and they wear the loveliest jumpers!" She nodded significantly.

"I do love a good sweater," Charlotte offered, a bit weakly.

"Just as well you're not Tallulah, I suppose," Nadine said, shaking her head. "Do you know, I saw the most *horrible* story in the *Daily Mail*"—Charlotte didn't know much about the British press, but she already knew that nothing good had ever followed that opening to a sentence—"about how the actress who plays Tallulah is a *Wiccan* who hates Christmas so much that she derailed an entire sequel film!" She looked scandalized.

"Shocking," Graham agreed with a somber shake of the head.

At that moment, a lifeline in the form of the inn owner appeared. "Morning, loves," she said to Graham and Charlotte. "Tea or coffee? And do you know what you'd like for breakfast?"

In the time it took Charlotte and Graham to order a full English and a veggie breakfast, Nadine had been sucked into a discussion with her companions, and Charlotte briefly experienced a moment of hope that she had escaped further conversation. She had not accounted, however, for the fact that chattiness seemed to be a common trait among amateur touring Christmas carolers, because the man sitting at the table to their right leaned toward them now.

"What brings you to town, if it isn't to see us perform?" he asked curiously.

"Do you have many groupies?" Charlotte asked, the notion that she and Graham would have traveled to a tiny hamlet in Buckinghamshire specifically to see a troupe of carol singers frankly astonishing to her.

"A fair few," said the woman next to him proudly; she, like her companion, was middle-aged, and was wearing a bright red dress that had enough boning in the bodice to make Charlotte wince in sympathy. "There was a lady last season who became *obsessed* with Rajesh," she said, nodding at her breakfast companion. "She came to *three separate villages* in a row, she did, and was always chatting with him after the performances—I finally had to put my foot down, tell her that we'd been married for *fifteen years* and if she thought that just because it was Christmas, he'd be susceptible to her vixen charms, well, she had another thing coming."

Graham's eyebrows were somewhere in the vicinity of his hairline by this point, while Charlotte was suddenly feeling that this breakfast situation had taken a turn for the better.

"Do you find that men are particularly susceptible to vixen charms at Christmastime?" she asked earnestly, leaning across Graham to address the woman directly.

The woman nodded solemnly. "Why do you think they make all those romances set at Christmas?" she asked. "It's the most lustful time of year."

Graham coughed on his tea, and Charlotte thumped him on the back.

"Anjali and I met at Christmas!" Rajesh added, smiling fondly at his wife. "I took one look at her, glowing in the lights of the skating rink at the Natural History Museum—"

"May she rest in peace," Anjali added sadly.

"The skating rink," Graham clarified, seeing Charlotte's confused look, having evidently cleared all the tea out of his windpipe. "They stopped doing it for environmental reasons."

"The very notion!" Anjali said, indignant now. "As if we should be thinking about global warming at *Christmas*, of all things!"

"It's true," Rajesh said seriously. "There's a time and a place for everything, you know."

"I . . . see," Charlotte said, before mercifully being rescued by the sight of her breakfast materializing. She and Graham occupied themselves for some time by shoveling massive quantities of toast and beans and eggs and mushrooms and tomatoes and—god, she got tired even trying to list them all; this country did not joke around with their fried breakfasts—anyway, the point was, by the time they were capable of speech, the carolers had already finished their own breakfasts and were preparing to depart for their first caroling stop.

"We pick several locations, you see," Nadine confided as she tied her bonnet more securely beneath her chin. "Wouldn't want anyone in the village to miss out!"

"How thoughtful," Charlotte managed, and waved them off while sipping her coffee. As soon as the room was empty, she turned to Graham.

"Fifty pounds says they are outside this fucking cottage I need to draw."

"Not taking that bet," he said, polishing off his final piece of toast.

❄

Sure enough, an hour later, once they'd checked out of the inn, moved the car to a different parking spot, and set off on foot, they found themselves being . . .

Well, serenaded.

"Didn't think we'd see you two again so soon!" Anjali said cheerfully once she saw Graham and Charlotte materialize, just as the troupe was finishing a stirring rendition of "God Rest Ye, Merry Gentlemen." They were assembled on the high street, a short walk down the road from the inn and the assortment of shops, directly outside the cottage that was Charlotte and Graham's destination; the cottage in question was predictably adorable, with a thatched roof and an ivy-covered trellis and a garden that, in the summer, was probably overflowing with roses. Despite its position directly on the main road, the village was so small that it had the feel of a peaceful retreat, with a view of lush green fields rising behind it. There was a fully dressed Christmas tree in the front yard, too, a feature that Charlotte understood was key to the cottage's appeal in the film. With a resigned sigh, she pulled her sketchbook from her bag, noting with amusement the small sign that had been affixed to the front gate, which read, *PRIVATE RESIDENCE—TRESPASSERS WILL BE PROSECUTED!* As she retrieved her supplies, she entertained herself with the soothing thought of megafans of *The Christmas Cottage* being hauled away in handcuffs after attempting to sneak onto the property.

"Lucy's an artist," Graham said, with a nod in her direction. "She loves Christmas so much that she's determined to do watercolors for every iconic English Christmas film spot, as we catch her up on all the classics."

"Excuse me?" she asked, freezing in the act of rummaging for her pouch of drawing pencils.

"You know," he said, smiling innocently at her as he slung an arm around her shoulders, "I've been trying to tell you that this might be too much—surely you can't be *that passionate* about Christmas films, of all things—but you've been undeterred."

"Isn't that lovely!" said Anjali, misty-eyed.

"Which Christmas film is your favorite?" Nadine asked eagerly. "I personally *love* the one about the girl who inherits that mansion in Sloane Square! Just imagine!"

"*Christmas, Truly* is my favorite," Rajesh confided. "The best bit is when the sweethearts from secondary school who had been separated by the war spend their last Christmas together in the same nursing home!" He blinked back tears.

"I will murder you in your sleep," Charlotte informed Graham.

"Back to London tonight!" he said easily, dropping his arm and taking a few steps back as a precautionary measure. "Won't have much opportunity!"

"I know where you live," she reminded him. "And Ava knows how to pick locks."

"Dare I ask *why* your sister has such a charmingly criminal hobby?"

"I don't ask too many questions."

"You would have done well under a totalitarian regime. Shouldn't you be sketching?"

"I'm too busy trying to defend my reputation from slander," she told him through gritted teeth.

"We don't want to interrupt, of course," Rajesh said, looking impressed as he watched her extract her preferred pencil and turn her attention to the cottage before her. "Only, I've never seen an artist at work before, and it *does* seem awfully fascinating."

He paused, and an expectant silence fell, as if the entire caroling troupe expected her to narrate her creative process to them as she worked. She cast Graham a pleading look, and, mercifully, he took the hint.

"I'm afraid you won't be able to see her at work now, either, if we don't give her some space. A watched kettle and all that."

There was some impressed murmuring—clearly the carolers now viewed Charlotte as some sort of eccentric creative genius whose methods they could not understand, an impression she was not going to dispute if it meant that they would leave her alone so that she could actually get some work done.

"We'll just be down the road," Nadine said brightly. "We've found that the acoustics of the intersection back there lend themselves particularly well to 'It Came Upon a Midnight Clear.' Makes us sound especially angelic, you see."

"Must take advantage," Graham agreed. "I look forward to listening to your angelic offerings from a distance."

This, apparently, was a suitably rapturous response to permit Graham and Charlotte to now be left in peace, and Charlotte sagged slightly against the stone wall she was resting her hip upon.

"This village is terrifying," she murmured, her eyes on the sketch slowly forming beneath her pencil. They were, admittedly, currently standing in front of a row of stone cottages with charmingly rustic little wooden signs on their gates, all proclaiming the cottages' names to be things like *Honeysuckle Cottage* and *Our Evergreen Nook*, but still: terrifying.

"I do sort of feel like I've wandered into the pages of *Cold Comfort Farm*," Graham agreed. "I cannot express to you enough how abnormal this is. I grew up in a small village, and nothing quirky or charming happened there. We just bought snacks at the corner shop and rode our bicycles around a lot."

"I could do with about 75 percent less quirk and charm," Charlotte said darkly, before lapsing into silence. She hastily created a series of thumbnail sketches, done from slightly different angles, before deciding on the best option and flipping to a new page in her sketchbook. She spent a while working on a sketch of the exterior, then created a few more sketches of some of the details of the window frames and features in the garden, and finally took a series of photographs of the cottage and the surrounding village lane that she could refer to later.

Once again, Graham was quiet while she worked; she glanced over at him at one point to find that he was replying to an email on his phone, his brow furrowed as he tapped away. A weak winter sun had crept above the roofs of the village at some point, and he'd replaced his usual glasses with a pair of sunglasses; these, combined with the second-day stubble and the vaguely tousled hair, created an overall look that was a bit rougher around the edges than his usual oxford-shirt-and-well-tailored-trousers vibe. She didn't hate it.

At last, she was done, and she replaced her pencil pouch and sketchbook in her bag with some relief. "Let's go," she said to Graham, and he glanced up at her, slipping his phone back into the pocket of his jeans. "If we walk fast, we might be able to slip past the carolers without them noticing us."

This turned out to be wishful thinking on Charlotte's part—they *almost* made it, but Nadine (of course it was Nadine) spotted them as they scurried past, and called out, "Don't tell us you're leaving so soon! Stay for a carol or two!"

And, of course, her pleas were immediately joined by Anjali, and Rajesh, and half of the caroling troupe, which meant that Charlotte and Graham had little choice but to stand politely among a crowd of delighted schoolchildren while "Rudolph the Red-Nosed Reindeer" was sung three times in a row (because the children kept screeching, "Again! Again!" and Nadine, who seemed to be in charge of the troupe's song selection, was incapable of standing up to a bunch of seven-year-olds).

Eventually, however, they were free—though not without having received a flyer advertising the troupe's upcoming tour stops (Cambridge and Bury St. Edmunds, this coming weekend), with copious use of some sort of deliberately old-fashioned-looking font and the overly liberal deployment of clip-art Christmas trees. ("A fascinating historical text," Graham had deemed it, rescuing it when Charlotte was about to throw it in a trash can next to their parking spot. "You're just worried Nadine will see us tossing it," Charlotte shot back.)

Now they were once again ensconced within the cozy confines of the Mini Cooper, having made it down all the winding country lanes (sans sheep-induced traffic jams today) while cheerfully abusing the vocal stylings of the Jingle Janglers. It was only now, on the highway, that they'd exhausted this topic and a slightly uncomfortable silence fell.

Charlotte decided to address the elephant in the Mini Cooper.

"So," she said, would-be casual, "I suppose we should discuss whether we plan to continue having oral sex in showers for the rest of my time in England."

"You know, when your conversation partner is driving a car at sixty miles an hour might *not* be the best time to utter that sentence." Despite this, his grip on the steering wheel was firm, the car's path steady.

"You're fine," Charlotte said dismissively. "If I thought you were the type to crash a car over the mention of cunnilingus, I'd have waited, but I knew you were made of sterner stuff."

"Your confidence in me is flattering." His eyes were still on the road, but she could tell, just from watching him in profile, seeing the telltale dimple attempt to make its presence known in his cheek, that he was amused. She *loved* amusing him, she realized in a rush; this was a somewhat disconcerting realization, because Charlotte had never spent much time going out of her way to make people laugh. The rest of her family loved to entertain, to put on a show for whoever they were with; Charlotte was quieter, steadier than that. But when Graham laughed at something she said, it made her feel like he saw her—*knew* her—in a way that many people didn't.

And she liked it.

"Seriously, though," she said, not willing to drop this. "Obviously I'm leaving at New Year's, and it sounds like you got out of a pretty long relationship recently—"

"Not recently," he interrupted, his eyes still on the road. "It was before my dad died."

Which had been, Charlotte recalled, a couple of years ago. She shouldn't have cared that this woman, whoever she was, was long in his past . . . but something within her eased, knowing that he wasn't hung up on her. That this wasn't a rebound.

He seemed to sense her curiosity, because he glanced sideways at her, quickly, before looking back at the road. "Her name was Francesca. We dated for . . ." He paused, clearly doing some rapid mental math. "Six years."

Charlotte stared out the window, unseeing. That was . . . so long. As long as Ava and Kit had been together, and they were married. With a *baby*. Instead of offering this unhelpful observation, though, she asked, "What happened?"

She heard him sigh, even as she continued gazing out the window. "We met through friends, when I'd been working in London for a year or two after uni. I was at a point in my life where it felt like I was . . . I don't know. Ticking things off a list. She was getting a law degree, so she was studying all the time, and I was working all the time—and then when she got her degree, she was working all the time too. We moved into a flat in Notting Hill and talked about getting a dog, except that neither of us had time to take care of it. I worked twelve-hour days and I was exhausted, and I never had time to go visit my parents, or to help my dad with upkeep on the house, and would always offer to send checks instead."

The self-loathing in his voice, on this last, was palpable, and Charlotte unthinkingly reached over to rest a hand on his where it sat on his thigh.

"Why did you break up?"

"We were almost thirty—both so busy with work that we hadn't really had time to properly think about getting married. It was sort of assumed that we'd do it . . . someday. Buy a house farther out from central London. Have kids. But it never felt pressing. And then my dad got sick." He paused, a long, heavy silence that she didn't want to break. "I was going home a lot more often, obviously—and my dad was in and out of hospital in London, so I was spending time there, whenever I could. I took leave from my job, for a few months so I could take him to appointments, give my mum a break. He went home, eventually . . . but he never got well again. And I'd come home, after these long days with my dad, feeling scared, but not knowing how to process it, and just feeling *lonely*, thinking about what my life would be like, if he died . . . and when I got home, sometimes she was there waiting for me, and sometimes she wasn't—but I realized . . . well, I guess I realized that she didn't make me feel any less lonely when she was there than when she was away."

Charlotte swallowed around a lump in her throat at the ache in his voice—and at the bone-deep recognition she felt, at his description of that feeling.

"She was—is—a good person," he said quietly. "I don't blame her—I felt like a bastard about the whole thing, to tell the truth. There was nothing *wrong*. But it just wasn't right. If my dad hadn't got sick, I might have never realized—might have married her and thought I was happy. But something like cancer really puts things into perspective, and I realized that if I were in my dad's shoes, spending days in hospital, going to endless appointments, frightened, tired, feeling like shit . . . she wasn't the person I'd want waiting for me at home."

He laughed then, under his breath—a low, derisive laugh. "This probably makes me sound like a complete ass. I was with her for *six years*, and then realized that I didn't love her enough to marry her?"

"It doesn't," Charlotte said softly, blinking into the darkness. "It just makes you sound . . . human."

"Well, the fact that she met someone six months later, and married him another six months after that, does make me feel a bit less guilty about it," he added, and Charlotte let out a surprised laugh. "They moved to Hampstead and just had twins and, from all I hear from mutual friends, are blissfully happy, so clearly she's well shot of me."

"No," she said, squeezing his hand, and then removing hers. "It just wasn't right. And besides . . ." Here, she hesitated. Felt the words forming in her mouth, considered swallowing them down again. But instead—here in the cozy confines of the car, with no one to hear but him—she said, "I've lived in the same city for most of my life—I have friends. A best friend. A whole *life*. But I've been feeling lonely lately, too—and I think that the thing that would make it so much worse, totally unbearable, would be feeling this way even if I was coming home to someone at the end of the day. Almost anything's better than that, I think."

It was his turn to glance at her quickly, his eyes unreadable behind his dark sunglasses. All he said, however, after another long silence was a soft "I think you're right."

Silence fell within the car, Graham's eyes on the road and Charlotte watching the rolling hills flash by, church steeples visible in the distant villages. It was a comfortable silence—more comfortable than any silence Charlotte had ever experienced with someone she'd slept with for the first time less than twenty-four hours earlier. This thought reminded her of her original question, which he hadn't answered.

"So," she said, "what's the verdict, then? Is this a thing now? Are we doing this?" She kept her tone light and breezy, as if the emotional revelations of last night—of the past five minutes—meant nothing.

"Preferably not in the shower," he said with a slight grimace. She glanced at him, grinning. "Not sure my knees can take that again."

"No one made you get down on your knees."

"I know. Horniness got in the way of common sense."

"You'd just told me, like, two minutes before that having sex on a *rug* was a bad idea, but then you decided that going down on me in a shower was better?"

"Lane. Your point has been noted. I wasn't thinking with my brain."

"Listen, *Calloway*," she said, offering his last name in an exagger-atedly posh English accent, "I'm here for three more weeks. Meaning that if you'd like to fuck me somewhere that isn't going to cause you to need knee replacement surgery later, your days are limited." She kept her voice light, almost dismissive, as though what they were doing was no different from any of the other casual flings she'd had in recent years—fun, yes. But not something that mattered.

"Is this how you attract all of your men?" he asked. "Lure them in with sexy discussions of their rapidly failing bodies?"

"No," she said, gleeful at the realization she was about to share. "Because I've never slept with someone over thirty before."

This *did* nearly make him crash the car.

"Not the Mini Cooper!" she howled dramatically, clutching the dashboard.

"You cannot be serious," he said, jerking the steering wheel so that the car swerved back into its lane. "You're *twenty-nine*—have you been trolling the local secondary schools for dates?"

"Ha. No, it's been a bit of a dry spell for the past year or so, and then before that . . ." She shrugged. "It wasn't intentional, obviously, but I've always been a bit wary of older men—my dad is ten years older than my mom, and I think I just instinctively thought that anything that was a feature in their marriage wasn't something that I wanted to replicate."

"I'm honored that you aren't too horrified by my age to be interested."

"Honestly, the gray hair kind of does it for me. Who knew?" She gazed fondly at the half dozen or so strands of gray that were visible at his temples.

"Christ," he muttered under his breath, but there was a smile tugging at the corners of his mouth.

And she realized, in a brief, terrifying moment of realization, that she was *happy*—happy in the sort of giddy, carefree way that she associated with a first crush, or childhood, or the day she'd made her first sale to someone she didn't know. Happy in the sort of way that she did not remember ever being, in the years she dated Craig—or with any

of the men who had come since. Happy in a way she shouldn't neces-
sarily be, barreling down an English motorway under a gray winter
sky, sitting next to—okay, yes, a very handsome man with a gifted
tongue, but *still.*

She was leaving in three weeks, she reminded herself. She lived
in New York—ran a business there, had friends, a *life*. She couldn't
let herself get attached—not when she'd tried, for so long now, to
ensure that she was immune to heartbreak, to needing, really *needing*,
another person.

"Stay at mine tonight?" he asked, sliding a glance toward her a
moment later, and she realized that he was, in his own way, answering
her question.

And then—despite the fact that she knew that there was absolutely,
positively no way this would end well—she couldn't help but say,
"Okay."

She was twenty-nine, she reminded herself. It had been *four years*
since her last heartbreak—she was older, wiser, and wouldn't be
making those same mistakes again.

Perhaps if she repeated it to herself often enough, she'd start to
believe it.

CHAPTER FIFTEEN

"So let me get this straight," Ava said on Friday morning, watching as Charlotte stared at her laptop screen with a furrowed brow. "You fled America in a tizzy because of *Christmas, Truly*—"

"I'm not sure I've ever been in a tizzy in my life," Charlotte objected mildly, glancing up at her sister.

"—only to start doing the horizontal tango every night with a man whose family's livelihood is tied to *Christmas, Truly*?"

Charlotte grimaced, then returned her attention to the screen before her; she'd scanned the first couple of her Christmas house watercolors, and was in the process of editing them digitally. "Please never call it that again."

"I'm a mother now, Charlotte," Ava said, looking martyred. "I cannot have inappropriate language around my precious daughter." She peered, limpid-eyed, down at Alice, who was—for once—sleeping peacefully in her mother's arms. At that precise moment, there came the sound of the front door opening, followed by a thunderous crash, a muffled curse—Charlotte recognized Kit's voice—and, predictably, Alice woke up and immediately burst into furious tears.

"*Christopher Adeoye, for fuck's sake!*" Ava screeched.

"Mmm, yes," Charlotte murmured, refocusing her attention on her laptop screen.

No one heard her over the general hubbub, which turned out to be Kit and his mother attempting to smuggle an entire dollhouse into the flat, which they'd assembled upstairs and now thought to hide in Charlotte's bedroom (of course).

"She's a goddamn *baby*," Ava snapped. "She wouldn't have known the difference if you'd assembled it six inches away from her."

"I wanted it to be a surprise," Kit said mournfully as he attempted to scoop up the dollhouse's various furnishings.

Ava's expression softened as she regarded her husband, currently on his hands and knees trying to fish a doll-sized bed out from underneath the coat tree by the door. She glanced at Charlotte, who had wandered out into the hallway to survey the general chaos (and to help Simone wrangle the dollhouse through the narrow doorway into the guest room).

"I bet Graham's good at assembling children's toys," Ava said slyly.

And Charlotte—thinking of adolescent Graham, sitting on the sofa next to his little sister, watching *Beauty and the Beast* over and over again—very much feared that Ava was right.

*

"Jesus Christ, I'm going to move to an abandoned island."

It was the evening of the same day, and Charlotte was back at Graham's; he'd texted her that afternoon, asking if she had dinner plans, and she had shamelessly appeared at his door with an overnight bag, not bothering with pretense. So far, however, their evening had been distressingly chaste: they'd watched several episodes of *The Traitors* (Charlotte had never seen the UK version, and was begrudgingly forced to admit that it was superior), and Graham had made them some sort of cabbage, potato, and cheese gratin that had tasted significantly more delicious than Charlotte had thought it possible for cabbage to taste.

Her own cooking skills generally extended to heating up leftovers and the occasional salad or sandwich. Now, she was sitting cross-legged on his floor, sketchpad and pencils before her, attempting a rough sketch of the Havanese puppies a client had sent her a photo of for their commission. She frowned; why did all of her attempts make them look like shaggy root vegetables? These dogs shouldn't exist.

Graham, who had stepped into the kitchen when his phone rang, walked back into the living room, scrubbing a weary hand over his face.

"What's wrong?" she asked.

"Mum just found out that the artist for the ornament workshop is unavailable at the last minute." He tossed his phone onto the couch and slumped down next to it. He looked tired—which, well, he probably *was*; the past couple of nights had not involved much sleep. But his wasn't the happy-but-smug tiredness of someone who had missed out on sleep for a very good reason; rather, he looked worried and exhausted. "Because we needed something else to go wrong."

"Wait," she said. "When is this workshop?"

"Sunday," he said darkly, resting a hand over his eyes. "So we've got about thirty-six hours to find someone else to run it, or maybe we should just cancel—"

"Graham," she said, fighting back the ridiculous urge to laugh, "you do realize who you're talking to?"

He lowered his hand, blinking down at her.

"*I'll* run your workshop for you," she said slowly, enunciating each word and still trying not to laugh at the expression of dawning relief on his face. Her mind was already buzzing with possibilities—the previous year, she'd actually briefly considered doing a limited run of Christmas ornaments, but the thought of spending the months leading up to the holidays *also* thinking about the holidays was, frankly, more than she could stomach. It was bad enough when Christmas

was everywhere *at* Christmas. It would be even worse to be surrounded by Christmas decorations in August.

"Oh god, you have no idea how much easier you just made my life,"
he said with a relieved laugh. "I *promise* you wouldn't have wanted to
see my attempts at art. Why do you think I ended up studying finance?"

"Because it's a requirement for emotionally repressed English boys
who live in countryside manors to find a career that cannot possibly
bring them any joy or passion, all so that a nice boy or girl can come
along to teach them how to feel," Charlotte said without missing a beat.

"I think I've read that one," Graham said, and Charlotte couldn't
help smiling.

"You and Padma both." At his frown, she clarified, "My best friend
in New York. She's basically the opposite of me—extremely soft-
hearted, loves romances, gives extreme Bambi vibes when you first
meet her."

"Not the first description that would spring to mind for you," he
agreed.

"Her secret is that she's actually terrifying—she's a lawyer, an absolute badass, but you'd never guess it, if you met her outside of work."
Charlotte sighed ruefully. "I should probably learn from her ways—
people *love* her when they meet her—but I've just never been able
to . . . I don't know. Charm people?"

"Hmm." Graham's tone was thoughtful, and she glanced over at
him, slumped on the couch, his elbow braced against one of the sofa's
arms as he looked at her. "I don't think you *try* to charm people. But I
wanted to know more about you, from the moment I met you."

Charlotte frowned, thinking back to their first, ridiculous meeting. "I have no idea why—I spent several minutes complaining about
you removing a reindeer suit, and then fled in a bit of a huff."

Graham's mouth curved up. "Exactly. It was fascinating."

Charlotte rolled her eyes, and pushed up onto her knees so that she could rest her forearms on the edge of the couch, close enough to reach out and touch him, if she wanted. "You were just interested because usually you flash your little smile and wear your—your *glasses*—"

"My glasses," he repeated, sounding bemused.

"—and then people find you *so* handsome and *so* charming and *so* English—"

"You do realize that I live in England, yes? I don't think the accent is that interesting to the natives."

Charlotte waved an impatient hand. "Whatever. You know what I mean."

Graham straightened, then leaned forward deliberately, reaching out his hands to rest on hers. "Yes, I do: you're furious because you like me."

Like.

The word hovered between them, and Charlotte reached for it like a life raft. "Like," she could handle. "Like" felt safe.

"I might be," she admitted, glancing down to where his hands covered hers. "I haven't let myself like anyone in a long time." She second-guessed herself as soon as the words were out of her mouth—it felt like she was skating close to the sort of vulnerability she didn't usually allow herself, and certainly not with someone she was casually dating.

The problem was that this, whatever it was, between her and Graham, didn't *feel* all that casual.

She could hear the frown in his voice as he said, "Why?"

She hesitated; it had been so long ago, now. More than four years. She hadn't told anyone the story in a long time—avoided spending too much time thinking about it, even. But here, with Graham, in his dark, quiet living room . . .

She found she wanted to.

She glanced up and met his eyes. "Craig—my last boyfriend—he and I dated for a few years, right after I moved back to the city after college. We met at a party, and he was a few years older than me, already established in his career at a start-up. Worked long hours, went to the gym at five in the morning, out late on weekends—that sort. Very responsible."

"I know them well," he said dryly, and she wondered what she would have thought of Graham if she'd met him years earlier, when he, too, was chasing the constant highs of money, late nights, the markers of a successful young urbanite. It was hard to reconcile that idea with the version of him that she knew.

"He was smart, though—so smart. And funny. And just . . . I don't know. Reliable. He felt safe, I guess. He wasn't at all like anyone in my family, and that felt so nice to me. For a while."

"What happened?" he asked, his gaze steady on her.

She grimaced slightly, unable to help herself. "He was busy, but I was, too, trying to get my business off the ground, so I didn't care that he worked late. But eventually, I started to realize how . . . frustrated he was, I guess. I never complained about his hours—I'm not a child, I don't need constant company, it was fine. But when he'd come home early, and I'd be on deadline for a commission and couldn't drop everything to go out to dinner with him—or when we'd go to a party, and I'd need to leave early, because I had to get up early the next morning to catch up on work—he *hated* it. And I finally realized that he liked the *idea* of a girlfriend who was an artist much more than the reality. He liked how it looked—him, with his desk job and the blonde girlfriend he could take to parties and tell everyone, 'She's an artist,' as if my job were some sort of quirky thing he could use to . . . burnish his own image?" She shook her head. "I don't know—I've thought about it a lot since then. I don't know if I was being unfair to him, ultimately. But that's how it *felt*—and it's just no way to live, in a relationship that makes you feel that way."

Graham's mouth was set in a thin line. "He sounds like a prick."

Charlotte sighed. "Padma agrees—she never liked him that much. The first time I ever did a collaboration, I was twenty-five, it was three years into starting my business, and a restaurant in New York invited me to design their menus, do all the art for their website. It was a great opportunity, and I worked really hard on it. And then I found out that the restaurant's investors were a group of Hollywood people." She pressed her lips together. "Friends of my dad. No one had told me—he got me the job. And after working so hard to do it all on my own, to have him just . . . go behind my back like that, I guess, even though I know he meant well. I got into a huge fight with him at the restaurant's soft opening—we had to go outside, I was crying, it was just . . . awful. And then I went home with Craig, and I could tell the whole way that he was upset, but I *thought* he was, like, upset on my behalf—but he told me that I needed to get over it. That I was being *dramatic*. That he didn't even recognize me. We'd been together nearly three years, and this was the first time I'd ever made a scene about anything, and he told me that he wanted to break up."

"What the fuck." Graham's cheeks were red, his eyes burning. "I just—I can't—." He was, she realized, actually struggling for words, he was so furious.

"The thing is, I think I *did* overreact," she said, glancing down at the couch. "I know that—it wasn't my best moment. But I've spent my entire life never causing a scene, never being a bother, and to suddenly be dumped the first time I was an inconvenience to him . . ." She shook her head. "That relationship needed to end, and I was starting to realize that myself, but it was such a shitty way to end things."

"You're allowed to lean on people occasionally, you know," he said, his voice calmer now. He slipped his hands beneath hers, gripping them, and then gently urged her up onto the couch next to him. She sat with her back against the arm of the sofa, her knees raised, and he leaned forward to rest his arm on her knees, the sort of casual, intimate gesture she had half forgotten about, after years of one-night stands, of refusing to allow anyone too close.

"The whole thing . . . spooked me, I guess. It made me question my own judgment, for a long time. And it made me really, really determined to never be a worry to anyone, ever again. To never *need* anyone. So I haven't."

"You were—what, twenty-four? Twenty-five?" At her nod, he continued, "I don't think you need to swear off relationships for the rest of your life just because you dated one wanker when you were young."

Charlotte laughed. "You sounded *so* English just then."

"Do I have to remind you yet again that *I am*?" But his dimple appeared in his cheek, and she knew he was trying not to smile, and she couldn't help herself, and leaned up to kiss him. It was the sort of kiss that was warm, and comfortable, and not intended to lead to anything further—and it was the sort of kiss that she hadn't had with someone since she was with Craig. Graham pulled back after a moment. "There's nothing wrong with needing people, Lane," he said quietly, meeting her eyes directly.

"I know," she agreed, even though she wasn't sure that she did. Or, rather, she knew it, academically, but still didn't *feel* it—for all that he made her want to believe it. Made her more nervous by the day, worrying that she was coming dangerously close to needing *him*.

"For the record," he added, his tone lighter now, "the fact that you're an artist isn't the most interesting thing about you."

"I know," she agreed seriously. "It's the fact that I was in *Christmas, Truly*."

He grinned. "Not that, either—though who among us can resist the plucky charms of . . ." He trailed off, his forehead wrinkling.

"Tallulah, you idiot!" she said, reaching for a throw pillow and whacking him on the shoulder with it. "It was filmed at *your house* and you've *still* never seen it?"

He scrubbed his hands over his face, settling back against the sofa again; Charlotte leaned forward to wrap her arms around her knees. "That'll change soon enough, if this film screening goes off."

"If?" she repeated curiously.

"Eloise rang, just before you got here. We've only sold half the tickets."

Charlotte frowned, then opened her mouth. Shut it again. Considered. And then said, slowly, "What if you told people that I was going to be there?"

Graham turned his head sharply. "No."

"Why not?" Charlotte said, instantly defensive. "You *know* it would make more people sign up."

"Because," he said incredulously, "you've already been recognized by *Christmas, Truly* fans multiple times since I met you—imagine how much worse it would be if we advertised your presence in advance!"

"But," Charlotte said, in the interest of fairness, "none of them have really bothered me." This was actually true, she realized—even the blonde, swearing woman at the lights switch-on had been basically harmless. She pointed this out to Graham now, but he still looked unconvinced.

"Are you forgetting the hysterical teenager in New York?"

Charlotte waved a dismissive hand. "But that was weeks ago now— I'm sure no one cares that much anymore—look." She leaned down to scoop her phone off the coffee table, and pulled up Instagram, then tapped into her DMs. Graham leaned over her shoulder to watch. "This time a month ago, I got literally *hundreds* of messages every day about that *Variety* article—not all of them insane, to be clear, but some definitely were. But let's see how many I have today." Another tap to her message requests. A quick scan showed that only a minority were related to the reboot—many more were simply tags from people sharing one of her posts, or reacting to one of her stories, or asking about her art, or even posting about *Christmas, Truly* in general, but not her current role as internet villain. The angry contingent was still there—but there were definitely fewer of them.

"See?" she said to him now. "It's dying down. People are starting to move on—it's the week before Christmas; they have better things to do than be mad about a failed reboot of a twenty-year-old movie."

"A movie that *you hate*," he reminded her. "Even if everyone who shows up to this event is perfectly kind, you still don't like to be reminded of it."

"No, but . . ." she began, and then trailed off, the words sticking in her throat. *No, but I like you* was what she'd wanted to say. *Still* wanted to say.

She liked Graham more than she hated *Christmas, Truly.*

She couldn't say this to him, though—not when she'd just explained how she'd spent the past four years studiously avoiding all relationships. Not when she had that meeting on her calendar in New York, inching closer each day. Not when telling him that might make him think that she was *serious* about this—that she wanted something more permanent, wanted to somehow figure out the logistics of a long-distance, international relationship.

Not when she'd worked so hard to build her own life in New York, separate from anything to do with her family, or that movie, or anything that wasn't *hers*.

Even though the more time she spent with Graham, the more she wondered if perhaps that life was starting to feel a bit small.

Instead, she simply said, "But I don't want you to lose your house, Graham," and his expression softened, and she knew she had him. And so she reached out, and kissed him again, and distracted them both enough that neither of them could spend much time thinking about the fact that something between them had shifted.

CHAPTER SIXTEEN

London ten days before Christmas was hell.

"There are"—Charlotte said breathlessly, bursting through the door into Ava and Kit's flat laden down with packages—"so many people in this city that it should actually be illegal."

"Charlotte, darling, you live in New York," Simone said from the couch, where she was bouncing Alice on her knee. Alice was emitting the sort of high-pitched squeals that Charlotte had learned from hard experience to be very wary of, as they tended to slip from glee into absolute fury without more than three seconds' warning. "Every time I set foot in your city, I feel as though there's someone sweating on me. It's very unhygienic."

"If we weren't all wearing coats, I guarantee I would also be covered in other people's sweat," Charlotte said grimly, dumping the bags on an empty chair. "I feel like I just escaped some sort of horror movie. There was Christmas music playing *everywhere*."

"It's December," Ava said, wafting into the room, wearing a caftan and looking strangely relaxed for a woman who was spending ten hours a day with her mother-in-law *and* whose baby was almost certainly about to begin howling so loudly that there was a real possibility the police would be summoned. "There's *supposed* to be Christmas music. Hear it?" she added beatifically, tilting her head to the side, and Charlotte caught the unfortunately unmistakable sound of Mariah Carey coming from the kitchen speakers. Charlotte sighed. Ava beamed.

"Why are you so happy?" Charlotte asked suspiciously.

"Because I gave her one of your little marijuana gummies, darling," Simone said casually, still smiling at her granddaughter.

Charlotte nearly fell off her perch on the arm of the chair. "I didn't bring edibles into a foreign country! I don't want to get arrested!"

Simone waved a hand dismissively, which resulted in Alice teetering wildly on her knee; this merely made the unhinged cadence of her squeal more pronounced. Charlotte felt a premonition of doom.

"Not yours as in *yours*, Charlotte; don't be so literal," Simone said severely. "But yours as in *yours*. Your generation."

"I don't think millennials invented weed, Simone."

"No," Simone said thoughtfully, "I suppose you're right. I had a very torrid night in Paris with John when we first started dating, you know, and if memory serves, there were some substances at play."

"I am so glad I ate that gummy so that I'm not bothered by the sound of my mother-in-law describing a torrid weekend," Ava said cheerfully.

There was a thump from the master bedroom down the hall. "I'm fine!" came Kit's muffled voice a moment later.

"Thanks, babe!" Ava called back at him.

"I got everything on your list," Charlotte informed her sister now, mustering the strength to reach for the bags to continue her journey into the kitchen. "I continue to be incapable of remembering where to find eggs in grocery stores here. I wandered up and down five aisles before I found them."

"I don't buy eggs," Ava said serenely.

Charlotte frowned at her. "They were on the list."

"Yes." Ava nodded, looking pleased. "*You* bought eggs."

"But . . ." Charlotte was beginning to wonder if *she* had taken an edible without realizing it. "I'm usually not here to go grocery shopping for you. You can't *never* eat eggs."

"First of all, vegans exist, Charlotte," Ava said, sounding remarkably self-righteous for a woman who Charlotte had personally watched eat an entire cheeseburger the night before. "But also, husbands exist. Kit buys the eggs."

"So when you go grocery shopping—"

"No eggs," Ava confirmed. "I even avoid the aisle they're on. Just seeing them sitting there in their little cartons on the shelves like they're canned beans is horrifying."

"You do realize that these eggs were on those shelves, right?" Charlotte said cautiously. "I didn't fly to America to buy refrigerated eggs."

Ava waved a hand in a gesture eerily reminiscent of Simone. "I just need to not see it with my own eyes. I can *pretend* these aren't unnatural European room-temperature eggs, so long as I don't have to see them on the shelf."

"This is insane," Charlotte said. "Just so we're clear on that."

There was another, louder thump from down the hall.

"Fine!" Kit called again, though his voice sounded a bit more strained this time.

"Any blood?" Ava hollered back.

"Not much!" Kit yelled, sounding disturbingly cheerful for such a proclamation.

"Does Kit need help with . . . whatever he's doing?" Charlotte asked as she dragged the grocery bags into the kitchen and began unloading them, her sister trailing behind her.

"Nope," Ava said, at least bestirring herself enough to open the fridge and begin unpacking the bag that was overflowing with various cheeses. "He's wrapping presents. It's like Santa's workshop in there. Full of secrets. We're not allowed anywhere close."

"What can he *possibly* be wrapping that's making so much noise?" Charlotte asked curiously as she attempted to rearrange the contents of Ava's cabinets enough to allow room for more canned goods.

"The collection of erotic garden statuary I found for Simone, probably," Ava said, putting a carton of milk in the fridge door.

Charlotte blinked, opened her mouth, and then decided it was probably best not to reply. "You remember that I won't be home for dinner tonight, right?" she said instead.

"Yes, yes," Ava said absently, frowning down at the packet of extremely expensive French butter in her hand. "You're going to a sexy ornament workshop."

"No," Charlotte said severely. "I'm going to a very professional work opportunity that I am being compensated for. Not sexy in the least."

"Hmmm. Being compensated for at your normal rate?" Ava asked slyly, to which Charlotte had no good reply. "As I thought. The rest of your fee is being rendered in *other services*."

"Ava, for god's sake." Charlotte was torn between exasperation and the insane desire to laugh. At that moment, at the exact same time, there was a third, even more ominous thump from the bedroom, what sounded suspiciously like a yelp of pain from Kit, and, as predicted, a shriek from Alice that veered suddenly from delighted to enraged.

"Charlotte?" came Kit's sheepish voice from the hallway. "Could you fetch me a plaster?"

As Ava wafted away into the living room to retrieve her baby, Charlotte rummaged in a drawer in the hallway bathroom until she found a box of *Bluey*-themed bandages (Alice was not permitted screen time yet, but Kit had gotten weirdly hooked on the show, which Charlotte found both worrying and adorable at the same time), which she carried to Kit, who was hovering just outside his bedroom door, holding one hand in the other, trying not to drip blood on the rug.

"I'm about to leave for Eden Priory," Charlotte told him, taking a bandage out of the box and unwrapping it for him.

"You'll miss all the fun!" Kit said earnestly, looking distressed. From the living room, Alice's howling grew louder, mingled with the sound of Simone singing her what Charlotte *thought* might be, mystifyingly, a sea shanty. "My dad's just off buying a blowtorch, and then we're going to try our hand at making crème brûlée this afternoon!"

Charlotte, privately, could not think of a less wise idea than introducing complicated French cooking and open flames into a situation that already involved one (1) demon-possessed baby, and one (1) mother of said baby who was currently in an altered state, as well as one (1) father of said baby who was bleeding copiously from his right hand, but she decided that this was not going to be her problem today, and instead offered a smile and a nod as she waved him off and went to her room to grab her coat and bag.

When Graham knocked on the door and she opened it, she informed him, quite seriously, "It will be a miracle if anyone in this flat is still alive when I return tonight. Ready to paint some ornaments?"

Eden Priory was in a state of frenzied activity when they arrived. Eloise and Lizzie were both present, but Charlotte barely had the chance to say anything beyond the briefest of hellos to them before Lizzie was swept off to the kitchen, where there was some sort of large-scale shortbread-making operation in progress. The ornament workshop was due to start in an hour, but there had evidently been some delay with the arrival of the supplies—"I don't want to tell you how long I spent on the phone dealing with it yesterday," Graham said darkly—and so things were being set up at the last minute.

Eloise beamed as Graham left Charlotte with a squeeze of the hand to go off in search of his mother, who was evidently looking for him. "I'll show you where we're setting up."

Eloise led her into a room that Charlotte thought might have once been used as a ballroom, but which now had been cleared out and was arranged with several smaller tables clustered in a loose circle. The room itself was spectacular: high-ceilinged, with a wood floor that looked to have been recently polished to a shine; enormous windows allowed the weak winter sun to pour in; bunting and fairy lights were strung from the ceiling. A tree—smaller than the iconic tree in the entrance hall, but still enormous for a regular-sized house—was strung with lights and beautiful glass ornaments, and unseen speakers were piping in (sigh) Christmas carols.

The workshop had been only partially set up thus far: boxes of ornaments, paints, and paintbrushes had been scattered around but not yet unloaded; along one wall, a couple of battered chests of drawers had been repurposed into refreshment stations, covered in platters offering a number of cakes, shortbread, and some sort of delicious-looking pastry that smelled strongly of cinnamon. There were a few cut-glass bowls laid out, presumably awaiting mulled wine and other drink options, and there were mismatched teacups and tumblers to choose from.

Eloise made a beeline for the boxes now as Charlotte set her bag down behind a chair at the front of the room and unloaded the sample ornaments she'd carefully wrapped in newspaper for the journey down, having spent the past couple of days practicing various designs on a pack of cheap ornaments she'd found at a craft shop in London. She then crossed the room to help Eloise finish unloading the boxes, setting up an array of craft supplies at each table.

"This is pretty casual," Eloise explained as they worked. "Nancy— our usual instructor—is just a lady in the village; we've known her for ages. She's lovely, but she's got to be at least eighty by now, and is a bit scattered. She tends to spend most of her time during the workshop downing mugs of wine—most of the people who show up for this are just looking for an afternoon out, so you don't need to worry too much about teaching proper *technique* or whatever to anyone."

"Got it," Charlotte said, setting a last cup of paintbrushes on one of the tables and stepping back to survey the room. "I did make some sample ornaments, though, just in case anyone wants to use those as examples." Eloise scampered over to look at the ornaments in question and squealed in delight.

"These are *incredible*; gosh, maybe we should have had you teach a proper course or something—"

"Too late now," Charlotte cautioned, and Eloise laughed.

"I'm just glad we didn't have to cancel it—the tickets don't cost that much, but Graham would've been stressed if we'd had to refund people their money. More than he's already stressed these days, I mean," she clarified with an eye roll. "We also had loads of messages from people at the last minute, saying they were going to come!" Eloise added happily. "I think it was your face on the Instagram post I made yesterday that did it."

Charlotte blinked. "My . . . face?" she asked a bit cautiously.

Eloise beamed, distracted, as she whipped her phone out to take a few photographs of the room. "Yes! Graham told me that you were willing to help us advertise the film screening, so I figured it wouldn't hurt to use you for this, too! So I posted that the star of *Christmas, Truly* herself would be running the workshop—that's when I started getting messages from people asking if they needed to book tickets in advance, that sort of thing."

She sounded delighted by this, which made Charlotte feel guilty about the swooping feeling of dread in her stomach. She *had* told Graham that they could use her to market the *Christmas, Truly* screening, after all; was this really so different? Why should this bother her so much?

Because, said a petulant voice in her head, the one that represented the darkest, worst parts of herself, *it's my art, the thing I'm actually good at, and now that stupid movie is ruining that too.*

But she didn't want to listen to that voice—not today, not when she so desperately wanted this to go well, for Graham's sake. So she shoved it—and all of her misgivings—aside, and offered Eloise the best smile that she could manage, determined that *Christmas, Truly* of all things was not—*not*—going to spoil her day.

❄

Graham found her later, as she was packing leftover supplies into the boxes they'd arrived in.

"How'd it go?" he asked, the sudden sound of his voice in the empty room making her startle, not having heard his approach. She glanced up to see him leaning against the doorjamb, arms crossed over his chest, watching her cushion unused ornaments in bubble wrap. She carefully placed the last one in the box, then straightened.

"It was fine," she said cautiously. "I thought I saw you a couple of times, during?"

He nodded. "I was in and out, trying to keep an eye on the food and drink. Best turnout we've had in a few years, I think—thank you so much for stepping in."

She bit her lip, weighing whether to tell him *why*, precisely, the turnout had been so good—something about the way Eloise had phrased it made her think that this had been an executive decision she'd made that Graham might not be aware of. Given all the disagreement between Graham and Eloise on the future of Eden Priory, she didn't want to be the person who tossed a grenade into an already tense situation.

He, however, must have read something in her expression, because he took a couple of steps toward her. "What's wrong?"

She decided to tell *a* truth, a small part of the larger one. "There were some *Christmas, Truly* fans."

A frown darkened his face, and he reached out to take her hand. "Were any of them rude?"

"No." She shook her head quickly, and his frown eased slightly. "They wanted to take selfies—one of them asked me about the reboot, but she was chill about it." She shrugged. "It was . . . fine."

It *had* been fine, was the thing; she hadn't realized how much the unending wave of messages on social media, the run-in with the teenager in New York, the constant feeling that she was some sort of Christmas movie villain, had been wearing on her. Until now. Until she met some people who'd seen a movie and liked her character and said some nice things, and then got back to painting their Christmas ornaments like it . . . wasn't that big of a deal.

Because it wasn't.

Which meant that she definitely didn't want to make things worse between Eloise and Graham by informing him how, exactly, it was that these people had come to this ornament workshop in the first place.

"That's good, then," he said hesitantly, still holding her hand. He was searching her face, clearly a bit puzzled by her mood. "Isn't it? Unless you're having second thoughts about the film screening? It would be fine if you didn't want to come, you know—I think Eloise has already posted about it, but it's easy enough for her to put out another message on Instagram, telling everyone you were canceling."

She smiled at him. "The film screening will be fine," she said firmly. "These people today weren't out for my blood, which feels like an encouraging sign."

"All right, then," he said slowly, still looking at her a bit oddly. "You'll let me know if you change your mind, though?" She nodded, squeezing his hand. "Mum wants to know if we'll stay for dinner," he added now, dropping her hand and reaching out to lift one of the boxes of leftover supplies. "She's ordered a full Sunday roast from the village pub—if we eat soon, we'll not be too late in getting back to London."

"All right," she said, turning to pick up another box. "I look forward to observing a vegetarian eat a Sunday roast, by the way."

As it turned out, Graham could eat more *without* eating meat than Charlotte could as an omnivore. She watched in frank astonishment an hour later as he polished off his second Yorkshire pudding, using it to mop up the remaining gravy on his plate.

"I don't want to be a jerk," she said, "but . . . gravy?"

Lizzie cackled. "He's the laziest vegetarian! At least when *I* do it, I do it properly."

Graham cast a baleful look in his sister's direction. "But *you* do it for about six months at a time every third year or so, whereas I actually manage it on a nonstop basis, so I'm not sure you're in a position to throw stones."

"I was doing so well the last time, too," Lizzie said mournfully—though not mournfully enough to have prevented her from eating every morsel of roast beef on her plate, Charlotte noticed. "But then I happened to walk into a restaurant *just* as someone was having a rasher of bacon set down before them, and I was doomed."

"An inspiring tale of moral courage," Graham said dryly.

"Charlotte," said Mrs. Calloway, seeming determined to prevent her children from veering into a philosophical debate at the dinner table, "Eloise showed me some of the pieces you're working on for us to sell in the shop at Christmas next year—they're beautiful. You're very talented."

"Thank you," Charlotte said, smiling at her. She was a tall woman—taller than either daughter, though still a bit shorter than her son—in her early sixties, willowy, with hair that had gone completely gray, which she kept cropped to her chin, glasses that were remarkably similar to Graham's, and extremely kind eyes.

"I wonder if we should unveil one of them at the film screening," Eloise said thoughtfully now. "Perhaps show everyone a peek of one of the ones you've done at Eden Priory, as a teaser for next year?"

After further consultation, Charlotte and Eloise had decided that Charlotte should do two pieces featuring Eden Priory—one of the exterior of the house, to match the others in the print series, and one of the famous interior from the movie, featuring the Christmas tree and the settee, which she'd already started working on, based on the sketches she'd made the day of the switch-on. During spare moments before and after the ornament workshop today, she'd made sketches of the exterior and taken some photos.

"We could collect email addresses from people who want to be alerted when they're available for order next fall," Graham said thoughtfully. "Even offer some sort of small presale discount for the people on that list?"

"Graham," Eloise said, startled, "that's very clever."

"I do have the occasional good idea, you know," he said with a wry smile at his sister.

"Not where *Christmas, Truly* is concerned," she muttered, and he frowned slightly at her.

"I've agreed to the film screening—and to the prints for the gift shop," he said, his voice low. "What else is it that I'm supposed to be signing on to now?"

"Well," Eloise said, pouncing on this opening, "I *have* been think-ing that perhaps we could offer *Christmas, Truly* tours next year! Let people see the specific spots within the house that were used in film-ing, that sort of thing!"

Graham sighed. "Eloise, isn't it enough that half the house is already full of informational placards about Christian Calloway? Do we need to turn this place into *more* of a public commodity?"

"Maybe," she said, a bit testily, "doing so would result in a few more visitors. We already get people coming here solely because they know it was used in the film—let's try to attract more of them! Have you noticed many Christian Calloway enthusiasts popping by lately?"

"I don't think we need to discuss this over dinner," Mrs. Calloway said brightly, a note of steel in her voice. Lizzie was staring determinedly at her water glass.

"It's the perfect time to discuss it," Eloise said sharply. "Since we're all here at once. I know Charlotte won't mind us talking business for a moment—will you, Charlotte?" She flashed a sunny smile at Charlotte, who offered a weak attempt at a smile in return. In truth, she'd been trying to sink lower in her chair in the hopes that the members of the family would just . . . forget she was there? It hadn't been her most well-thought-out escape plan.

"I had a call from our solicitor," Mrs. Calloway said now, looking at each of her children in turn. This was enough to make Graham and Eloise stop staring daggers at each other and look at their mother curiously, and even Lizzie glanced up. "There's been interest from someone at the BBC who wants to use the house's grounds for a couple of weeks in the autumn for a period drama they're shooting. They wouldn't need to do any interior shots, so it wouldn't be terribly invasive—"

"No." Graham's voice was curt.

"Graham," Eloise said, throwing up her hands in exasperation. "Have you lost your mind?"

"Dad hated—"

"Dad's dead," Lizzie said quietly, speaking for the first time during this argument. "He's dead," she repeated, her voice even and calm, "so I don't know that his opinions matter quite as much as ours do." She seemed, suddenly, very adult—older than twenty-two. Graham and Eloise both looked somewhat taken aback, but Graham quickly rallied.

"Yeah, he is," he said, looking at his sister, affection and stubbornness warring for dominance in his expression. "Which is why I don't think we should immediately do the *one thing* he swore he'd never do again."

"Graham, love," Mrs. Calloway said, more gently than she'd yet spoken to him. "You know I love your father, too, but—well, he wasn't right about everything. You fought with him often enough, after all."

"Yeah, I did." Graham stood abruptly, making a great show of gathering the dishes and beginning to stack them carefully. "And I can't do anything about those fights, now that he's gone—but I can do something about this."

And with that, he vanished with a teetering stack of plates into the kitchen—a clear signal that, to him, there was nothing more to discuss.

The drive back to London passed largely in silence. Graham had turned on the radio as soon as they got in the car, and Charlotte was therefore treated to a never-ending array of Christmas hits on the drive north. She would have thought that he was doing it deliberately to troll her (an impulse that she would have begrudgingly respected), but she could see from the tight set of his jaw, the firm grip of his hands on the steering wheel, that his thoughts were not on taking advantage of her Christmas-averse tendencies to annoy her.

It was toward the end of the trip, as they got off the motorway and began weaving their way slowly through West London, that she decided to address the elephant in the room.

"I'm guessing this isn't the first time you've had this argument with your family."

She kept her eyes fixed out the window at the lights of the city as she spoke, but out of the corner of her eye she caught a flicker of motion, as if he'd suddenly turned toward her before glancing ahead again.

"No." The word was short, tense, though not precisely angry.

"Would it really be so terrible?" she asked carefully. "It sounds like it wouldn't be at all invasive to your mom, living at the house, and while I'm sure the BBC doesn't pay as well as Hollywood, the money would definitely help."

She felt like she was badly overstepping, but if she'd been forced to sit through a weirdly tense dinner with someone else's family, through no fault of her own, then it didn't seem completely unreasonable that she be allowed to offer an opinion on it.

"My dad would've hated it," he said, quietly enough that she could barely hear him over the noise of the road. "He felt this responsibility to the legacy of Christian Calloway—he admired his work so fiercely, and he felt like he was failing—if the house was losing money under his watch, it meant that he wasn't worthy, I guess, of caring for the family heritage."

"You realize that's patriarchal bullshit, right?" Charlotte asked conversationally. "This enormous, drafty, impossible-to-heat house has been passed down to the eldest son in each generation like we're living in a Jane Austen novel, and your dad somehow internalized this to mean that it was his *destiny* to preserve the house, or whatever?" She shook her head, feeling annoyed with the whole thing. "It's ridiculous."

"Ridiculous or not," Graham said, his jaw now so tight that she wondered how he was getting words out, "it was important to him, and I don't want to be the ass that waltzes in after his dad's untimely death and tosses out everything he cared about." He blew out a frustrated breath, and glanced over at her again. "I'm sorry. I'm not angry with you, I just—we've had this conversation a dozen times, and I feel like they're not listening to me."

Charlotte hesitated, torn between saying what she really thought, and not wanting to argue with him any further. In the end, however, as it so often did with her, honesty won. "I think they're listening," she said slowly. "I just think they're coming to a different conclusion, when presented with the same set of facts. And you guys will have to figure out how to reconcile it."

"Right," he said, and then laughed under his breath—a dark, bitter laugh that signaled nothing so much as bone-deep weariness. "Happy fucking Christmas, everyone."

And to that, Charlotte didn't have any response.

FIVE DAYS
TO CHRISTMAS

CHAPTER SEVENTEEN

On Friday, she put the finishing touches on the final commission she was working on for the year, then stood at Ava's kitchen sink, rolling her shoulders as she washed her paintbrushes and carefully packed them away. The rest of the morning passed in a haze of end-of-workweek admin—she was trying to dig her way out of preholiday emails, and she had a lunchtime call with her assistant (still in her pajamas, given the hour of the morning on the East Coast) as they prepared to close down the shop on Charlotte's website next week for a brief, much-needed hiatus to recover from the holiday rush.

"And I think that's it," Sarah said, looking down at the list on her iPad that she was consulting. "I'll keep monitoring the customer service email for the website and let you know if anything comes up over the weekend, but we've mainly been getting questions about Christmas shipping, so I've been referring them to the printing service that handles fulfillment, and I've added a banner that says that anything ordered after Monday won't be shipped until after the new year. Oh..." She frowned down at her iPad. "I forgot—we got an inquiry from someone named Jamie Dyer—claims he knows your mom? He wants to commission invitations for an event. The lead time isn't nearly enough, given how long your wait list is, but since there was a family connection, I thought I should check with you. Want me to forward you the email?"

Charlotte sighed, running a hand through her hair. "Yeah, send it to me and I'll take a look." She was mildly surprised that her mom had had the follow-through to relay her message to Dyer in a timely manner. It felt almost . . . considerate. As though she were actually trying to help.

Huh.

"Okay," Sarah said, making a note on the iPad and setting it aside. "Then I think that's all I have for today."

"Perfect," Charlotte said, stretching; she was in leggings and a cashmere pullover, hunched over her laptop on her bed at Ava's like a weird troll. She'd barely ventured out of her room all morning, except to fetch coffee and a banana, and she was now feeling the vague sense that it might be nice to approximate something of a normal human existence for the rest of the day.

Sarah smiled at her. "How's London? All the pictures I see online make it look like a Christmas wonderland."

"It is," Charlotte said darkly. "Please understand I don't consider that a compliment."

"Because you're an emotionally deficient Grinch who refuses to embrace the magic of the season," Sarah said, without the slightest hint of awareness that Charlotte was, you know, the person who paid her.

"Sarah. You're Jewish," Charlotte pointed out.

"But I can still appreciate some nice Christmas decorations because I'm not a holiday movie villain," Sarah said cheerfully. "Good luck avoiding doing anything that would make your heart grow three sizes."

"Thank you," Charlotte said dryly. "I'll talk to you on Monday to wrap up any loose ends, all right?"

She waited for Sarah to wave goodbye before disconnecting the call, then closed her laptop. She might not like Christmas, but she *did* like the knowledge that her workload would be considerably lighter for the next couple of weeks, particularly once they closed the shop on Monday night. She wouldn't be fully relaxing—she needed to finish her sample materials for her meeting with Perfect Paper—but at least she wouldn't have other deadlines to worry about. (And, crucially, could step back from Instagram a bit, which would offer a nice respite from the slowing-but-still-active trickle of DMs from people accusing her of hating all forms of joy.) Once this meeting was behind her, whatever the outcome, she planned to spend January working on a new set of prints to unveil, though she hadn't decided what the theme was going to be—she liked to release small collections all centered on a given theme and hadn't picked her next one yet. Usually, by this time, she had it all in mind, had been sketching away as ideas struck her, but she was feeling a bit flat this year. Though, considering how much she'd had going on lately—avoiding deranged teenagers in Central Park; cohabitating with demon-possessed babies; having sex with emotionally repressed British men—she thought it was understandable that she was a bit off her game.

She pondered this further as she showered, blew her hair dry, and put on a green wool dress that she was very sure made her legs look incredible—not that there was anyone around at the moment to appreciate them. Ava, John, and Simone had strapped a protesting Alice into her stroller and gone to watch Kit don a Santa suit and run a 5K, surrounded by a bunch of other people in Santa suits, which was one of those events that Charlotte would *love* to watch someone attempt to explain to an alien visiting the planet.

Now, she found herself alone, with an entire afternoon to fill stretching before her. This felt strangely luxurious. She thought for a moment of texting Graham, but something gave her pause. She'd spent most nights this week at his flat: he'd cook her dinner, if she arrived early enough; they'd watch TV together; in the mornings, he'd wake her up with a mug of coffee and a kiss. She told herself that she was there for the sex—and the sex was undeniably fantastic—but something within her worried that this was more than that. The sight of him, first thing in the morning, with bedhead and a crease from the pillow on his cheek, did weird things to her chest, and she didn't trust it—didn't trust this feeling. On the mornings she wasn't at his flat, he was the first person she wanted to text upon awakening—and for this reason, she didn't let herself text him now. She had a free afternoon, and she was going to spend it alone—she *liked* being alone. She shouldn't have had to remind herself of that fact.

She pulled on her coat, shoved her phone and a credit card into her smallest purse, and set off on foot. She stopped into a café for a sandwich, then browsed in a bookshop, relishing the feeling of being alone, with an afternoon free, no deadlines weighing on her mind. Eventually she hopped on a bus and made her way to the Victoria and Albert Museum. She loved the V&A and made a point of visiting each time she came to see Ava, but hadn't yet popped in on this trip. It was crowded, but everywhere in London was crowded and nauseatingly festive at the moment, so at least being surrounded by artwork made the preponderance of plaid and Christmas sweaters a bit easier to ignore. She lingered for a while at the fashion exhibit, which was always one of her favorites—they were currently displaying a Regency-era waistcoat in a yellow paisley pattern that was quite honestly one of the ugliest articles of clothing she'd ever seen—and then spent a while on the Islamic art, reading every single placard and suddenly gripped with a strong desire to buy new pottery for her apartment in New York.

It was only later, as she was browsing in the gift shop on the way out, that she spotted it: a stylish-looking biography, the cover art showcasing a famous pattern she recognized all too well.

Christian Calloway: An Intimate Biography.

She hesitated for only a split second before taking it to the till.

And then took it home and, while she was enjoying an afternoon glass of brandy-laced apple cider, began to read.

And read.

And read.

And by the time she was done, she was feeling remarkably *angry*.

Which was why it was now December 22, at 6 p.m., and she found herself on Graham's front steps, clutching a book, a bottle of wine, and the shreds of her righteous indignation.

"Hi," he said as he opened the door. He'd been down at Eden Priory all day Saturday and half of today, and this was the first time she'd seen him since Friday morning, when she'd left his flat. She had at least texted to make sure he was home and free tonight, and he'd responded right away, inviting her for dinner.

"Hello," she said, sweeping past him into his flat, her moral outrage withering somewhat under the smell of something absolutely *incredible* coming from the kitchen. "I hope you're prepared for an evening of cinema."

"I—what?" He trailed after her as she made her way to the kitchen, setting down the bottle of wine on the counter and reaching for the corkscrew she knew he kept in a particular drawer.

"I've been doing some reading, you see," she said, nodding at the biography she'd tossed imperiously onto the kitchen island. "And I have a *lot* of thoughts."

Graham picked up the book, frowning down at the cover. "I remember this one," he said slowly, flipping it over so he could read the back jacket copy. "I think my dad was interviewed by the author."

"He was," Charlotte confirmed. "He's quoted several times."

"Did you *read* this?" he asked, glancing up from the book to raise an eyebrow at her.

She uncorked the wine and nodded, reaching for wineglasses from a cabinet. "The entire thing. I've been like a kid on summer break for the past couple of days, just holed up in Ava's flat reading nonstop. It's been weird."

"Dare I ask *why*?" he asked, a slightly impatient note to his voice.

"Well," she said slowly as she poured, "at first, I was curious— I realized I didn't know that much about Calloway's personal life, and I thought it might be interesting to learn more, especially now that I've visited his house."

"But?"

"But soon, I was motivated by rage," she said, handing him a glass of wine and turning to pour one for herself. "Because I'm not sure you're aware, but Christian Calloway was *an ass*."

Behind her, she heard a faint choking sound, and turned in time to see Graham coughing on a mouthful of wine. "Sorry," she said sweetly, "but you cannot *possibly* be unaware of this fact."

He recovered enough to breathe normally, which seemed like an encouraging sign. "He wasn't someone I'd personally like to go to the pub with, no," he agreed, taking a more cautious sip of wine.

"Graham!" Her voice was approaching a pitch that only dogs could hear, so she deliberately paused, took a calming breath, and tried again. "Graham, that is the understatement of the *year*. He had a mistress who lived *in the same house as his wife*."

Graham winced. "Yes. Poor Minnie."

"Poor Minnie *and* poor Adelaide—that's the mistress's name, you know."

"Yes. I tried to convince my dad that we should add an extra section to the exhibition rooms at Eden Priory to sort of examine his complicated legacy, but—"

"Let me guess, your dad wouldn't go for it?"

He sighed, scrubbing his hands over his face. "He wasn't entirely opposed, but he never really prioritized it . . . but I should do it, now that he's gone."

She walked toward him and impulsively reached out to take his hand. "You don't have to make that decision alone. Your mom and sisters are *right there* and clearly have their own ideas—and those ideas matter just as much as yours. Stop turning the family business into some weird tortured-romance-hero-with-daddy-issues subplot."

"A *what*?"

"Don't worry about it," she said, waving a hand. "Not relevant. Graham, the future of Eden Priory *is not up to you.*"

"I know," he said heavily. "I know you're right, but I just keep thinking about every change that we've made that he would have hated, and I feel like I . . . owe it to him. To try to be a voice for him, now that he's gone. Especially since—" Here, he broke off, swallowing. "Since there were all those years when I could've come home more often, to help around the house, but everything about my life in London, my job, felt so much more important—"

"I'm sorry, you mean the job that you got specifically so that you'd be able to support the house?" Charlotte interrupted, not having *any* of this, hating the bitterness in his voice. "Graham, you're doing *the best you can*. You always have been. And your dad did the best that *he* could, while he was alive. And now it's up to you, and your mom, and your sisters, to figure out what the best thing for Eden Priory is now." She reached for his hand, and he laced his fingers through hers. "Your dad is dead, and I'm so sorry, and I know that's more painful than I can even imagine—but you don't owe him Eden Priory's future. Not when your mom and sisters are still here, loving you, loving this house, and you're letting this come between you and them."

He frowned, but not like he was mad at her—more like he was thinking.

"You're trying to prove yourself to a ghost, and there are plenty of living people who love you who would appreciate you proving yourself to *them* instead. Or," she added, thinking of the years he'd spent working long hours at a job he didn't love, a job that ate up all the hours of the day and brought him no joy, "maybe don't try to prove yourself to anyone. Just yourself."

A silence fell after this, and Charlotte—feeling, honestly, torn between pleased with herself and mildly nauseated at how badly she'd overstepped—took a large sip of wine to steady herself. As soon as she set her glass down, however, Graham tugged her closer.

"Thank you," he said, lowering his head to hers. "I think I've needed someone to say that to me for—Christ, for two years, I suppose. I've been an ass."

"No," she said, shaking her head. "Well, yes, a bit, but mainly you've been a person in pain who isn't perfect." She blinked. "I swear to god, I have never been half this wise in my entire life. I sound like a life coach. What a wild career pivot."

"Lane?"

"Yes?"

"Please shut up."

"Make me."

So he did.

After the kitchen island wine-and-emotional-reckoning portion of the evening's agenda, they relocated to the couch for the next, more enjoyable item on the schedule: coconut curry and *Christmas, Truly*.

"Please, please explain to me why we're doing this," Graham said, slumped on the couch with a tumbler of whiskey, neat, in his hand.

This would have looked considerably more Don Draper and badass had he not been wearing a cable-knit sweater and gray sweatpants.

"It's part of your healing journey," Charlotte informed him, topping up her glass of wine. "And, I don't know, maybe mine? I got death threats on the internet and yelled at by a teenager because of this movie; I guess it's probably time I revisited it."

"What a promising beginning," he murmured, but gamely reached for the remote and hit play.

For the next two hours, they were—well, they were kind of transfixed. It wasn't that *Christmas, Truly* was going to make any lists of all-time classic films anytime soon—no movie that contained the line "Christmas, truly, is all that we need," uttered in complete earnestness, could lay a claim to that designation—but there *was* something strangely watchable about it. It was just a bunch of attractive, upper-middle-class, carefully-diverse-but-not-*too*-diverse-in-the-way-of-the-early-aughts people on both sides of the Atlantic having romantic problems while running around New York and London in nice sweaters. (Nadine really wasn't kidding about the sweaters.) By the time the credits rolled, she felt like she'd had her brain ironed, but in a nice way? (That might also have been the wine.)

Graham clicked off the TV and turned to her.

"Oh my god." She leaned forward on her knees. "Are you *crying*?"

"The woman with the dying husband who hoped to spend one last Christmas with her was *sad*."

"Oh boy, we have *got* to watch *The Notebook* together—I do not think you'd be able to handle it."

"Is that the one where Ryan Gosling does a Southern accent and then there are elderly people with dementia?"

"Confirmed."

"Seen it." She raised an eyebrow at him. "Sisters," he reminded her.

"And? Did you cry?"

"I might have," he said, looking a bit shifty. "I can't remember."

"Ha! I knew it!" She flopped back onto the couch, satisfied, then turned her head to meet his gaze. "So?"

"So, what?"

"So, what do you think? Do you agree with your dad that that was such an embarrassment to the entire concept of film that the use of Eden Priory as a filming location for *one* set of scenes was enough to sully the legacy of your jackass of an ancestor forevermore?"

"I mean, to be clear, it wasn't *Citizen Kane*."

"My good sir, you are preaching to the choir. Have you forgotten that I derailed an entire reboot due to my distaste for this piece of cinema?"

"Fair enough."

"But answer my question."

He sighed, scrubbing a hand over his face. "No, Dad was wrong. It doesn't matter."

"Exactly," Charlotte said smugly, cradling her glass of wine in a protective manner against her chest.

"I rather enjoyed it, actually."

"Well, I don't know that I'd go that far," Charlotte said hastily. "But my point remains: one movie does not a legacy destroy."

"Yes, yes."

"One *might* say that siring five children out of wedlock but refusing to allow them to use your last name while still allowing them to live in the same house as you destroys a legacy."

"You've made your point, Lane." He paused, brow furrowed. "Actually, I'm not sure I remembered that detail."

"I am your newly minted resident Christian Calloway expert," Charlotte said cheerfully. "Anything horrifying you want to know about him, I'm your girl."

"We've really got to get to work on that addition to the exhibition," he muttered, but reached over to take her hand.

"Yes, you do."

He turned to her then, his eyes still a bit red, his hair disheveled due to the fifteen minutes he'd spent gripping it in dismay during the portion of the movie in which Tallulah had thought that her pen pal, Pip, had abandoned her forever after failing to respond to her last letter, and cried herself to sleep each night in the hair of her pet rabbit. "Lane," he said softly, and something in his tone, the way he said her name, made her heart kick up a rapid beat in her chest. "What are we doing?"

"Watching a mediocre Christmas movie and then hooking up on your sofa?" she asked hopefully.

"You leave in . . ." He paused, mentally counting. "Ten days."

She felt every one of those ten days like a weight in her stomach. "I know."

"Does this feel like a holiday romance to you?"

"You know, it's funny because it is *both* a holiday romance, because that's what you call a vacation, and *also* a *literal* holiday romance, because it's three days before Christmas and my life appears to be sponsored by the Hallmark Channel now."

"Charlotte."

She sighed. "No," she said softly. "But . . . well, I didn't come here looking for this."

His mouth quirked up. "I promise you I didn't escape into my favorite hiding place at Eden Priory last month looking for this, either. But . . ."

"But?" she asked, trying to keep her voice neutral, not as though she were hoping for him to say anything in particular—because, still, she didn't quite understand *what* she wanted him to say.

"But I don't want this to end," he said, and she wished, in that moment, that she'd been brave enough to say it first—because no sooner were the words out of his mouth than she realized that she felt the exact same way.

"I have to go back to New York," she said, her heart racing at the intensity carved into every line of his face as he looked at her. "This meeting—it's important. I can't miss it. And my whole life is there." Except, of course, it wasn't. Ava and Kit were here; her parents were in LA; even Padma and Andrew were no longer close enough for impromptu weeknight hangouts. Parts of her life were in New York—but she wondered, now, if she wasn't using that as an excuse, because she was too afraid of what this might be between them, of the fact that an increasingly large part of her life might be *here* instead.

"I know that," he said, reaching out to take her hand. His thumb rubbed a soothing pattern against her palm, and she felt, in this moment, that she would do anything—give anything—if only he wouldn't let go of her hand again. "I don't want you to give up your life—I don't want you to give up *anything*," he said fiercely. "I'm not . . ." He trailed off, clearly weighing his words, and then said, "I'm not your ex. I don't want you because of what you do. I don't want you because your family is famous, or you were in a film once, or you're a *brilliant*, talented artist who has created her own business no matter what her family thinks. I like all of those things about you, but . . . I just want you because you're *you*." His grip on her hand was tight, now, but she still didn't want him to let go—and she couldn't bring herself to look away.

She swallowed against all the words rising in her throat, trying to work out how to say what it was that she truly meant, in a way that he'd understand. And then realized—*trusted*—that he'd understand anyway, even if she didn't get it out perfectly, because he was like that. And because he knew her.

And that, she was realizing now, was what she'd been longing for, for so long.

"After Craig and I broke up," she said quietly, never moving her eyes from his face, "for a long time, I sort of . . . retreated back into myself. I was determined to never put myself in a situation like that ever again—I was going to do everything myself, not rely on anyone else, not be a . . . a *burden* to anyone, ever. And it was good for me, for a while—I felt like I'd built a life of my own, without a partner, and I was determined to not risk anything that might ruin that. But . . ." She paused, considering her words carefully, but he didn't press her—just watched her quietly, his hand still holding hers.

"But after a while," she continued at last, "I think it started to feel . . . *too* safe. And when Padma got married and moved to the suburbs earlier this year, it really knocked me off-balance, because it felt like things were changing, were unsettled, and I hadn't agreed to it. This might be why the *Christmas, Truly* thing freaked me out so badly—I was already feeling sort of unsettled." She shrugged. "I've been realizing this all, since I've been here—this is the longest I've spent away from New York since I moved back from college. And I miss my apartment, and my friends, and my life—because I *do* like it, and I'm proud of the life I've built for myself, but . . ." She glanced down, then glanced back up at him again, very directly. "It's just *a* life. It's been a good one in my twenties, but it doesn't have to be forever. If something—someone—came along and made me want to change it. Maybe take a risk or two."

"I don't want to be a risk, you know," he said, leaning forward now to cup her cheek with his hand, his expression almost unbearably tender. "I don't want to hurt you—I don't want to be some ass who blows up your life."

"I know you don't," she agreed. "Or I wouldn't be here right now."

"But," he added, "I don't want you to be afraid to—to need me. To lean on me. I don't like you because I think you're calm, or steady, or whatever role it is you played in your family, in that relationship. I want to be with you, whatever you're feeling."

"It feels . . . risky," she said softly, looking down at her lap. "I haven't let myself need anyone else for so long—I'm scared to get used to it, I guess." She took a deep breath, and glanced up to meet his eyes again. "But I think . . . I'm willing to risk it. For you."

"Good," he said in a low voice. "Because I already worked out, about a week ago, that there's not much I wouldn't risk for you." It was so quiet, so simple, so sneakily devastating that it took a moment for the ache in her chest to even register. He wiped her cheek with his thumb.

"I'm not crying," she informed him as he lowered his face to hers.

"Not anymore," he agreed, and then he kissed her and made the words true.

CHRISTMAS EVE

CHAPTER EIGHTEEN

H i, Charlotte." Lizzie met her at the door to Eden Priory on Tuesday afternoon, wearing all black and looking somewhat glum.

"Hi, Lizzie," Charlotte said, a bit hesitant. "Everything all right?"

Lizzie heaved a dramatic sigh. "I thought we should have shown *The Nightmare Before Christmas* for this."

Charlotte blinked. "A Halloween movie?"

Lizzie looked outraged. "It's not a *Halloween* film, it's a *Christmas* film!"

Charlotte shook her head. "It's not. It's a Halloween movie with a bit of Christmas mixed in—because no one wants a Christmas movie with Halloween mixed in."

"*I* do," Lizzie insisted, which was fair enough, Charlotte supposed.

It was midafternoon on Christmas Eve; Graham had driven down to Hampshire that morning, but Charlotte had felt that some display of family holiday spirit was required, so she'd spent the morning with Ava and Simone, going out for pastries and taking Alice on a long walk, while Kit and John had labored mysteriously—and, occasionally, alarmingly noisily—in the kitchen. After lunch, Charlotte had caught the train to Upper Larkspur—which, even with a connecting train, took only about an hour and a half—and then a taxi from the train station to Eden Priory. The film screening was due to begin at three, and at half past two, the crowds were already flooding in.

Deciding to change tack, Charlotte glanced down at the potted plant she held. "I brought a poinsettia?"

Lizzie visibly brightened at this, and reached out to claim it. "Ooh! I'll take you to the kitchen. I think Eloise wanted to speak to you for a moment."

"Should you be abandoning your post?" Charlotte asked, eyeing the headlights farther down the gravel drive, a sure sign of more *Christmas, Truly* watchers on the way.

Looking untroubled by this, Lizzie unceremoniously ushered Charlotte inside and closed the heavy wooden door. "Waiting in the cold will heighten their anticipation!" she informed Charlotte cheerfully, and Charlotte decided not to argue with this extremely dubious logic.

She followed Lizzie into the house, weaving her way around happily chattering families in the entrance hall (and smiling gamely in response to the occasional "Tallulah!" called in her direction). They were screening the movie in this room, to fully lean into the *Christmas, Truly* vibes, and a giant screen had been set up against one wall, most of the floor space having been taken up with folding chairs. (The settee next to the Christmas tree was currently mobbed by people taking selfies sitting on it, most of them pretending to write letters, which *was* funny, Charlotte had to admit.)

There was a table bearing paper bags of popcorn at the base of the stairs, and Graham was currently stationed behind it, handing popcorn to parents and hastily snatching a bag back from a small child who was attempting to stick it under her sweater. He glanced up, as if sensing Charlotte's presence, and met her eyes with a smile; Charlotte waved at him, but he was quickly distracted by a second child joining the first would-be thief with similarly larcenous intentions, and Charlotte trotted to catch up with Lizzie.

Lizzie led her through one of the doorways marked PRIVATE and into the kitchen, where the rest of the Calloway family was currently located, and which smelled, at the moment, overpoweringly of popcorn.

"Mum, Charlotte's brought us a plant!" Lizzie said. "I'm naming it Gertrude, just so we're all clear on that."

"Why've you never named any of the flowers *I* brought you from my garden?" Eloise asked, sounding vaguely disgruntled as she filled a paper bag with popcorn from the enormous popcorn machine currently set up on the kitchen island. She added the bag to what looked to be a tea trolley that had been repurposed for popcorn-carting duties.

"Those are cut flowers," Lizzie said, sounding extremely unimpressed. "Flower corpses, basically."

"Lizzie," Mrs. Calloway said, sounding a bit shocked. She was standing at the stove, stirring an enormous pot filled with what Charlotte suspected was hot chocolate, based on the smell. "That's a rather dark way of looking at it, darling."

"I'm just speaking my truth, Mum," Lizzie said with a shrug, before absconding with the poinsettia and vanishing through a doorway.

"Can I do anything to help?" Charlotte asked; the kitchen was not a place she tended to feel at home, but she at least had the basic skills required for the current tasks. She hoped.

"Mum, if you want to wheel this cart out to Graham, we can start pouring the hot chocolate," Eloise called to her mother, who happily relinquished her place at the hob. Eloise took over the stirring, directing Charlotte to find a bag of paper cups hidden in one cabinet. Once these had been procured, they commenced a fairly seamless operation of cup filling, with Charlotte carefully placing the filled cups on the counter while she waited for Mrs. Calloway to return with the cart.

"It seems like a good crowd," she said, handing Eloise an empty cup.

"Yes!" Eloise said brightly. "We had a lot of people sign up after—well—"

"After I told Graham to shamelessly cash in on my child stardom?" Charlotte asked dryly, and Eloise looked sheepish.

"Well, yes," she said, trading a full cup for an empty one. She bit her lip as she carefully ladled another serving of hot chocolate, looking more uneasy than Charlotte had ever seen her in their brief acquaintance.

"What's wrong?" Charlotte asked warily, accepting the full cup and lining it up next to the others on the counter.

"I'm feeling a bit like a horrible person," Eloise said, handing her another full cup and waiting while Charlotte reached for another empty one.

Charlotte froze in the act of reaching for the empty cup. "Why?"

"You and Graham seem so happy!" Eloise burst out. "And after Francesca, I wasn't sure I'd ever see him *happy* like this again."

Charlotte blinked. "And that's . . . a bad thing?" She handed Eloise the empty cup.

"No, no," Eloise said, ladling out more hot chocolate. "I just feel bad because I nearly ruined it!"

Charlotte accepted the cup and set it down slowly, frowning. "What do you mean?"

Eloise set down the ladle and wiped her hands on a tea towel, then turned to face Charlotte directly. "I recognized you, the day of the lights switch-on."

"Okay," Charlotte said slowly, trying to remember their initial conversation in the car.

"Not immediately," Eloise clarified, "but while we were talking in the car, I kept thinking you looked familiar, and when you mentioned your art, I looked you up, and worked it out."

"And you didn't say anything?" Nothing about this made sense to Charlotte—she couldn't figure out what Eloise was building up to here.

"Well, if you didn't want to admit to it, when I mentioned the film, I thought it would be sort of rude to bring it up," Eloise said, which seemed reasonable enough, but she wasn't done yet. "But once I'd mentioned the idea for the commission, I started thinking . . . that if we could . . . befriend you, I suppose? Then maybe you'd be willing to do something related to the film, for us."

"Like," Charlotte said, a sinking feeling in her stomach, "letting you use me to publicize this film screening?"

Eloise pressed her lips together. "It might have crossed my mind."

"Right," Charlotte said, her mind already working in overdrive, thinking back on every conversation she'd had with Graham about *Christmas, Truly*—about Eden Priory—about . . . everything.

"But," she said slowly, "this was *my* idea. I had to convince Graham."

Eloise nodded, relief flooding her face. "I know! He wouldn't do it—he said that our arrangement with you for the commission would be it, and that we weren't going to ask you to do anything else for us—I wasn't even supposed to ever mention *Christmas, Truly* around you."

This was, admittedly, somewhat reassuring—she would have felt pretty freaked out if Graham had somehow manipulated her into offering to do something he'd been angling for all the while, but . . . why didn't she *feel* that reassured?

"When I finally told him about *Christmas, Truly*," she said, still trying to work out the sequence of events in her mind, "he already knew?"

The relief slowly faded from Eloise's expression now, as if she was belatedly realizing that this confession might not be as straightforward a *we'll laugh about it later* sort of thing as she'd expected.

"Um," Eloise said. "I reckon so. He didn't recognize you himself! I had to tell him!"

Of course he hadn't—he'd never seen the movie. There was, Charlotte admitted to herself now, a small part of herself that had been attracted to him specifically because of this fact. After the couple of weeks she'd had before meeting him, there was something deeply relaxing about being around someone who knew absolutely nothing about *Christmas, Truly*, and couldn't have cared less that she once had worn round glasses and lisped charmingly and been, briefly, adored by millions of people.

Except, as it turned out, that wasn't true. Not entirely, at least.

"My point was that I'm so glad Graham didn't listen to me," Eloise said now, stumbling over her own words in her rush to get them out. "I'm so happy about the two of you—*he* seems so happy—and I'm so glad I didn't manage to mess it all up!" She looked, suddenly, incredibly anxious—which seemed about right, Charlotte thought darkly. She would look anxious, too, if she was gripped with the dawning realization that she'd just massively fucked up her sibling's love life.

At that exact moment, Mrs. Calloway returned with the empty tea trolley. "Shall we send out a round of hot chocolate?" she asked brightly, oblivious to the tension that filled the kitchen. She hummed "Jingle Bells" to herself as she began moving the full cups from the counter to the trolley; Charlotte began to help her, carefully avoiding Eloise's eyes as she worked.

The conversation she needed to have with Graham—the argument that was brewing, the anger burning beneath her skin—would have to wait.

But not for long.

By six, the house was empty again, nothing but popcorn kernels and a few sticky hot chocolate spills remaining.

Charlotte was helping Mrs. Calloway break down folding chairs, lining them up against a wall to be collected in a few days by the company they'd been rented from, when Graham approached. "Let me give you a lift to the train station—your ticket is for six thirty, right?"

"Right." Charlotte straightened, brushing her hands against her skirt (black; she'd paired it with a black turtleneck, because there was absolutely no chance she was wearing anything remotely Christmassy to a screening of *Christmas, Truly*; she had to draw the line somewhere). She had managed to avoid Graham for the entirety of the event; once she'd helped Mrs. Calloway deliver the hot chocolate to the refreshment stand, she'd found herself swept into a number of interactions with enthusiastic-but-basically-benign strangers, who wanted a selfie with Tallulah, or to ask her what filming the movie had been like, or to ask if she'd visited any of the other filming locations. And, yeah, a few people asked her about the reboot—a line of inquiry that she politely but firmly shut down each time—but she could sense that the collective cultural attention had moved on.

And, honestly, the whole thing had been *fine*. It was a few hours out of her life, it involved cringe-watching her own (in her opinion, somewhat questionable) child acting, but the room was packed, everyone seemed happy, and she knew the ticket sales would be a huge boon to Eden Priory.

It should have felt like some sort of record-scratch moment—an afternoon during which she made her peace with the *Christmas, Truly* thing, once and for all—but after that conversation with Eloise in the kitchen, she'd barely been able to focus on anything happening around her. She'd tucked herself away in a corner, once the movie had started, in a spot where it would have been impossible for Graham to reach her without disturbing about twenty other people in the process, and so she'd seen him vanish into the kitchen instead, presumably to help his mom with cleanup.

But now, there was no avoiding the conversation they needed to have.

She managed to make it through the leave-taking while behaving more or less normally—perhaps her one childhood foray into acting had been worthwhile after all?—and it was only when they were in Graham's car, headed to the train station in the village, that he at last seemed to realize something was wrong. To his credit, it was only about fifteen seconds into the drive—enough time for Charlotte to offer one monosyllabic reply, and for him to catch a proper look at her expression—that he caught on.

"What's wrong?" he asked, wariness writ plain in his voice.

"Did you cozy up to me to use me to promote Eden Priory?" she asked, not mincing words. She'd never been one to beat around the bush, even under the best of circumstances, and she was not exactly in a diplomatic frame of mind at the moment.

To Graham's credit, he didn't lie. There were plenty of men she'd dated in the past that she knew would have offered some sort of excuse at this point, tried to weasel their way out of trouble. Graham, however, simply let a long, painful beat of silence elapse before he reached over to switch off the radio.

"Did Eloise tell you that?" he asked at last, his voice quiet.

"She did," she responded, equally quiet, trying not to let any of the hurt gnawing at her chest creep into her voice. If Graham had just explained, early on, what had happened, she could have forgiven him—probably would have found it funny, in fact. But this deliberate, ongoing deceit? She had a much harder time swallowing that.

"Then let me provide a bit of context that she might not have added," he said.

"Oh, there was zero context," she said, her voice sounding bitter to her own ears now.

"Eloise recognized you the evening we met you," he said, his voice carefully even, his eyes on the road ahead. "And she had just read that goddamn article a few days earlier, so she knew you were—um . . ." He hesitated, clearly looking for a delicate way to say *hated by an unhinged faction of people on the internet*. ". . . on the minds of people, at that moment."

Charlotte snorted at this, and his mouth twitched.

"So she was thinking that if we all became friends somehow, you might agree to do us a favor. And when she cooked up the idea of the prints to sell at the gift shop, she thought it would be killing two birds with one stone if we could also . . . befriend you."

"Befriend," she repeated, incredulous.

"I swear, that's all it was," he said, glancing over at her. "This isn't a bad novel, and she didn't ask me to play a Jane Austen villain and try to seduce you for my own gains, or whatever. It doesn't matter, in any case, because I initially said no—it seemed invasive and sort of disturbing."

"And then you slept on it, and used your little accountant brain, and realized that this was too good a possibility to pass up?" she asked with considerable acid in her voice.

"No." He shook his head vehemently. "I wasn't lying to you in the coffee shop that day. I looked up your website and was truly impressed by your work—it had nothing to do with your name, and I genuinely thought it was a good opportunity for both us and you. It's why I came to discuss it with you, rather than Eloise; I told her point-blank that I wasn't going to try to—I dunno—weasel my way into your affections, or whatever the fuck she had in mind."

"So you're expecting me to believe that everything that happened between us was real, and you just happened to fall for the person who your sister had specifically targeted for, like, some sort of weird publicity scheme?"

"Why do you think I never asked you to do anything?" he asked, sounding frustrated. "Why do you think I seemed so reluctant when you offered to let Eloise use your photo for the film screening?"

"Guilty conscience?"

"Well, yeah—and because it just all seemed extremely fucking creepy, honestly. I didn't want anything that was happening between us to be . . . *tainted*, I guess."

He fell silent then, and Charlotte turned in her seat to study him for a long moment. She could believe him, largely; she didn't think he was some sort of sociopathic mastermind who had been hunting her down for his purposes, despite what her initial thoughts had been. She thought he was human, and he made mistakes, and he'd made a big one, this time, and had handled it the best way he could see to do so.

But . . .

"Why didn't you tell me?" she asked softly. Sadly.

He didn't respond for a long moment, his eyes on the road ahead, the increasingly bright lights of the village as they approached the high street.

"I couldn't work out a way to tell you that you'd believe," he said at last, turning at a roundabout to head to the train station.

"If you'd been honest, I'd have believed you," she said as he slid the car into one of the parallel spots in front of the station. He pulled up the parking brake and turned off the car, but she was already unclicking her seat belt, her hand on the door handle. "Lane—Charlotte," he said, the slightest pleading note entering his voice for the first time. "I should have told you sooner, I know that—but please don't leave like this."

She looked at him for a long moment—at his stupid, handsome

face. She noted how tired he looked, with dark circles beneath his eyes, visible even behind his glasses. She wondered how many sleepless nights he'd spent poring over Eden Priory's finances, trying to work out a way to save this place that he loved so much.

"I've spent twenty years trying to escape *Christmas, Truly*," she said. "I literally *came here* because I didn't want anything to do with it—because I'm sick of even talking about it, Jesus Christ. It would be nice to *not* have to think about something I did when I was nine years old for more than a week at a time, you know. And now, with this . . . I'd always think about it, when I thought of you. Of us." She shook her head. "I can't let this be something else that it hangs over. I just . . . can't do this."

And then, feeling like a bit of a coward, she opened her door and fled into the station before he had time to reply.

And told herself, as she stood on the platform, awaiting her train, that she didn't care what he would have said anyway.

But deep down, she knew it wasn't true.

CHRISTMAS DAY

CHAPTER NINETEEN

In an ideal world, she wouldn't have spent Christmas morning slightly drunk, but this, clearly, was not an ideal world.

She had managed, somehow, to come home the night before and behave like some semblance of a normal human being. Ava and Kit had been too caught up in the Christmas Eve festivities to ask too many questions about Charlotte's suspiciously red eyes. There had been the last-minute flurry of gift wrapping, of making a dessert for the following day, of—much to Charlotte's dismay—a forced viewing of *It's a Wonderful Life*, which on the one hand was terrible because it was the longest movie ever made, but on the other hand at least viewed Christmas through about as cheerful a lens as she did, which had always been a point in its favor.

Given the length of the movie, she hadn't gone to bed until late, though, mercifully, she'd been able to sleep until a humane hour this morning, because Alice—say what you liked about her (and Charlotte had said plenty)—had one enormous factor in her favor: She was a *baby*, which meant that *she didn't know it was Christmas*.

Charlotte was certain that in future years, she'd be awoken by a mercenary cackle at five a.m., but this year, blessedly, the demon baby slept until seven.

"I think you're being a *bit* melodramatic," Charlotte said, as Ava literally kissed the floor upon finally wandering into the living room that morning.

"I'm not," Ava retorted, wincing as she climbed back to her feet—it was one of the least-graceful motions Charlotte had ever seen her sister make. "Just wait until you have a baby."

"Pass," Charlotte said without missing a beat.

"Probably a good call," Ava said, although her face did brighten at the sight of Kit wandering into the living room with Alice in his arms; he was wearing a pair of pajamas in a matching print to Alice's onesie. It was pretty adorable. Though—

"Did you not get the matching-PJs memo?" Charlotte asked her sister, gesturing at Ava's pajamas—a silk tank-and-shorts set that, knowing Ava, had cost at least $300. It was completed with a pink silk robe. She looked significantly more glamorous than anyone had a right to look before eight in the morning, but she was decidedly *not* completing the picture of a family in matching Christmas harmony.

"I got it, and I ignored it," Ava said, lifting her nose. "I accidentally logged into Facebook last year at Christmas—"

"How do you *accidentally* log into Facebook?" Charlotte asked skeptically.

"It wasn't an accident," Kit said cheerfully. "We were arguing about whether her last boyfriend before me was fit or not—"

Charlotte closed her eyes. "I don't think I want to hear this story anymore."

Kit was undeterred. "—and so she had to log in to prove to me that he was, which was wonderful because it was how she learned that he'd converted to become a Mormon—"

This had taken an unexpected turn. "I'm sorry," Charlotte said. "He what now?"

"—and had four children and they all wore matching Christmas pajamas."

"It was harrowing," Ava said with a shudder. "But then I did a bit of digging, since I was already logged in, and discovered absolute *hordes* of boring people I used to know who are now happily married and popping out offspring—"

"Like you," Charlotte pointed out, in the interest of fairness.

"—and this matching-pajamas thing seems to be some sort of plague. You cannot *imagine* how many people do it." Ava crossed her arms. "So I refuse to participate."

"Mum will be disappointed," Kit said, "since she's the one who bought them for us."

"She won't," Ava said serenely. "Because I gave the pair she got me back to her, and she's going to wear them instead."

At precisely this moment, there was the sound of a key in the door, the door opening, and a cheerful "Happy Christmas!" trilled from the entryway. Simone and John appeared in the living room a moment later, both wearing matching pajamas of their own, with Simone brandishing a bottle of champagne in her hand.

"Bubbles?" she asked brightly.

"Please," said Charlotte.

From that point, the morning became a bit of a blur: there was a round of mimosas, then the absurdity of a bunch of adults sitting with bated breath as an unimpressed baby played with a ball of wrapping paper rather than any of the gifts that it had been used to wrap. There was a Christmas lunch, and a round of charades, and Christmas crackers—one of the few Christmas traditions that Charlotte actually enjoyed, since she liked to wait until someone was deep in conversation and then pull a cracker directly next to them, just to see them jump.

But throughout all of this, there was a constant whine of misery humming just below the surface for her—one she didn't want to think about, to consider too carefully, scared of what it would tell her. About herself, about Graham, about what she might feel for him.

Might have felt, she corrected herself mentally. *Past tense.*

But she didn't believe this, really.

She thought she was doing a decent job of hiding this, since no one seemed to notice anything out of the ordinary, but it turned out that Ava had just been choosing her moment to strike.

"What the hell is wrong with you?" Ava asked without any warning that afternoon as she and Charlotte were loading the dishwasher. "You look like you're going to a funeral. I know Christmas isn't your thing, but this seems extreme."

"I do not," Charlotte objected, scrubbing at a particularly stuck-on bit of food on the plate in her hand.

"Oh my god, you *don't have to wash the dish first*," Ava said, plucking the plate out of her hand and sliding it into a free spot in the dishwasher.

"It helps to loosen up the tough spots!" Charlotte said; this was a rehash of an argument they'd had at least twenty times in their adult lives, but it was comforting in its familiarity, like a favorite—if slightly annoying—pair of shoes.

"Do not try to distract me, Charlotte Rose Lane," Ava said severely, crossing her arms and leaning against the counter. "What's wrong?"

"Nothing," Charlotte hedged, then quailed under her sister's narrow-eyed gaze. "I had a fight with Graham," she confessed reluctantly, trying not to be offended when Ava's face brightened at this news. "Why do you look *happy* about that?"

"Because," Ava said, "it means you *like* him."

"We fought, and are possibly never going to speak to each other again, but you think this is a *good* thing for the relationship?"

Ava waved a dismissive hand. "You'll make up—but the fact that you're this upset about it means that you really care about him. Which, to be clear, I definitely knew," she added, sounding extremely pleased with herself.

"Well, maybe save the smug self-congratulations until you know what we fought about," Charlotte said grimly, before giving her sister a brief rundown of the argument with Graham.

Annoyingly, by the time she was done, Ava was frowning thoughtfully, rather than seething with righteous indignation, as Charlotte might have hoped.

"So," she said slowly, adding a scoop of detergent to the dishwasher and closing the door, "you're mad at him because of something his sister did?"

"No!" Charlotte hung a dish towel on its hook on the wall and turned to face her sister, leaning her hip against the counter. "I'm mad because he pretended not to know who I was, and never mentioned the fact that his entire reason for getting to know me was because of *Christmas, Truly.*"

"Hmm," Ava said, pressing the button to start the dishwasher and then crossing her arms over her chest. "I think *that's* what you're really mad about."

"What?"

"*Christmas, Truly.* Not Graham."

"They're completely connected in this situation."

Ava shrugged. "Sort of. But the problem here isn't really Graham, who, from what his sister said, seems to have gone out of his way not to do anything manipulative or creepy in this whole series of events. The problem is that you are so *insanely touchy* about *Christmas, Truly.*"

Charlotte, ridiculously, felt this accusation like a blow to the chest. "I think I have cause to be touchy."

Ava sighed impatiently. "I'm not denying that the fallout from that *Variety* article was a bit intense, and I don't blame you for being freaked out by it. But you're blowing this out of proportion, because you're mad that you're more famous for that movie than you are for your art."

"I'm not—" Charlotte began heatedly, but Ava wasn't done yet.

"Remember when you were interviewed for that article about your stationery line, and the headline called you Tallulah?"

"Vividly."

"You complained about it for months."

"I didn't—"

"You *did*. You were joking, sort of, but you also mentioned it a lot. Because that movie is a sore spot, and you haven't fully sorted out how you feel about it, and the way those feelings are all tied up in the way you feel about Mom and Dad."

"Ava, what the hell." Charlotte felt like her sister had transformed into a different person, even as she stood there before her.

Ava exhaled a frustrated breath; her long hair was loose, she was still wearing her bathrobe, and there was a smear on her neck where Alice had gotten a bit overly enthusiastic in trying to share some of her mashed avocado, but she looked imposing for all that—a reminder, in case Charlotte needed one, that Ava had spent the entirety of her adult life commanding the attention of sold-out theaters.

"Charlotte. I love you, and I know Mom and Dad are . . . difficult."

"Easy to say when you're the one who's done exactly what they wanted you to do with your life."

Ava let out a laugh—a sharp, biting laugh that Charlotte hadn't heard from her sister in a long time, since the worst fights of their teenage years. "Yes, please imagine how easy it is to try to create your own career in theater with Mom constantly breathing down your neck. Imagine how easy it is for your first major role to be in a play that Mom *wrote*—and of course she had plenty of notes on my performance." Ava sighed. "I'm lucky, I know that—I've obviously gotten a huge leg up in my career because of Mom, and I've had a much easier time of it than most people. But there are definite negatives that come along with it. So don't think that you're the only one who ever fights with Mom and Dad."

Charlotte was shamed into silence; she knew that her sister and mom fought sometimes, especially during the early years of Ava's career, but she hadn't spent too much time thinking about it—they were four years apart in age, just enough for them to each be very much caught up in their own lives. Ava had gotten her own apartment when Charlotte was still in high school. She wondered how many of the dynamics in their family, as she remembered them, weren't entirely accurate—the recollections of a child.

"None of this is really the point anyway," Ava said, more gently now. "I know that it's annoying to be incredibly talented, to be successful in your career, and to have people still bring up one thing that you did when you were a kid, twenty years ago—but come on. Hollywood is impossible to break into, and you were basically *handed* a role. Do you know how many people would kill for that—how many people I know, how many of my friends, would commit murder for the chance to be in a movie like *Christmas, Truly*? And it's not like you haven't benefited from it—that movie is the reason you were able to start your own business, without asking Mom and Dad for help. It's the reason you're able to more or less ignore them and do whatever you want. It gave you a leg up, just like Mom gave *me* a leg up. It's let you spend your adult life doing the thing you really want to do. So maybe . . . be just a little grateful for it?"

Charlotte had never thought of herself as ungrateful, exactly. She wasn't so self-centered or oblivious as to be unaware of the fact that her position was incredibly privileged, and that most people couldn't start a creative business in one of the most expensive cities on earth at the age of twenty-two. But still, whenever she'd done something that alluded to her *Christmas, Truly* fame—that article that Ava mentioned; the film screening yesterday, even—she'd viewed it as an unpleasant necessity, a way to get some benefit from an experience that she hadn't enjoyed. But maybe this was the wrong way of thinking about it.

She didn't have to *like* the movie . . . but it was one small moment in her life that had enabled a lot of other, great ones.

And suddenly, she *did* feel a little bit grateful.

"Thank you," she said to her sister now. "You're right, and I have some things to think about."

Ava nodded, pushing off the counter to come over and give Charlotte a quick, fierce hug. "Don't think too long. Because I'm guessing there's a handsome Englishman who's currently having an absolutely *miserable* Christmas in his fancy old house."

"Join the club," Charlotte muttered, reaching for a clean glass and turning on the tap. The problem, she thought as she filled her glass, was that everything Ava said made perfect sense . . . and yet. She couldn't shake the knee-jerk impulse she had to recoil at the thought that *Graham*, of all things, was tied up in *Christmas, Truly* too. She'd wanted this one thing for herself.

And she didn't know how to move past it.

Sometime later, their parents called. It was late in the afternoon by that point—not surprising, given the time difference—and Ava grimaced at the name on her phone screen when it lit up, waving it at Charlotte to catch her attention.

Charlotte groaned. "Please, no."

"It's Christmas—we have to!" Ava tossed her mane of hair over one shoulder, straightened as if bracing herself for battle, and answered. "Hi, Mom and Dad! Merry Christmas!"

"I didn't know her voice was capable of reaching that pitch," Simone said in an impressed whisper to Charlotte.

"It's all that training for the stage," Charlotte whispered back. "She has incredible vocal range."

"Yes, Alice is right here," Ava said now, in response to whatever their parents had said on the phone. She waved a hand at Kit, who was balancing Alice on his knee while trying to eat a sizable portion of Christmas pudding at the same time. He blinked at her, then proffered the baby, who Ava accepted. "Alice, do you want to say hello to Grandma and Grandpa?" Alice obligingly made some incoherent babbling noises, and then tried to tug Ava's necklace off. Ava paused, frowning, for a long moment as she waved her offspring in Kit's direction and listened intently. "Mom, Alice is six months old; she can't actually *speak*." Another, longer pause. "I think that's an unreasonable expectation of a baby, frankly." Yet another pause. "Let's let her learn English first before we start worrying about teaching her French."

Charlotte blinked at this, suddenly wishing that she were privy to both ends of this conversation—not an emotion she regularly experienced when it came to her parents. However, in a true case of "be careful what you wish for," at that precise moment Ava said brightly, "Did you want to talk to Charlotte? She's sitting right here!"

Charlotte frantically waved her arms at her sister, offering a cartoonish grimace in case her meaning wasn't already clear, but Ava pointedly ignored all this and merely brandished the phone at her.

Shooting her sister a look that promised retribution at some future date, Charlotte took the phone. "Hello, parents," she said, trying not to sound too weary already.

"Charlotte, do you know that I was asked about you at a party the other day?" her father asked without so much as a "Merry Christmas" to ease into things. "It was at Tom Gallagher's, and I ran into one of his old production partners, who wanted to know if there was anything they could do to persuade you about the *Christmas, Truly* reboot."

Charlotte counted to five before replying. "No, Dad, I think I made myself perfectly clear earlier. I'm not an actress, and I have too much work to do these days, anyway."

"Do you?" Her father sounded mildly surprised. "All those watercolors on Instagram keeping you busy?"

She took a slow breath; her instinct, previously, would have been to flare up and argue—they'd certainly spent enough Christmases doing just that, at whatever far-flung location they'd happened to land on that year.

Now, however, her earlier conversation with Ava crossed her mind, and so she took another breath, counted to three, and simply said, "Yes, they are. I actually have a meeting in New York next month with Perfect Paper—they're interested in me potentially designing a special line for them." She wouldn't ordinarily have mentioned something like this to her parents until the contract was signed and it was a definite reality, because confessing that it didn't work out later on would be absolutely insufferable, but it was Christmas and she was feeling . . . well, she wasn't quite feeling like herself.

"That's nice, honey," her dad said, sounding a bit surprised—and also a bit distracted—but also genuinely, mildly impressed. Charlotte frowned. Had he had a stroke? "You'll have to let us know when it's on sale—your mother has taken it into her head that we need a pool house, and I'm sure some wallpaper would look nice."

Charlotte frowned. "You don't have a pool." This had been a point of much discussion when they'd bought the house in LA; her mother did not believe in getting her head wet unless absolutely necessary, and so their backyard was occupied by a large patio and garden instead.

"Well, she hurt her knee traipsing around that farm in Vermont with the young man she met there, and her doctor seems to think that some low-impact exercise would be best going forward, so we're getting a pool."

"Well," Charlotte said, blinking. "That's nice."

"So you'll let us know about your wallpaper, then?" her dad continued, still sounding vaguely distracted; she could hear her mom's faint voice in the background, presumably occupying half of his attention. "And your mother says you could come see it, once it's installed."

And Charlotte realized, astonished, that this was a peace offering from her parents. So, too, was that email from her mom's friend, looking to commission her. If she stopped looking for the insult in everything they did, she could see it better—the intent behind it. They weren't thrilled that she hadn't done what they wanted her to do with her life; they likely never would be. And everything this year with the *Christmas, Truly* reboot had only reopened that old wound.

But this . . . this was them trying to salve it.

If she took the offer.

"I'd like that," she said, clearing her throat.

"Excellent!" her father said brightly. "And perhaps, when you're in town, if you wanted to swing by Tom's office to take a meeting—"

"Nope," Charlotte said cheerfully, without missing a beat.

Her dad sighed. "I guessed you'd say that. You really should reconsider, though, Charlotte—Tom sent us a *very* nice fruit basket for Christmas. Think of the pears you could be eating!"

"I can buy my own fruit, Dad," Charlotte said, but then, miraculously, the most incredible thing happened: she wanted to *laugh*. She couldn't stop herself imagining the expression on Graham's face if he overheard even a fraction of this conversation, and the urge to laugh was almost impossible to suppress. Her parents were absurd, but they were hers, and she was stuck with them, and they were going to continue behaving like absolute lunatics even from eight time zones away, so she may as well get used to it, and stop letting every single thing they said work its way beneath her skin.

"I suppose," her dad agreed, a bit mournfully, and Charlotte, suddenly, was gripped with the wildest desire to throw him a bone.

"Hey, Dad?" she asked.

"Yes?"

"If *you* wanted to send me some pears . . . I wouldn't hate it."

There was a long pause, and then, softly, her dad said, "I think I'll do that, Charlotte."

And Charlotte really believed that he would.

BETWIXTMAS

CHAPTER TWENTY

In a charity shop the day after Boxing Day, Charlotte found the mask.

She was in the back of the shop, past the clothing, rummaging through the odds and ends—mismatched dishes, single candlestick holders, novelty mugs from long-ago vacations—when she spotted it, tucked almost behind a chipped vase. It was black velvet, studded with paste jewels. It was campy and dramatic and *fun*, and it would look spectacular with the black dress she'd stolen from Ava's closet the week before, assuming that she had somewhere to be on New Year's Eve.

Without thinking too hard about it, she bought the mask—it cost only three pounds, after all—and shoved it in her bag, then took it back to Ava's flat, tossing it in her suitcase beneath a couple of sweaters, carefully out of sight. She felt far too aware of its presence, however, in the days that followed—as she spent time with Ava and Kit, lazing around in the weird liminal time between Christmas and New Year's that she'd learned the Brits referred to as "Betwixtmas." This involved a lot of sitting around the living room, trying to hold Alice without her screaming bloody murder as if she'd just been handed to a convicted criminal, and eating leftover mince pies, which Charlotte had decided were somehow disgusting *and* delicious at the same time.

During all that time, the mask haunted her with its presence, with its reminder of what she *should* have spent this week doing instead— namely, savoring every last moment with Graham, before her flight home on New Year's Day.

Eloise had texted her on Boxing Day, just a simple message apologizing for complicating things between Charlotte and Graham. Charlotte could tell just from reading it how carefully it had been considered—there was none of Eloise's usual breezy charm, but instead a cautiously worded apology, and then this:

> Graham doesn't know that I'm sending this, but
> you should know that he was very reluctant to do
> anything that would benefit Eden Priory if it involved
> asking anything of you. He's the most honourable
> person I know, and I just want you to know that.

Charlotte had stared down at the message for a long time, despite the fact that it hadn't contained anything out of the ordinary. One part of her brain argued that Eloise was just a sister trying to make up for accidentally having royally screwed up her brother's love life, but another part, one that she was having a hard time ignoring, was very well aware of the fact that until Christmas Eve, Charlotte herself would have agreed with that final sentence from Eloise.

She hadn't responded to the text—had let it sit on her phone for hours, glancing at it and then setting it aside, as she tried to work out how, exactly, to reply. The thing was, she liked Eloise. But she didn't feel particularly warm toward someone who apparently had set her up to be used solely for her name and her temporary viral infamy. The whole thing left a bad taste in her mouth—like everything she'd left New York to try to escape had followed her here instead.

That evening, she FaceTimed Padma, who was staying with Andrew's parents in Pennsylvania and apparently slowly dying of boredom, and explained the entire situation. She'd been attempting to keep her up-to-date via text, but finally sent her an SOS, feeling that a face-to-face session was required.

By the time she had finished talking her through everything, Padma's expression was a combination of outrage mixed with . . . delight?

"Why do you look so happy?" Charlotte demanded, after a silence of several seconds had fallen, during which Padma seemed to be struggling to formulate a reply.

"I'm not happy," Padma said hastily. "I'm full of righteous indignation on your behalf. I'm furious. I think we should burn Graham at the stake, on the grounds of his extremely large and historic country estate." She didn't even try to keep a wistful note from entering her voice at this last bit, and Charlotte knew immediately that she had lost her ally to that most ancient of lures: property.

"Padma, we don't sympathize with rich English people who inherit houses," she said sternly. "It's in the Constitution somewhere."

"Speak for yourself. I read a lot of romance novels, I'd be a complete hypocrite if I disliked Graham just because his ancestors were rich enough to build a big house."

Charlotte wanted to take issue with this argument, since she was pretty sure that this line of reasoning would crumble under the slightest provocation, but she decided to keep her attention focused on more important things. "We don't hate him because of the house," she reminded her friend. "We hate him because he spent a whole month lying to me while also making me f—"

She broke off abruptly, alarmed at where that sentence had almost led.

On-screen, Padma had crossed her arms over her chest and was regarding her with a severe expression, which was extremely effective since she rarely deployed this weapon outside of work. "Charlotte Rose Lane. You are not going to run away from this problem using the same excuse you always use," Padma said, her voice stern.

Charlotte crossed her arms in turn. "I don't think that's really fair, unless I'm forgetting another time that someone tried to cash in on my name and face without telling me, all while using sexual sorcery to ensure that I wouldn't realize what was happening?"

"Sexual sorcery, is it?" Padma asked excitedly. "Does he take his glasses off?" she added, without missing a beat.

"I'm not answering that."

"Aha!" Padma said triumphantly, pointing an accusatory finger at her through the screen. "Because you're still secretly hoping to work things out! You wouldn't care about spilling the beans if you never thought you'd sleep with him again!"

"That's not true," Charlotte protested. (It was, she feared, absolutely true.) "I'm just being . . . considerate."

"Yes," Padma said, nodding innocently. "You are always *so* considerate of your former paramours. The things I wish I didn't know about the bedroom habits of a certain subset of millennial men of Manhattan and Brooklyn—"

"We've got to find you other books to read," Charlotte muttered. "*Paramours?*"

"Andrew loves me for my vocabulary," Padma said fondly. "And don't change the subject!"

"*You* changed the subject!" Charlotte howled.

"Stop arguing, and answer me this question: If Graham had told you his sister's plan from the start, how would you have reacted?"

"I'd have understood and appreciated his maturity and honesty," Charlotte said.

Padma made a sound like a game show buzzer on a wrong answer. "Try again."

Charlotte sighed. "I would have been furious," she admitted. "I wouldn't have wanted to listen to his explanations. *But*," she added, holding up a hand before Padma could interrupt, "I think I would have eventually forgiven him, because I liked him so much."

"Or," Padma said thoughtfully, "you would have used it as an excuse to prevent anyone else from getting too close, just as you've done with everyone you've dated since Craig."

"If I recall correctly, you were *extremely* supportive when I announced my no-relationships stance," Charlotte objected.

"I'd had a lot of cocktails," Padma pointed out, which was fair. "Also, it was one night of tipsy venting in a bar *four years ago*—I didn't think you'd actually refuse to ever fall in love again, like, indefinitely."

"That breakup sucked," Charlotte said, shifting on her bed and trying not to dislodge the pillow she had her phone propped against. "Can you blame me?"

"Not all men are like Craig," Padma said simply. "And not every guy you meet is going to be some asshole who thinks it's cool and quirky to have an artist girlfriend from a famous family, and then bails the second you dare to have a moment when you actually *need* something from him and aren't just a low-maintenance piece of arm candy that makes him look cool." She paused, her eyes widening as her own words seemed to register. "Sorry. That was harsh . . . but, god, I hated that guy."

"I know," Charlotte said quietly. She *knew* Graham wasn't anything like Craig—knew that she was letting her own fears, her own past, get in the way here. But . . .

"I just hate the thought that there was anything about *Christmas, Truly* that was responsible for us getting together."

"Charlotte." Padma gave her a look through the screen that was half affection, half exasperation. "It will never *not* be *Christmas, Truly* that got you guys together. His family owns Pip's house! You're doing a commission that includes a scene *from the movie*! No matter what weird and sort of Machiavellian scheme his sister was cooking up, the movie *always* would have been part of the reason you guys started hanging out. *Christmas, Truly* is always going to be part of your story with him. Just like it's always going to be part of *your* story."

Charlotte was silent, feeling mildly stunned.

Because Padma was right.

"Of course I am," Padma said patiently, when Charlotte told her this. "I'm always right. That's why they pay me so much money."

"No, they pay you so much money because you're good at winning arguments." Charlotte paused, frowning. "Have I just been lawyered? Are you actually wrong and just concealing it well?"

"No," Padma said. "Because here's the thing—and this is the last thing I'll say about this, because Andrew is downstairs trying to teach his mom how to use TikTok, and I need to go intervene before something truly horrifying happens: I'm not trying to get you to forgive Graham for *his* sake. I'm doing it for *yours*."

"What do you mean?" Charlotte asked, honestly befuddled, and Padma rolled her eyes, which was about as big a display of impatience as she ever offered.

"I want you to forgive him," Padma explained, "because he messed up, and he apologized, and he'll try to do better next time—and if he doesn't, then you'll know. But you're falling in love with him—and *you* deserve another chance at that."

"I—hmm." This hadn't been exactly what Charlotte was expecting from this FaceTime; Padma was, among her many other excellent qualities, a friend who was loyal to the point of implausibility—Charlotte was pretty sure she could commit a crime directly in front of her and have Padma still protest her innocence. She'd expected Padma to be firmly on her side in this Graham-versus-Charlotte situation. "Why are you taking his side?" she asked, trying not to let a plaintive note creep into her voice, feeling more than a bit pathetic.

"I'm not," Padma said. "I'm taking *your* side, because I love you, and I want you to be happy. And I think Graham might make you happy."

And Charlotte didn't have any sort of reply to that—because she was pretty sure that Padma was right.

*

A couple of days later—the day after she bought the mask that she refused to think about, sitting in her suitcase—she saw Graham at the grocery store.

Her first thought was that he looked tired; he was wandering the aisles of Waitrose, a basket in hand, wearing jeans and a fisherman's sweater with a hole in the sleeve, his glasses slightly askew, his hair rumpled. While he didn't *exactly* look like a man who had vanished down a deep well of despair—which would have been extremely gratifying—he didn't appear to be thriving.

He also stopped in his tracks when he saw her, then slowly advanced, like someone approaching an unfamiliar cat they were afraid would start hissing if they attempted to pet it.

"Hello," he said.

"Hi," she said, affecting an air of breezy unconcern that probably would have been more convincing if she hadn't been wearing sweatpants and carrying a basket that currently contained only a bottle of merlot and a carton of the Cornish ice cream brand she'd become unfortunately obsessed with. She was acutely conscious of the fact that this seemed to practically scream, *I am heartbroken and pathetic!*, which was a message she generally went to great lengths to avoid conveying, but she *was* feeling, if not precisely heartbroken (or at least not that she would admit), at the very least extremely heart-*bruised*, and the fact that she had willingly left the house in sweatpants seemed to be all the evidence necessary in the "pathetic or not?" debate.

She was also feeling slightly terrified, because it had been four days since their argument on Christmas Eve, and she'd screened no fewer than five phone calls from him, and even more texts. Her conversations with Ava and Padma had given her a lot to think about—she'd lifted her phone to text him a number of times, and then set it down again, too nervous to follow through. Too unsure, still, of what she wanted to say to him. But now, the decision had been taken out of her hands, because here he was, with his rumpled hair and dark circles under his eyes, watching her with a combination of wariness and hope that made something in her chest ache.

"How have you been?" he asked, which was very polite but which she found extremely annoying because when, from the first moment of their very first meeting, had she and Graham ever been particularly polite to each other? To hear him now, attempting to exchange pleasantries with her in the grocery store like they were friendly neighbors, was depressing.

"Not great," she said; the fact that she was wearing sweatpants and a pullover that Alice had drooled copiously on that morning made the truth of that reply abundantly clear. She suddenly wondered, somewhat wildly, when she'd last washed her hair, then decided that this simply was not a thing she was going to worry about right now.

After a moment of sudden, surprised silence, though, Graham did the most remarkable thing:

He smiled.

She'd forgotten how much she loved that smile.

"Me either," he said, which Charlotte could tell, of course, but which it was still nice to hear confirmed. He took a step forward, and reached out a hand as if to extend it toward her, but then stopped, clearly realizing the mistake that this would be. "Lane—Charlotte—" he started, and then he stopped, looking at her almost helplessly, and she realized that this might be the first time she'd ever seen him struggle for words. "I'm so, so sorry. I was an idiot, and I just want you to know that I know it, and that I'm an ass, and that you deserve someone who wouldn't try to use your name to sell a few extra tickets to a goddamn film screening. I know how much you didn't want to risk getting hurt again, and I hurt you all the same, and I hate that— because you deserve better."

But the thing, Charlotte realized in that instant, was that she *did* know this—in no small part because of him. Because he'd told her that, shown her that, over the past five weeks. He'd made a mistake . . . but he was human. And hadn't she told him, more than once, that this was okay?

She stood there, silent for a long moment, failing to respond in a remotely socially acceptable way to anything he'd just said to her, because she was so floored by this realization.

While she was busy having minor epiphanies, however, he was apparently determined to say the rest of what he had to say—the reason he'd approached her in this grocery store. He reached into his pocket and pulled out his phone, tapping at the screen for a moment before glancing back up at her.

"The last thing I need you to know," he said, taking a step closer and dropping his voice a bit, making this entire conversation feel, suddenly, almost unbearably intimate, "is that, from the moment I met you, I wanted to know you for *you*. Not for any other reason." He extended his phone, and Charlotte glanced down at the screen. It was a text exchange between him and Eloise, from a few weeks before. She quickly did some mental math—it would have been the day after they'd seen each other at Kew Gardens.

Eloise: you and charlotte looked cosy last night
Eloise: ••

Graham: Not taking any questions from you along those lines.

Eloise: don't be boring. she seems nice!

Graham: She is.

Graham: Please don't fuck this up, E.

Graham: I like her. So please, please do not say a single thing to her, ever about anything to do with Eden Priory, or the film. I don't want her to ever feel like we're using her.

Eloise: because you want to USE HER in other ways 😏

Eloise: is this the first time you have EVER told me that you like someone?? jesus

Graham: Please.

Eloise: anything for young love! 🐶

Graham: I regret this conversation already.

Eloise: i can't tell you how happy i am to hear it

She glanced up at him, not bothering to control whatever expression was on her face, and saw that he was watching her closely.

"It was never about Eden Priory, when it came to you and me," he said in a low voice, his gaze locked with hers. "It was always more. And I thought you should know that." He pocketed his phone again. "I'm heading back down to Hampshire tonight, to spend time with my mum and sisters. We've a lot to talk about, I think—and it's because of you that I'm able to have those conversations, and if nothing else ever happens between us, I'll always be so grateful to you for that." He reached down to pick up his basket again, and then glanced back at her. "But if you're around on New Year's Eve . . . well, you'll know where to find me. And there's no one else I'd rather see that night—or ever again, I think."

And, with that, he turned and walked away.

NEW YEAR'S EVE

CHAPTER TWENTY-ONE

T his," Ava said cheerfully, "is *so* romantic."

"It's not, actually," Charlotte said patiently from her spot on the floor, folding up gift bags to be reused for next year's Christmas. They'd allowed the Christmas morning mess to linger in the living room in an unseemly pile next to the tree for close to a week, but Ava had awoken this morning in a strange fit of virtuous productivity and had put them all to work. Kit was currently vacuuming in the spare room with Alice strapped to his chest, which seemed like a recipe for disaster to Charlotte, but she'd refrained from offering commentary.

"But your one true love has apologized and laid his feelings bare, and now you are going to offer him a Grand Gesture!" Ava said dramatically.

"A what now?"

Ava sighed. "A Grand Gesture, obviously. Have you never watched a rom-com, Charlotte? Wait, what am I saying? You have a cold, dead heart and you don't believe in romance."

This struck close enough to home to flare a spark of anger in Charlotte. "That's not true," she said quietly. "Also," she added, "I'm friends with Padma, so of course I've seen a fucking rom-com. I've seen more of them than anyone should be required to see in their entire lifetime, in fact."

"Then you should be familiar with the Grand Gesture," Ava said impatiently.

"It's not a Grand Gesture," Charlotte objected. "It's a . . . declaration of feelings."

"At a ball, at midnight, in disguise," Ava said, snapping shut the lid on the rubber box that contained all the Christmas wrapping supplies.

"Almost none of that is true," Charlotte said. "Also, it's not a *ball*, it's a party. It's 2024. Get a grip."

"Hear me out, though," Ava said, looking delighted. "You show up at his ball in your mask, allowing the minutes to tick by, leaving him to believe you haven't shown up, and then you dramatically reveal yourself at an opportune moment and confess your love!"

"That seems unnecessarily dramatic," Charlotte said skeptically. Drama of any sort wasn't really her style, much to the dismay of every other member of her immediate family.

"It's a Grand Gesture!" Ava said impatiently. "That's what it's *for*!"

"Do I *need* a Grand Gesture, though?" Charlotte asked. "Since he was the one in the wrong, you know? With the lying and deception?"

Ava waved a hand. "Details. Have you considered nudity? Men love nudity."

Kit chose this convenient moment to switch off the vacuum cleaner, evidently in time to overhear this last comment. "It's true!" he shouted from the next room. "Big fan of nudity!"

Charlotte crumpled up a scrap of wrapping paper and lobbed it at her sister's head. "I'm never asking you for advice again."

"I think you're discounting this too quickly. A Grand Gesture on New Year's Eve—what could be better? It's the stuff holiday movies are made of!"

"Have I *ever* given you the impression that I want my life to look like a holiday movie?"

Ava sat back on her heels, a thoughtful expression on her face. "Actually," she said slowly, "don't you think that's *exactly* what your life has turned into, for the past month?"

"No," Charlotte said instinctively, without even pausing to consider.

"Yes," Ava said definitively, a gleeful smile crossing her face. "Do you remember all the things you told us you *hated* about Christmas movies?"

"Yes," Charlotte said slowly, feeling very certain that she did not like where this conversation was going.

"Well," Ava said, leaning forward and raising a finger to begin keeping count. "Meet-cute under implausible circumstances? Check."

"Not implausible," Charlotte argued. "Perfectly plausible!"

"Charlotte, he was removing a *felt reindeer suit*. Shut up." Duly chastened, Charlotte fell silent. Ava raised another finger. "Some sort of festive task that requires the hero and heroine to band together and discover the joy of Christmas? Check."

"Not check! Not check! There was no Christmas joy!"

"But you two certainly *banded together*, in every sense of the phrase," Ava said, with a lascivious eyebrow waggle. "Cast of charming supporting characters to egg the protagonists on toward their happily ever after?" Ava beamed, waving a hand at her own face. "Check."

"Check!" Kit echoed from the guest room.

"*Waaaaa!*" said Alice.

"Quirky, borderline-contrived Christmas rituals and activities? Let us not forget the roving caroling troupe. Check."

Charlotte was too worn down to even protest at this point.

"Third-act fight that casts our protagonists' happy holiday into doubt? Check. Ending with a Grand Gesture, and a kiss in front of the Christmas tree!" Ava finished happily, then straightened. "Charlotte, it's very important that you kiss him in front of the Christmas tree— it's the only thing you're missing!" She paused, frowning. "Except for some improbable, unexpected snowfall, I guess. Can't do much about that, though—this *is* England."

"Flurries forecast for tonight!" Kit called from the guest room, and Ava looked as delighted as anyone in human history has ever looked upon hearing a weather forecast.

"Charlotte Lane," she said, leaning forward and taking both of Charlotte's hands in hers. "Welcome to your holiday romance. Now go get your true love!"

"Can I take a shower first, at least?" Charlotte asked dryly.

"If you must," Ava said, sighing dejectedly.

Charlotte laughed, and continued tidying, and then eventually showered, dressed, did her makeup, prepared for an evening out— and not once did she tell Ava one key fact:

Charlotte had already *made* a Grand Gesture. And tonight, she was going to tell Graham about it.

❄

Her first mistake, Charlotte thought, a bit grumpily, several hours later, was allowing Ava and Kit to accompany her on this outing.

"A New Year's Eve out!" Ava said brightly, standing before her closet and surveying the many, many dresses she had to choose from. She held up a slinky green silk dress with a very high slit, pouting at herself in the mirror. "Do you think green makes me look sallow?"

"You wear green all the time," Charlotte said from Ava and Kit's en suite, where she was carefully pinning her hair up, an endeavor that required enough bobby pins to supply a small country.

"But what if I've been wrong all along? Alice has aged me, you know—"

"She's aged *all* of us," Charlotte muttered around a mouthful of bobby pins.

"—and what if my face can no longer tolerate green?"

"Ava?" Charlotte called, carefully extracting another bobby pin from between her teeth.

"Yes?"

"Please shut up."

Ava, miraculously, had complied—though she *had* ended up donning an off-the-shoulder red dress with an extremely low neckline, on the off chance that her fears about green were accurate—and by six they were on the road, slowly inching their way out of London holiday traffic, John and Simone having been left with a disgruntled Alice, who had appeared unamused to discover that both of her parents were leaving at once.

"We've not gone out together since she was born," Kit explained weepily to Charlotte as he eased the car away from the curb, his eyes red-rimmed. He frowned in the rearview mirror. "Perhaps I should stay—"

"No." Ava reached over and clamped a firm hand on her husband's forearm. "She's with your parents; she'll be fine. This is good. This is healthy. Charlotte, do you know of any secluded, unused bedrooms at Eden Priory?"

Kit brightened. "I do like the way you think, love."

"Oh my god," Charlotte said, and spent much of the rest of the car ride trying to ignore the waves of almost obscene anticipation emanating from her sister and brother-in-law.

They were at Eden Priory just after seven thirty, only half an hour late, but the car park was already nearly full, Charlotte noted. Hopefully they'd sold an absolute shit ton of tickets—anything that would alleviate Graham's stress she'd consider a positive, even if it did increase the odds that a *Christmas, Truly* megafan would be in attendance. She was pretty sure this was going to be an occupational hazard of dating Graham, going forward—and she was terrified by how unbothered by that fact she'd become.

The path leading up to the house was lit by a series of lanterns, and the house itself was ablaze with a warm light—candlelight, Charlotte realized, once they walked through the front doors and had their tickets scanned on their phones. Lizzie was on ticket duty and had immediately recognized Charlotte despite the half mask blocking much of Charlotte's face; Lizzie's jaw had dropped, an expression of dawning glee creeping across her face, and Charlotte had simply held a finger to her lips and smiled at Graham's sister.

The entrance hall was lit by candlesticks in sconces mounted on the walls, and the electric light of the Christmas tree and the white lights in the rafters above, but there were no other lamps in use, giving everything a cozy, romantic glow.

"Straight through to the ballroom!" Lizzie called behind them, sounding as cheerful as Charlotte had ever heard her, and they trailed behind a couple of men in sharp-looking suits, following the sound of music as they passed through a corridor and emerged into the ballroom. The last time Charlotte had seen this room had been on the day of the ornament workshop, and it had been transformed since then—lit with hundreds of candles and strings of lights, the tables that had occupied the room gone, the floor now cleared for dancing. A full bar appeared to be operating along one wall, staffed by a couple of bartenders in sequins and masks of their own, and a live band played at one end of the room. Potted plants—palms and ferns and even potted citrus trees, mixed in with the obligatory poinsettias and rosemary bushes that the season demanded—filled the corners of the room. Along the wall above the bar, several original

Christian Calloway pieces had been hung—sketches for patterns that would eventually be made into wallpaper; original versions of some of the illustrations he created for books; intimate portraits of his family, ones Charlotte had never seen before. The dance floor was crowded with couples and groups, everyone in suits and dresses of varying degrees of sparkle, and every single one of them was masked.

"This is a *vibe*," Ava said, impressed. She turned to Kit. "A dance, handsome masked stranger?"

Kit kissed her hand. "But of course, mysterious lady," and he led her onto the dance floor. Charlotte watched them walk away and be absorbed into the crowd of dancers, before she allowed herself to turn and look.

She spotted him almost instantly. He was at the far end of the room, arms crossed, face hidden by a simple black half mask that emphasized the sharp line of his jaw. He wasn't wearing his glasses, she realized. It made her feel a little unsteady, when she was preparing for a declaration of—of *something*, of a feeling she still, even to herself, in the quiet of her room late at night, struggled to name, because doing so made her feel so vulnerable—that he should look ever-so-slightly not like himself, not like her Graham.

Hers.

That was all she really wanted him to be.

That was what it felt like he already was.

Despite the fact that she couldn't have been in the room more than a minute, couldn't have hesitated, watching him, for more than twenty seconds, it was enough time for him to notice her. Across the room, he straightened, turned his head sharply, as if she'd called his name. His gaze landed on her, and she didn't doubt, even for a single second, even with her mask in place, that he'd recognize her.

Charlotte. She saw his lips form her name, unheard from this distance. She began to walk toward him, even as he began to elbow his way through the crowd . . .

Which is how she learned that this sort of thing looked *much* easier in movies than it was in real life.

"Ow," she muttered, as she was accidentally elbowed by a dancer for the second time. She dodged out of the way of a couple that was completely ignoring the jazzy take on "O Christmas Tree" currently being played by the band and instead doing some sort of modified swing dancing, and glanced up, trying to find Graham in the crowd again. He was tall enough, fortunately, that she was able to see him, even as she weaved among the dancing couples, avoiding more rogue elbows and nearly getting knocked over by a guy dipping his partner dramatically for a kiss. Just past them, she saw Ava and Kit making out like a couple of teenagers, and took a great amount of pleasure in howling, "Get a room!" at them.

But then she turned around—

And he was there.

Tall. Broad-shouldered. Rebellious curls threatening to break ranks from his carefully combed hair. *That jawline.* And, tellingly, a dimple in one cheek, a warning of the smile that he was trying hard to suppress.

"Lane."

"Calloway."

"Nice dress." His eyes dipped shamelessly to the neckline, which was plunging enough that Charlotte had to employ the liberal use of body tape to ensure that no one got more of a show than she intended.

"Nice contacts," she replied, which sounded cooler in her head than it did aloud. His dimple deepened.

"It's interesting," he said, oh-so-casually, tilting his head at her, "that you should be here tonight."

"Is it?" She frowned at him. "Did I completely misinterpret your romantic grocery store declaration?"

"No," he said quickly, reaching out to take her hand. "But I've had Lanes on the brain today, because I opened my inbox this morning and found an email from one Peter Lane, wishing me a happy new year and asking if I'd mind if he passed on my contact information to some industry friends who he knew were in the process of scouting filming locations for period pieces."

"That was fast," Charlotte said, impressed; her dad had sounded surprisingly pleased to help her out when she'd called him the evening of her run-in with Graham ("Anything for young love!" he'd said dramatically, then spent ten minutes telling her about the new film he was developing, in which, from what she understood of the plot, every single likable character died), but she hadn't expected him to spring into action so quickly. "You don't have to do it, if you don't want to," she added hurriedly. "I just told Dad to email you and ask— I didn't even give him your phone number; I wanted you to have time to think about it and not feel put on the spot. But . . ." Here, she took a breath, then squeezed his hand. "I know how much you love Eden Priory, and I don't want you to lose it. And I thought, after we watched *Christmas, Truly*, and had that conversation about your dad . . . I thought you might be more open to it. And I wanted to give you the chance, at least, to say yes—especially since the money would give you guys some breathing room, while you worked out the future of the house, and how to make it sustainable." She paused, then added, "Sustainable in a way that doesn't involve you working at a soulless job that is chipping away at you—at your life. Because, Graham, I—I think you deserve so much more than that, and it would break my heart to see you work a job like that again."

He drew her slowly toward him. "I had some long chats with Mum and Eloise and Lizzie this week, and I told Mum we should let the

BBC shoot on the grounds this autumn. And Eloise is going to come up with an idea for some sort of holiday-film-themed event program, next year, to go with your print collection's sale at the gift shop." He grimaced. "She wants to call it 'Twelve Days of *Christmas, Truly*,' but I told her we'd need to workshop that." Charlotte bit her lip to prevent a smile as he continued, "Some of the things we'll try, my dad probably wouldn't have liked, but . . ." He shrugged. "It's our house now, not Dad's. And we're going to do whatever it takes to save it. But this . . ." He waved his phone at her. "If this pans out, it would make everything else so much easier. I can't . . ." Here, he broke off, swallowing. "I can't thank you enough. And I can't believe you were willing to do this—to reach out to your dad, to call in these connections, given everything—especially after how we treated you."

"The thing is," Charlotte said slowly, "I think I overreacted, when Eloise told me about her scheme. She made it clear from the beginning that you'd had nothing to do with it, but I freaked out, because I always freak out whenever *Christmas, Truly* comes up—but I talked to Ava, and she helped me realize that maybe . . . maybe I should just be grateful for all it's given me." She inhaled, preparing to take the plunge. "And I *am* feeling grateful, because I guess . . . I guess, in a way, it gave me you."

"If my understanding of holiday film tropes is correct, this is Confession of Love time, isn't it?" he asked, smiling in earnest now, and her heart thumped heavily in her chest.

"I mean," she said, would-be casual, "Ava wisely pointed out to me this morning that I *do* seem to be living in a holiday romance at the moment." She glanced out the windows. "If you notice it start to snow, please let me know so that we can run and kiss under a gentle flurry."

"It's England. It's probably just drizzling, and you'd get your hair wet."

"Oh well. It was a nice dream." She sighed, mock-regretful. "My *point* is, it appears that I, Charlotte Lane, noted hater of Christmas romances, have come to the realization that I do not, in fact, hate a Christmas romance when it's my own."

"Shocking," he murmured, taking a step closer to her. "I think I *love* Christmas romances, actually."

"Do you?" She tipped her head up at him.

"Lane." His voice was quiet, his dark eyes steady on hers. "I love *you*."

She reached up and, in one quick motion, tugged his mask over his head. "Say it again. I want to see your face."

"I love you." He reached out with deft fingers and untied her own mask, the air of the room suddenly cool on her cheeks.

"I love you, too," she said, so softly he had to tip his head down to hear her. "And I have no idea how we're going to do this—with you here, and me in New York, and I'm terrible at relationships, and long-distance seems hard, and—"

"We'll work it out," he said quietly. Calmly.

And she nodded, because she knew they would. And on the days when it was hard—or she had a bad day—or she felt sad—or felt any sort of way that was any bit messy . . . it would be okay.

Because she would have him.

He reached down to cup her chin, his mouth already lowering, and she blurted out, just before his lips touched hers, "Just for the record, I'm going to need you to repeat that confession of love with your glasses on."

"I didn't realize you were so deeply perverted about glasses," he said, his smile widening, and he was still smiling when he kissed her. "I like it."

His mouth was warm and he tasted of mulled wine and his tongue was in her mouth and her hips were pressed to his, and she really didn't care at all that they were in a public space, until, dimly, she became aware of the fact that someone was tapping her on the shoulder.

"I would suggest you get a room," came Ava's voice, from far away, "but who am I to interrupt the dramatic conclusion to a holiday romance?" Charlotte pulled back enough to register her sister's presence; she was standing with Kit, watching Charlotte and Graham with an expression that could only honestly be described as "smug." "Unfortunately, Graham, your mom is looking for you—something about the eight-o'clock toast?"

Graham muttered a curse. "It's tradition," he said, looking at Charlotte sheepishly. "We do a toast, and then we turn over the first of four hourglasses, to run down the time until midnight. When the last one runs out, everyone removes their masks."

"This seems unnecessarily dramatic and showy," Charlotte said, tucking back a strand of hair that had been pulled loose when he'd plunged a hand into her hair. His eyes went darker as he looked at her.

"I think they can handle it without me this year," he muttered.

But she didn't want them to; dramatic and showy wasn't her vibe, but occasionally, for him, she'd make an exception.

"Oh, no," she said now, very serious, shaking her head. "Grand Gesture time is over. Confessions of Love time is over, too, and so is Dramatic Kiss by—oh, shit, we were supposed to do this by the Christmas tree. Never mind," she added hastily, waving a dismissive hand as his eyebrows inched toward his hairline. "My point is, it is now, um, Heartwarming Romantic Conclusion with Supporting Characters Present time, good sir, and we need to play our roles."

"I can't decide if your newfound enthusiasm for Christmas films is disturbing or attractive," he said, rubbing his jaw; his mouth was smudged with her lipstick, and she reached up to attempt to wipe it off.

"In the immortal words of *Christmas, Truly*, 'The only thing worse than the total agony of being in love is the total agony of *not* being in love at Christmas.'"

She straightened his collar, smoothed his hair, and added, as an afterthought, "Just so we're clear, I'm never quoting that fucking movie ever again."

"Lane," he said, pressing a quick, final kiss to her forehead and grinning down at her in a way that made her heart jump in her chest, "I would call a medical professional if you did."

"You know what the best thing about today is?" she asked as he slipped his hand into hers and began to pull her along with him toward the front of the room, where his mom and sisters awaited.

"The emotional reconciliation with your beloved?" he asked, offering her that satisfied smile that made her want to do extremely inappropriate things with him.

"The knowledge that it won't be Christmas for another fifty-one weeks," she said cheerfully, and then reached up to stop his laugh with a kiss.

ACKNOWLEDGMENTS

Writing a book is, as ever, a team effort—and this is especially true for a book that came together as unexpectedly as this one, immediately on the heels of a big, stressful international move. Endless thanks to:

Kaitlin Olson, my editor, for somehow thinking I could do this, and helping me turn this book into something I'm proud of.

Taylor Haggerty, my agent, for always being the calmest voice of reason.

Jasmine Brown and the rest of the Root Literary team, for being an absolute dream to work with.

Megan Rudloff, Zakiya Jamal, Ifeoma Anyoku, Morgan Pager, and everyone else at Atria—in production, art, subrights, audio, sales, and more—who worked so hard to make this book (and all my books) as successful as possible.

The people in the book world—booksellers, librarians, journalists, bloggers, and everyone active on bookish social media—who spread the word about what they've read and loved, and get books into the hands of readers who would appreciate them the most.

The author friends who kept me company—both here in London

and from afar—*and* kept me from (too much) panicking. Special shout-outs to Sarah Hogle, Kaitlyn Hill, Sarah Adler, Emma Theriault, Laura Sebastian, Alwyn Hamilton, and Sarah Chamberlain, among so many others. You make this job less lonely.

My family and friends—in Florida, in North Carolina, in Maine, and beyond—who have spent years listening to me sing Christmas carols at inappropriate times of the year. (Charlotte would be horrified.)

And you, if you are reading this. Thank you, if you are a new reader, for picking up this book; and thank you, if you are a longtime reader, for taking a chance on something a bit different from me. It's such an honor to get to continue telling you stories.

ABOUT THE AUTHOR

Martha Waters is the author of *Christmas Is All Around* and the Regency Vows series, which includes *To Have and to Hoax*, *To Love and to Loathe*, *To Marry and to Meddle*, *To Swoon and to Spar*, and *To Woo and to Wed*. She was born and raised in sunny South Florida and is a graduate of the University of North Carolina at Chapel Hill. She lives in London and loves sundresses, gin cocktails, and traveling.